BECOMING A KING

MARCI BOLDEN

PINK SAND
PRESS

[1]

I HELD my eyes closed as tightly as I could. Water lapped at the edges of the pool all around me as the late afternoon sun beat down, heating my shoulders. Crescent City, named for the curve of the bay that cut into the southern Rhode Island shoreline, tended to feel suffocating in the July heat. Today was no different.

Though a long, sweeping staircase led to the sandy beach, I preferred to cool off in the mosaic-tiled infinity pool that dominated the living area built specifically for entertaining friends, family, and a revolving door of business associates. The view from the edge of the pool seemed to go on forever, overlooking the boats that dotted Crescent Bay at all times.

The salty air stirred with the near-constant breeze. I held my breath and listened intently before calling out, "Marco."

"Polo," came a voice to my right.

I lurched toward the sound but came up empty. "Marco."

"Polo."

After my second attempt to tag my son failed, I grinned. I knew when Adam was being mischievous, and the thinly veiled giggle along with a drip of cold water on my forehead confirmed my suspicion. He was up to no good.

"Marco."

"Polo."

I tilted my head back and opened my eyes. Dangling a foot above my head, Adam broke into a fit of laughter.

"I'm not sure that's fair," I pointed out.

"It was Daddy's idea."

Garrett set him at the edge of the in-ground pool. "Go get Mom a towel, buddy." As soon as Adam darted off, Garrett looked down at me. "The gala starts in two hours. Don't you think it's time we got ready?"

I dramatically fell back into the water. The Annual Gala for the Fine Arts was just one of many events we attended to be seen along with everyone else who only showed up to be seen. For me, the worst part about running in the highest levels of society was that the networking never ended. If Garrett and I weren't hosting parties, we were attending them. And in between, we were attending fundraising galas or conducting business over nearly every meal.

Today, I just wanted to swim with my son. Adam was only six, but I knew from experience that every memory we made was precious. Playing Marco Polo on a hot summer day seemed far more important to me than dressing up and faking smiles all evening.

"Do we have to?" I asked.

"For the price we paid for those tickets? Yes. We have to. Come on."

Reaching down, Garrett waited until I grasped his hands, then pulled me from the pool almost as easily as he'd dangled Adam out of the water during our game. My husband was closing in on fifty faster than he wanted to admit, but he was fit, and pulling my thin frame from the water wasn't much of a challenge for him.

Another downfall of this world we lived in? Women, even those of us who were married and had children, were expected to look like supermodels. I didn't quite fit that mold —I chose work and family over hours spent with trainers— but no one in their right mind would ever consider me less than fit.

This afternoon might have been spent playing with Adam, but only after I'd swam laps until my muscles felt as if they'd melted inside my skin.

Garrett draped the fluffy towel Adam handed him over my shoulders and swatted my behind. "I'll get him settled while you take a shower. Mara," he said, pulling me to a stop before I walked away. "A *quick* shower, please."

"Fine," I said with another dramatic flair and headed inside.

I took a *quick* shower by my standards, but even so, enough steam escaped the glass-walled shower and settled on the wall-length mirror that filled the space above my vanity. I towel-dried my hair as I walked to where my robe hung on a hook, then wiped the condensation from the mirror so I could see enough to drag a brush through my long hair. As I opened the bathroom door, a burst of cold air enveloped me —a drastic change from the heat of the bathroom.

Garrett was already in his black slacks and buttoning his

tuxedo shirt. "I see we still need to work on your basic understanding of time."

I laughed as I headed for the closet to get my gown.

"Oh, darling," Garrett called. "I've got your dress right here."

I glanced to where he'd gestured. A strappy slip of material lay spread across our king-sized bed. The thin black dress was as much a contrast to the dress I'd picked out as the temperature between the bathroom and the bedroom—one hot and steamy, the other cool.

This was the dress I'd worn for our anniversary dinner in Paris. The gown had been a gift from Garrett. I never would have picked out something so revealing. And I'd only been brave enough to leave the hotel in that skimpy bit of material because no one I knew would see me. I had the body to pull it off—even without hours spent at the gym, my muscles were firm—but flaunting my body was outside my comfort zone.

The warmth of a blush touched my cheeks as I recalled how the low-cut material had barely covered my breasts and bordered on inappropriate in the back as well. Only a few sparkly straps ensured the dress didn't fall off. Not exactly what the other women at the art gala would be wearing.

"That's not what I bought for tonight."

"I know." He tilted his head and grinned. His dark-chocolate eyes didn't exactly change colors with his moods the way my blue eyes tended to betray me, but I could read him so well that just a look let me know what was on his mind.

He was manipulating me. I knew what was coming before he opened his mouth. Compliments. Gentle touches.

Light kisses. His sultry bedroom voice hypnotizing me until I gave in to him.

I closed my eyes and turned away, attempting to steel myself against his charms. I was weak, and after seven years of marriage, he knew all the right buttons to push. I finished my trek to the closet and pulled out the red sequined gown that covered far more of my body than the black one.

"You haven't even seen this dress, Garrett. I think you'll like it."

He slid his arms around my waist and pulled me against him. "So save it for the next fancy dinner. Tonight, I want my wife to be the sexiest woman in the room."

"Oh. And I'm only sexy if I'm scantily clad?"

He dragged his hand down my side and over my thigh until he couldn't reach any lower. "It's a full-length gown."

"That practically shows my tits."

He sagged a bit—not a full pout, but as close as he'd ever get. "I bought that dress for you, Mara."

"I know. And it's lovely."

He smiled as if all had been settled. "So wear it." Gripping my hand, he pulled me to the bed where I looked at the dress. He lightly brushed his hand over the front of my satin robe, taking a moment to circle my nipple before tugging the sash loose. The material opened, revealing me to him.

Running his hand over my stomach, he inhaled slowly. He slid his hand between my legs and stroked so lightly, I thought I could be imagining his touch. I wanted to tell him to stop, but something in me was determined to confirm his touch.

"Remember that night in Paris?" he whispered.

I jolted as he rubbed over my clitoris, and I knew I hadn't imagined anything. He was taking his usual manipulation a step further. Of course, we didn't have much time to do our usual back and forth before the gala started. If Garrett was going to get his way—and he always did—he'd need to convince me to wear his dress fast.

He became more assertive, slipping his fingers between my folds and pressing hard against my clit several times before shoving two fingers inside me as he nuzzled my neck.

"Remember how seeing you in that dress drove me so mad, we didn't even make it back to the hotel?"

Oh, I remembered all too well. The driver's tip that night had been watching me straddle my husband in the back seat as he pushed the bit of material aside and sucked my nipples while I rode him. That wasn't like me—that wasn't like me at all. But after too much wine and seeing my husband lust after me all through dinner, my head had definitely *not* been in the right place. Garrett never let me forget it, either. He got off on sex in strange places—his office, dressing rooms, cars driving through the streets of a foreign city. I didn't give in to his public sex fetish often, so he really clung to the times I had.

Like that night in Paris when I wore a skimpy black dress and let him get me off in a moving vehicle despite sharing the space with a driver who knew exactly what was happening behind him.

But I couldn't say that I'd minded. I liked knowing I could still please my husband. That was stupid considering the truth of our relationship.

We'd agreed to an open marriage six years ago. I'd been

six months pregnant when I'd first learned of his affairs. His stupid little assistant had walked into my office, the smell of sex emanating from between her legs and filling the room, to let me know she'd just fucked my husband. I'd confronted Garrett, and he admitted what he'd done. I'd been crushed—my heart and hopes for our future and family shattered.

I had gone straight home and packed a suitcase. I hadn't been born to the same world as Garrett, so I didn't know how this game was played. My parents had been average, and I lived an average life until they'd died unexpectedly. The courts had found some relation—second cousin twice removed, or something—to take me in.

Aunt Victoria became the only mother I'd known for most of my life, and when she frowned as I told her what had happened, I expected her to tell me I'd done the right thing.

Instead, she schooled me on the reality of being married to a man who had his choice of women and enough money to buy them all. She'd sat, with a bored look on her face, as she explained that Garrett's assistant had done me a favor. Most wives pretended not to know what their husbands were doing, but he'd confessed his sins.

"You have that man by the balls," she'd said, surprising me with her vulgarity. Aunt Victoria was as prim and proper a lady as I'd ever seen, but now, she lifted her frail hand and made a fist in the air. "Squeeze them. Twist them. Pull as hard as you can. Do you think I got all this"—she spread her arms as she sank back on her pristine white sofa—"by storming out when my husband sought pleasures elsewhere? No. When a man fucks up—and they *all* fuck up—you don't forgive and forget, darling. You take them for all they are worth."

Before I'd left that night to go home, she'd coached me on all the things to say. I'd been sick to my stomach as I presented my stipulation to my husband: He could have his women, but if any came forward again, if any became pregnant, or if he ever gave me any kind of venereal disease, I would divorce him, and he would agree to give me everything. He'd lose the house, the company, and our child.

He was furious. He tried to negotiate, but eventually he agreed, and by the end of the week, we'd signed a contract allowing both parties to take lovers—so long as no one else ever knew.

While I had yet to take advantage of our agreement—I was too busy being a hands-on mother and vice president of our property-development company—Garrett wasn't exactly sex-starved. I had no doubt any number of women were happy to indulge in his fetish. He didn't need me to fulfill those needs.

Even so, when he slipped his fingers deeper inside me and whispered, "I want to relive that night," I felt myself give in to him.

WALKING INTO THE GALA IN GARRETT'S DRESS WAS A BIT like walking into the lion's den after rolling around on a steak. Contemporary art lined the walls of the enormous gallery, and women wearing gowns that cost as much as a year of college tuition walked around the sculptures scattered about the room while tuxedo-clad men stood in small groups, talking business.

I held my head high as I ignored the whispering behind my scantily covered back. I was actually used to the gossip. The women may or may not have intended me to hear what they thought of my dress, but the high ceiling bounced their voices back to me.

I gave Garrett an accusing side-eye.

He smirked and patted my hand before leaning close. "Forget them, darling. They're just upset that their husbands are staring at you."

And they *were* staring. More specifically at the assets that made me different from them.

When I first joined this level of society, I was the poor girl who hit the jackpot when her parents died. When I chose college over marriage, I was the girl too good to follow social expectations. When Garrett hired me, I was the girl screwing her way to the top. When he married me, I was the girl who manipulated the most eligible bachelor around.

Now, rather than having facials and going shopping, I spent my time raising my son with minimal help from his nanny and working hard at King Incorporated.

Though Garrett was born and bred in higher ranks of society, his father insisted he make his own way. His father fronted him the money to start King Inc., but it had been up to Garrett to make it succeed. And Garrett had.

But his company had plateaued until, as part of our marital contract, he put me in the role of VP and had to start listening to me. Since then, King Inc. had become a power-house in the property development industry, and I'd more than proven I belonged amongst the business elite. I demanded to be respected for my brains and business savvy, not just as Mrs. Garrett King.

So, walking into the room in Garrett's dress made me feel like I'd just lost most of the gains I'd managed to make over the years.

Even as the vice president of our company and Garrett's wife, I had to work twice as hard as the men around me to earn respect. Most assumed Garrett had given me the position because I demanded it. Which, truth be told, I had.

The night I'd gone back home and laid down the law of our marriage, part of the package was giving me the role of second in command. But I had what it took to be in that position.

The only difference between me and the other people in high-level executive positions was the fact that I had tits and a vagina. Sadly, all the work that I'd done to prove those didn't matter was probably out the window. This dress was clearly reminding them all that I did, in fact, have tits. Which would also remind them that I should be at the spa with their wives instead of negotiating contracts in the boardroom.

Garrett, however, seemed as pleased as a man with a trophy wife could be. I wasn't as young as some of the wives draping off their husbands, but at thirty-two, I still qualified as a member of that club. For a few more years anyway. The difference between me and the others was that Garrett couldn't trade me for another model. Not without giving me everything. That gave me a leg up on the others. They'd likely fade away in the next five to seven years. I'd still be there to see their younger, perkier replacements.

Even so, Garrett repeatedly said, "You remember my wife," as if we hadn't known the same people for years.

And they all took a moment to glance at the abundant cleavage I was flashing before meeting my eyes and smiling.

Yes. I'd definitely shot myself in the foot with this dress. Damn it.

Frustrated, more with myself for caving in than Garrett for manipulating me, I accepted a glass of champagne from a waiter expertly holding a tray of fresh drinks. He bowed slightly and moved on to the next person.

We all stood around silently judging everyone while smiling and pretending we were all the best of friends and that raising funds for the art gallery somehow proved we weren't as shallow as we all knew we were. Nights like this made me wonder what my parents would think of who I'd become.

"Work hard, Mara," my father used to say. "That's the most important thing."

I did work hard. I worked hard every day and most weekends. I was born to a humble home. Humble parents who worked hard. Who strived to do better. To make me better. And here I was, dressed like my husband's prize and smiling prettily at his side instead of asserting myself like I'd been raised to do. I hated myself in that moment.

I was about to suggest we leave, even though the evening had barely gotten started, when Jake Decker called out to Garrett. We had been working closely with Jake's company, JD Construction, to edge Carter Enterprises out of the property development game. Carter had long been our strongest competitor, but their vice president had embezzled millions and had gotten the company caught in a legal web that was dragging them down.

We needed to move fast while the president, Albert Carter, was off balance. We'd teamed up with Jake to kick the company while it was down. He'd help us buy and construct as quickly as possible while Carter Enterprises was trying to get back on their feet. By the time they were, King Inc. would be the top company in the industry, and eventually, we'd buy Carter out and hold an even larger market.

All was going well until Garrett muddied the waters by utilizing our open marriage agreement on Jake's wife. I was sure Jake hadn't realized yet, but the way Megan was looking at my husband—like a cougar stalking her prey—he was about to find out.

They approached us, and Megan put her hand to Garrett's chest and batted her eyelashes as she leaned in and planted a far-too-friendly kiss on his cheek.

I ignored her move and gave her husband a proper hello —a quick kiss on the cheek. Though Jake was attractive, I hadn't really taken too much note of him. He'd told me once that he'd been the coxswain on his college row team and still took a boat out into the bay regularly to stay in shape. I believed him.

He wasn't bad to look at. I just wasn't interested, and I'd never considered that he might be interested in me until his gaze lingered on my plunging neckline. I couldn't really hold that against him. I practically had *stare at me* written across my chest.

Garrett pulled away from Megan's hand as he slithered his arm around my waist and tugged me closer. The stupid woman's smile fell as if she thought he would be receptive to her blatant flirting in front of his wife. Not to mention her husband and our business partner was standing right there watching the show.

Jake seemed oblivious, however, even when Megan reached out and stroked Garrett's lapel as if she were his date.

Wow. She seemed intent on staking some kind of claim on my husband in public.

I wondered then if the Deckers had the same agreement I had with Garrett. I imagined open marriages weren't as unheard of in our circle as one might like to believe. The men needed their egos stroked more than average males, and the women needed to be kept in their plush lifestyles. As Aunt Victoria so wisely told me, marriage was a contract, a give and take—the women gave their dignity and took the money. And that seemed to work well for most of them.

But my agreement with Garrett clearly stated that our open marriage and any lovers were to be kept away from public view. Megan Decker apparently hadn't been made aware of this. Or she just didn't care.

Garrett took her hand and politely dropped it, causing her jaw to tense. She drank down the champagne in her glass faster than any person could metabolize alcohol. I'm sure Garrett noticed as well because he excused us much more quickly than he normally would. The last thing either of us wanted was one of his lovers making a scene.

"I would suggest you get her under control," I said through a fake smile as we walked away.

"I will."

Turning to him, I met his gaze and held it. "If she ruins our deal with Jake—"

"She won't."

"You'd better be sure about that."

In response, Garrett nodded toward another small cluster of well-to-dos. "Who is that? Talking to the Carters."

I spotted a man in a perfectly filled-out tuxedo. His dark hair was a bit longer than most men in his position would wear. I didn't know if he intended that to be as rebellious as it seemed, but that was enough to pique my interest. Anyone who didn't toe the rigid lines laid by this group lit a spark of curiosity in me.

"That's Michael Redmond, the new vice president of operations for Carter Enterprises. He owned a smaller company that Albert bought out last year. When Albert was in need of a new VP, he called this guy in. Something about him having small-town integrity. Clearly a calculated move to convince his stockholders he was taking the embezzlement issue to heart."

Garrett nodded. "Right. I knew he looked familiar. Where was it that we met him?"

"The Carters' anniversary party in April. On Albert's yacht. His wife passed away last year in a car accident. He has a son Adam's age." I closed my eyes for a moment, scanning the recesses of my memory. "William, but he calls him Will."

Garrett patted my hand in a sign of his appreciation. I hated when he did that. I wasn't a goddamned poodle. Even so, I put on my show-dog face—a plastered smile and eyes filled with faux excitement as he led me to the group.

"Albert," Garrett said as he shook Carter's hand. "So good to see you."

I kissed his wife's cheeks as she gushed over how beautiful my gown was. As Grace gave the compliment, her smile remained frozen around her obvious lie. She hated the dress almost as much as I did.

"Mara," Albert cooed with a friendly tone as he took a lingering glance at my chest. He'd always had a fat, rounded nose, long ears, and deep-set eyes that seemed to carry a natural air of suspicion. At the moment, though, those eyes had more lust than doubt. "You look lovely this evening."

I returned Albert's compliments as he pecked my cheek. I wasn't familiar enough with Mr. Redmond to do more than accept his handshake, but I did notice that he was the first man we'd spoken to who didn't seem the least bit tempted by the generous amount of flesh I was showing. That was as refreshing as the length of hair brushing his collar.

I almost resented Grace's presence. When it was just me and the men, we could talk business, but when the wives were present, I was delegated to entertaining them while Garrett got to talk about the interesting things. Grace and I smiled and chatted politely about the art and artists while the men conversed.

Albert barely took his attention off me. I tried not to notice, or to let it get to me, but I loathed when men openly gawked at me—even when my dress was inviting their stares.

Garrett pulled Grace and me back into the conversation by gripping my hand. "Did you hear Albert, darling?"

"Oh, I'm sorry." I smiled at the man who licked his wrinkled lips and didn't bother to hide the fact that he was looking like he could dive into my chest at any moment. I moved closer to Garrett, holding his arm more tightly, blocking Albert's view.

"Albert would like us to join him at his beach house this weekend."

"No worries." Albert smiled. "It won't be all work. There'll be plenty of time for swimming and sunbathing."

I forced my smile to stay firmly in place. I just bet he'd like to see me sunbathing. Pervert.

"Oh, shoot," I said as if I was really disappointed. "Adam has a swimming competition this weekend."

Garrett and I had long ago learned to not counter each other's lies, so instead of calling me out, he said, "Perhaps we could miss just one. I'm sure the nanny could take him."

"That's what nannies are for," Albert said, skimming over me again.

I crossed my arm over my chest, putting my hand on Garrett's bicep, effectively blocking what was left of Albert's view. "Darling," I said to my husband, "you know how upset he gets when we miss his events."

He patted my hand and shrugged at Albert. "Perhaps another time."

Albert toasted me. "I'd love to have you. Whenever you're ready."

Seriously?

I hugged Garrett's arm a bit more closely. "Well, there's no need to wait for me. I'm sure Garrett wouldn't mind a break from familial obligations. A gentleman's retreat might be the answer."

"Not a bad idea," Garrett said. "Something to think about, Albert."

"I'm sure Mr. Redmond wouldn't mind an opportunity to get better acquainted with our competition," Albert said and offered a fake laugh that we all joined in. But then he looked at me again. "We'll have to plan a time for us all to get together. The boys can entertain each other while the adults partake in other activities."

My smile nearly faltered at that, but I managed to keep the curve of my lips plastered in place. I looked at Grace who couldn't look more bored. She'd likely seen her husband play these games a thousand times over the years.

I was again thankful for the rule that Garrett and I put into place forbidding blatant flirtations. I would be prone to stabbing him if he tried to pick someone up in front of me as openly as Albert.

"Grace, what do you enjoy doing at the beach house?" I asked.

"Grace doesn't go," Albert offered. "She hates the sand. And the wind. And the water."

"And the *other* activities," Grace offered.

I wanted to apologize to her, but really, it wasn't my fault she'd married a pig.

"Sounds like the boys would have a wonderful time," Mr. Redmond said.

"Well," I said, smiling at the only man in the room who seemed to be able to look at my face, "perhaps we'll have to consider joining in some other time, then. In the meantime, I'm afraid we must bid you goodnight." I usually waited for Garrett to usher us along, but I'd had enough ogling from

Albert Carter to last a lifetime. "I absolutely must say good evening to my aunt, or she'd never let me hear the end of it."

I pushed Garrett along.

"Would you care to explain yourself?" he asked as we moved out of hearing range.

I simply lifted a brow at him.

"Adam isn't even on a swim team, Mara."

"Did you see the way that old man was looking at me?"

The smirk on Garrett's face said it all. Much like our son, I could see when my husband was up to no good.

"Oh, dear God, Garrett. Is that why I'm wearing this dress?"

"I was testing the old coot."

"To determine how little respect he has for his wife?"

"No. To determine how much he wants to fuck mine."

I narrowed my eyes at him, and he steered me toward the balcony. The curved space was large enough to hold half a dozen tables, and several were filled with people sipping champagne and enjoying the city skyline. Garrett turned us toward a corner away from everyone else.

As soon as we were alone, my fake smile fell into an angry frown. "What the hell are you playing at?"

He lifted his hands as if to surrender. The pacifying move pissed me off even more.

"I'm not your personal prostitute, Garrett."

"Mara." He put his hands to my face and kissed me lightly. "I'm not whoring you out."

"Then why am I dressed like this? Why did you stand there and let him look at me like he could buy me? Did you hear what he said to me?"

"Shh." He kissed me again. "Calm down," he whispered.

I swallowed and looked away, then took a deep breath as my stomach knotted. "I don't like when men look at me like that."

The first time I'd seen a look like that on a man was at one of Aunt Victoria's parties. There'd been too much alcohol and not enough supervision of a curious twelve-year-old girl. I'd never seen women in dresses like they'd worn that night. The scene was like in one of the black-and-white movies my mother had loved so much. I thought Ingrid Bergman would come sweeping in at any moment.

I sat on the stairs, partially hidden, as I peered into the ballroom, soaking in as much of the party as I could. As the evening wore on, and the party thinned out, the guests drank more and laughed louder...and touched each other more.

My parents had been affectionate, but not in the way that I was witnessing as I hid on the dimly lit stairway that night. Men openly kissed women—women they hadn't come to the party with—and touched their breasts and backsides in a way that shocked me. But I couldn't stop watching.

I hadn't noticed a man coming toward me until he was so close that when he stroked my hair, I nearly jumped from my skin. The smile that curved his lips set me on edge. I'd never felt fear like that before. Though I'd been caught where I wasn't supposed to be, watching things I wasn't intended to see, instinctually, I knew his intentions weren't to chastise me for that.

I sat frozen, unable to run away.

"Like what you see?" he had asked, and my heart nearly exploded. The hand that had stroked over my hair then touched my shoulder, and his eyes lowered over my cotton nightgown, settling on my budding breasts.

"Have you ever had a man kiss you like that?" He licked his lips.

And I threw up all over his shoes as he leaned closer to me.

I never told Victoria why I was there or what the man had said, but I suspected she knew—or guessed. He yelled. I cried. She rushed out of the party and called for a servant to clean up the mess as she rushed me off to bed.

I never saw that man at one of her parties again. But I also never spied on the adults again. Whenever she had a gathering of friends, I stayed in my room behind a locked door. The only other soul who knew about that night was Garrett.

"Okay," he soothed. Pulling me into his arms, he hugged me. "I'm sorry. You know I'd never let anyone hurt you."

I buried my face in his chest. Despite his casual attitude toward fidelity, he was quite protective. I was *his* wife. *His* woman. And while he didn't mind showing me off, I did believe him when he said he'd never let anyone hurt me. He knew I was haunted by that night, by what could have happened if my stomach hadn't responded to the fear that had caused me to freeze.

Garrett hugged me tighter. "I should have told you my plan."

"What plan?" I leaned back, making sure I could see his face when he answered.

He lightly ran his hand over my bare arm. "I've caught Albert looking at you more than once, sweetheart. He's used to getting any woman he wants, but you don't even notice him. You're the rabbit and he's the greyhound, just waiting to be released so he can sink his teeth into you."

"That's an appealing thought," I said dryly.

"You distract him." He brushed his hand up my arm, this time discreetly dragging his thumb over my nipple.

I immediately glanced around to make sure no one could see. We were alone. Even so, I pushed his hand away.

"Don't do that."

"What?"

"Manipulate me into agreeing to whatever you're trying to get me to do."

He had the grace not to deny what we both knew he was doing. Instead, he clutched my hand and kissed my knuckles —an unspoken apology. "He's been far too focused on business lately. Carter is bouncing back much more quickly than predicted."

"Perhaps that's due to the new VP. I hear vice presidents can be quite effective when allowed to fully apply themselves to their jobs."

He smirked at my jab. "You are living proof. Look what you've done for my lowly little business."

I didn't respond. King Inc. had plateaued until I took over a larger role, but I wasn't egotistical enough to think I was solely responsible. The company would have rebounded without me. I just helped push it along a bit faster.

"I need him focused on something else," Garrett said. "I need time to secure a few more deals. I'm not asking you to sleep with the old geezer...unless you want to."

I rolled my eyes and pulled away from him.

"I'm kidding." Wrapping his arm around my waist, he tugged my body to his. "Mara, I know you are brilliant. But you are also incredibly sexy. It's the sexy part that has Albert tripping over himself whenever you are near. I'm asking you to utilize that within the confines of your comfort level to give our company an edge over his."

I shook my head. "You have no idea how difficult it is for a woman to succeed at business without prostituting herself, but I've done it. Garrett, I've done it, whether people believe that or not. But here you are, my husband, asking me to start now. Do you know how cheap that makes me feel?"

Putting his hands to my face, he looked into my eyes. "That is not what I'm asking. Mara, this is for us. For Adam's future."

"Oh, my God, Garrett. Really? You want me to flash my tits at a dirty old man for my son's sake?"

"Yes," he said without hesitation. "To secure his future. To make this company as strong as it can be. Don't stand on some feministic soapbox, Mara. You're smarter than that. Pool boys, martial arts instructors, rich businessmen. We've all been put on display as much as you have. If that man were into dick, I'd be happy to accidentally flash him a peek if it achieved what I needed. You think women are the only ones sexualized?"

I exhaled heavily and frowned at him.

"You don't even have to flirt with him, darling. Just seeing you is enough to give him something to think about." He nuzzled my neck. "Just let him imagine. That's half the fun for him."

"It's the other half that I'm worried about."

He kissed me lightly. "Perhaps Megan would like to go to his beach house."

"Only if she got to scream from the rooftops that she's sucking your dick."

He chuckled. "She couldn't scream, darling. Her mouth would be full the entire weekend."

I punched him playfully, and he laughed outright.

"I deserve better than this, Garrett. I'm not a piece of meat."

He stroked his hand over my hair. "I agree. One hundred percent. And I'll make it up to you."

"How?"

"However you want."

A faithful husband? A real marriage?

Neither of those would happen. But it didn't hurt to have Garrett owe me something. Taking a breath, I held it for a moment. "Fine. He can look, but if he touches, I'll break his fingers."

Garrett grinned. "And I'll break his arm." He lifted his elbow out, a silent request for me to take it. Only this time when he led me into the lion's den, I felt like that steak had been tied around my neck.

[2]

Garrett and I rode home to our French-château-inspired mansion in silence. Garrett didn't wait for Tomas, our driver, to open the door. He climbed out and held his hand back to me, assisting me to my feet, and slammed the door of the sleek black Town Car we rode in to events such as the one we'd attended tonight.

Garrett tucked my hand into the crook of his elbow, as any gentleman would, and led me up the sweeping staircase toward the arched glass doors with hand-scrolled wrought-iron fanlights that opened into a two-story foyer. That same pattern carried throughout the entire design of the house, from window coverings to the banister that prevented someone from falling off the numerous balconies in and outside the estate. The chandelier, made in the same style but covered with hundreds of crystals, filled the space with crisp white light that reflected prisms high on the walls.

Once inside, I pulled from Garrett and headed up the set of stairs to the right side of the foyer—not that it mattered, since both sets curved to meet at the second-floor balcony, but the bedrooms were to the right.

Easing the door to Adam's room open, I silently moved to his bed, smiling at his sleeping face. Touching his blond hair, the same golden shade as mine, I kissed his head and stepped away from my sleeping boy. My breath hitched when I crunched a toy under my black satin-covered heel. Glancing to the bed, confirming Adam was still asleep, I bent down and snagged the broken car. Carrying it with me, I eased his door closed and jolted at the feel of a hand on my hip.

"He asleep?" Garrett asked softly.

I turned and smiled. "Like an angel."

"He *is* an angel. He gets that from you."

"I stepped on his Camaro." I held up the broken toy as evidence.

"Uh-oh."

"Another one bites the dust." Slipping around him, I walked into the bedroom across the hall. Adam's room wasn't small by any means—he had more room than many full-grown adults who chose to rent apartments in large cities, but our room was massive.

I felt Garrett watching me as I crossed to the sitting area. Setting the broken toy on the table, I put my fingertips on the surface to balance myself as I slipped out of the shoes that had been pinching my toes for far too long.

I grinned at Garrett as his blatant gaze skimmed over my legs. "See something you like, Mr. King?"

He closed the distance between us in a few long strides and pulled me into a hard kiss. As much as I insisted I was an independent woman who deserved respect, I couldn't help but melt when Garrett tried to possess me. His kiss was hot and demanding. After a night of watching other men wanting me, he was staking his claim on my mouth, and I loved it.

He was breathless when he broke away. "Do you know how many men I caught staring at you tonight? You were driving them crazy in this dress." He ran his nose along my neck, inhaling deeply. "Every time you'd move, your nipples would perk up, and just a little more cleavage would sneak out. Every man in that room was captivated, hoping to catch a glimpse at what you were hiding just out of view. It was glorious."

He got far more enjoyment from their responses than I did. He loved knowing that while I was admired by others, I would be going home with him. And I loved that I could still turn him on to the point of ravishing me. I didn't like to admit that it made me just as twisted as he was. I preferred to think he was the one who was fucked up, but the fact that I let him touch me even though his lovers said things about me that I didn't want to consider.

But then he lowered his hand over my hip to the high-cut slit that had flashed hints of sun-kissed flesh all evening, and any self-loathing fell away. His hand was hot against my skin and would be hotter when he touched me in the places he'd teased to get me into the dress he'd wanted me to wear. The games we played, the emotional manipulations and physical teasing we partook in, seemed to be a fetish of its own, but I would never call it that.

He pressed his body against mine and whispered, "It's been too long, Mara."

"You've been busy elsewhere."

I reminded him of this only because he'd come to expect it. If I gave in too easily to his seduction, he'd lose interest. Hard to get. That's how he wanted me. He wanted me to be disinterested so he could turn me on, bend me to his bidding, prove he was still stronger than me. And I let him.

Dipping his head down, he lightly kissed my neck. "That doesn't mean I don't still desire my queen."

I grinned despite my intent to make him work a bit harder for what he wanted. I could still recall so vividly the first time he'd called me his queen. He'd walked into my office well after most of the staff had gone home. I was the head of development, and he, of course, was the CEO.

Like many executives, we always worked late, so his barging in wasn't unexpected. However, the wicker picnic basket and neatly folded tartan blanket were. I sat back as he closed the office door and smiled at me with all the excitement of a boy at an airshow.

"What are you doing?" I'd asked with a surprised laugh as he spread the blanket out on my office floor.

"Come," he'd directed. "It's dinnertime."

We hadn't exactly been discreet about our relationship, but we hadn't announced it either. There were rumors, but we tried to keep the fact that we were dating out of the office. Garrett hadn't cared what people thought, but I had. I was hyperaware, in fact. I didn't want to be accused of sleeping my way to the top.

When I'd started at King Inc., I walked in much higher up the pecking order than many felt I deserved. They were right. I'm certain my aunt had talked to Garrett, who had talked to his HR department, who, in turn, placed me in a position much higher than what I'd applied to get.

I hadn't complained. Who would? I'd jumped right in, kept my head above water, and gained Garrett's attention in the process. I'd rebuffed his advances, refusing to be *that* woman. But he was persistent, and I admit to being weak. I did maintain some standards, though, and refused his attempts at office sex.

That night, however, with him spreading a picnic out before my desk, I had no doubt what he was up to. He was going to lay the seduction on thick, and it would take everything I had not to end up naked on the floor making love to him.

But I was in for a bigger surprise. After a dinner of meats, cheeses, and some of the best champagne I'd ever had, Garrett pulled a ring from his pocket. My heart dropped. I'd seen a lot of oversized diamonds since moving to Aunt Victoria's estate, but they paled in comparison to the emerald cut perched on the gem-encrusted band he presented to me.

He didn't ask me to marry him. Garrett rarely asked for what he wanted. He simply staked his claim as he tended to do. He slipped the ring on my finger, smiled warmly, and announced, "You're my queen, Mara. Now and forever."

I could barely remember how to breathe. I hadn't expected to marry Garrett King. In fact, I suspected our affair would end with me finding another job at another company when he was done with me. That's how these affairs usually ended.

But there I was, wearing his ring and finally giving in to his in-office seduction. On a soft blanket in the middle of the floor of my office at King Inc., I'd let him seduce me into fulfilling his desire—not only to become his queen, but to let him fuck me in the office.

He continued to seduce me to his will even now. Even though I was on to his games. On to his manipulations. I still gave in more than I should, but now without a lot of personal benefit.

I gasped as he ran his fingers over my panties and gently nipped my neck.

I was seconds from begging for more when our bedroom door flew open.

"Mommy!" Adam screamed, running toward me, and I pushed Garrett away. "I can't find my car!"

I widened my eyes at Garrett—secret parent code for him to cover for me—as I stepped around him. Sinking to my knees, I distracted Adam while Garrett got rid of the broken car.

"Did you check under the covers?" I asked.

"Yes."

"And under the bed?"

"Yes." His eyes, blue like mine, filled with tears. "It's gone."

I looked up at Garrett. "Let Daddy check. I bet he can find it."

Garrett ruffled the boy's hair and left the room, heading for the stock of backup dark-blue miniature Camaros I'd bought after the first time Adam's toy car had gotten broken and he was inconsolable.

The toys were cheap and poorly made, but they meant the world to him. A large section of his room was made to look like a racetrack, and he had a shelf filled with tiny cars, but the Camaro was his favorite and shared a special place on his pillow each night. Some kids wanted teddy bears—Adam just needed the small metal vehicle to keep him company.

I dried Adam's face and smiled reassuringly at him. "You know the car never goes far."

He leaned in and hugged me tight, and my love for him swelled. I dreaded the day this little boy would outgrow hugging his mommy. It would break my heart. Until then, I would cherish each squeeze.

"Look here," Garrett announced a few moments later. "Daddy saves the day again."

Adam pulled from me and ran for the toy. Moments like this made me forget that my marriage was a farce. I felt like a real wife as Garrett gestured for me to join in getting Adam back to bed. We took turns kissing his head, but I was the one who tucked the blankets just right around him and stroked his hair until his eyes drifted shut. I managed to leave without breaking any of his cherished toys this time.

"You're such an amazing mother to him," Garrett whispered as we walked back into our room.

I closed the door and pulled him closer, pinning myself between the solid wood of our bedroom door and his body. I took a moment to turn the lock so Adam couldn't barge in again.

"Where were we?"

Fire lit in Garrett's eyes as he leaned down and kissed me. Parting my lips, I let his tongue invade my mouth as I clung to him. While he wasn't as faithful as I'd always thought a husband should be, I couldn't deny that his experience with a woman's body was beneficial to me. He was an amazing lover.

He turned his kisses to my neck, then pushed the strap of my dress down until he could free my breast. I bit my lip and fisted his hair as he dove in, assaulting my nipple like he was starving for me. He suckled for a moment, then pressed his teeth into the sensitive peak. The sensation shot straight to my clit and made my body arch into him. He licked at the pebbled flesh, soothing the slight sting from his bite as he once again parted the slit in my dress. His mouth pressed to mine as he went right for my center.

No more teasing. No more hard-to-get. No more games.

He was ready, and I wasn't going to stop him.

He breathed my name as he found his way inside the waistband of my barely there panties.

"So wet," he whispered.

Rolling my head back, I put my hands to his shoulders and pushed him down. He didn't resist. A moment later, he was on his knees before me, pushing my satin gown open and tugging my underwear down. I gasped as he tasted me—his mouth just as masterful there as when he'd been kissing me. His fingers slid deep inside my body, curving to press against that magical spot as he sucked at my clit.

I put one leg over his shoulder, pulling him closer, demanding more. I was no longer too shy in the bedroom to take what I wanted. When we'd first become lovers, I was intimidated by how forward Garrett could be. My innocence amused him. That was probably what drew him to me. But

I'd blossomed over the last six years—the timid girl he'd married was long gone.

Even so, sometimes I surprised myself with my boldness. He seemed to love those moments when I pushed the edges of my comfort zone just a bit further as much as he enjoyed pushing them without my realizing it.

This moment was no different. As soon as I took control, he became more eager. Hungrier. Draping my leg over his shoulder, opening myself to him, only made his mouth move faster, his sucking harder.

I dug my hands in his hair, fisting the strands, and gasped.

He gripped my ass, digging his fingers into the flesh almost to the point of causing me discomfort. I didn't complain. I rolled my head back, bit my lip, and let the pain highlight the pleasure.

The way I always did with Garrett.

He fingered me deeper, sucked me harder, moaned louder, letting me know he was enjoying this as much, if not more, than I was. My muscles tightened in response, and I cried out as I came.

Standing, Garrett pulled me from the door and into his arms. He held my head as he put a forceful kiss to my mouth and guided us across the room. I hadn't even realized he'd released the zipper down my back until he easily slipped my dress from my body. The black material pooled at my feet, leaving me standing in my skimpy underwear, but he deftly removed those as well.

While I slipped into the bed, he tugged his tux jacket off and started working on his bowtie. He groaned as I put my hand between my legs and toyed with the bundle of nerves he'd already set on edge. By the time he lowered his body over mine, I was ready to orgasm again.

"Uh-uh," I warned, tightening my thighs on his hips before he could plunge into me. "You know the rule."

"Mara," he breathed.

I lifted a brow, and he sighed as he reached for the nightstand. I would not have unprotected sex with him when he had a lover. And he always had a lover—or three. He tore the packet open dramatically and then sheathed his erection.

"May I fuck you now?" he asked.

I smirked. "Yes, you may."

"Thank God."

I curved my hips up to meet him as he dove into me, hissing as he invaded my body. He filled me in all the right ways, and he moved just how I needed him to. Spreading my legs and lifting my hips, I gave him better access so he could thrust deeper. He slammed into me until I came, which didn't take long.

Pushing him onto his back, I straddled his hips. Easing my body over his, I slowed the pace from fucking to making love. I'd had two powerful orgasms. Now I wanted a few minutes of feeling wanted for more than just my body. Rotating my hips slowly, I kissed him gently, letting him know the mood had shifted.

He took my cue and slid his arms around me, moving with me, loving me like he used to. Before our contract, before I'd become the type of wife I loathed, I had made Garrett treat me like a lady in the bedroom as well as out of it. I refused to acknowledge that fucking could be as good as making love.

After I found out about his indiscretions, I thought if I gave him what he wanted, and stopped being a sexual prude, that he'd stop needing other women. I'd given in, tried things I hadn't before. And it thrilled Garrett. But not enough to be faithful.

Slowly, over the last six years, I took more control in the bedroom. I didn't have a plethora of lovers to turn to. I took my pleasure with my husband, and I made sure I took it how I wanted it. He could have his whores give him what he wanted. This was my time, and he'd yet to complain about my change in attitude toward our sex life.

This time when he breathed my name, it was filled with the emotion that had a way of reminding me that, despite everything, he did indeed love me. I never doubted that. He just had a different view of marriage than I did.

Hearing him say my name like that melted me a bit, softened some of the bitterness that tended to seep into my heart. I kissed him, slowly and deeply, as he gripped my hips and started thrusting harder.

"You are my queen," he whispered. "My only queen."

He hugged me tightly to him as he stiffened. I came with him, then collapsed onto his chest. He slid his arms around me, and for a moment, I felt content.

Then his phone rang.

"Don't," I said, but he pushed me off him and reached for his discarded slacks.

"This is Garrett," he said.

I closed my eyes at the sound of a distinctly female voice

coming from his phone. I couldn't quite make out what was said, but I recognized the tone. A disgruntled lover. Probably Megan Decker.

"I'm busy right now," he said.

The woman's voice grew louder, angrier.

Garrett sighed.

And I knew he was going to leave me.

"Fine," he said. "I'll be there in twenty minutes."

I scoffed and rolled off the bed. In the bathroom, I looked at my reflection as I yanked the pins holding my long hair in a bun. My blond strands uncoiled as I raked my fingers through them. I was climbing into the shower to wash away the smell of sex when he came into the bathroom.

"I'm sorry," he called as I closed the glass door.

"Sleep in another room when you get home. I don't want you to wake me."

"I just need to put her in her place."

"I suggest you do." I finally turned to him, not trying to hide my anger. "Or I will."

My aunt and I sat under the oversized umbrella on the patio, protecting our skin from the sun as Adam's swim instructor carefully watched the boy holding his breath under the water.

There was a covered section of the tiled patio where the breakfast table sat, but I liked to keep a close eye on Adam when he was in the water, even when he was with his instructor, so we sat at the smaller wrought-iron and tempered-glass table. Just a step away from the water's edge in case Adam ever needed assistance.

It was my own engrained fear, and I didn't deny it. He was safe with Julio always within arm's reach, but I was convinced no one could ever protect Adam from harm like I could.

"If you keep frowning like that, you'll need Botox before you're forty," Aunt Victoria warned. "What's happened?"

I shook my head slightly. The last thing I wanted was a lecture about how stupid it was to still care for Garrett. I couldn't help that I hadn't completely closed my heart off to the man. The desire to have a marriage like my parents had was stupid. I knew that. I'd never have what I wanted. I knew that too.

And just in case I ever doubted it, Garrett was more than happy to casually mention one of his lovers to remind me. Or run off to put one *in her place* before we'd even had a chance to catch our breath after having sex.

But I did love him. And he loved me. In his own way. I just wished his way didn't have to come with such a sharp knife.

"Oh, dear God, Mara. You let that man touch you again, didn't you?"

I laughed softly. "Every now and then, I like being touched."

"So fuck the pool boy like everyone else."

I darted my gaze across the table. "Aunt Victoria, please. It's so jarring when you speak like that."

"I'm sorry, darling. So fuck the *water recreation manager* like everyone else."

I shouldn't encourage my aunt, but I tossed my head back as laughter burst from me. "You are impossible. And for your information, this isn't about Garrett. Not exactly, anyway."

"You've finally taken a lover."

"No." I looked back to the pool, making sure Adam wasn't listening. "That damned dress I wore to the gala last night."

"Is that what that was? I thought you lost a wrestling match with a pack of dental floss."

I frowned at her. "Garrett bought that for me in Paris last year. He insisted I wear it even though I didn't want to. I gave in, of course."

"As you do."

My scowl returned. She could at least try to be support-ive. "He said he wanted to see me in the dress he bought me. Turns out, he wanted *Albert Carter* to see me in the dress he bought me. He used me—my body—to test his theory that the old man can't think straight when faced with a pair of boobs."

"He was right, I'm sure."

I shuddered, remembering how Albert had looked at me. "I felt so dirty when I realized what Garrett was doing."

"What *was* he doing?"

"Albert is rebuilding his business faster than we can expand ours. Garrett thinks if Albert has something else on his mind, it will give him the time he needs to get ahead on some deals."

"He wants you to seduce Albert?"

"No. He said I don't even have to flirt with him. Just flaunt a bit. Let him look."

"Oh. Well, what's the harm in that, darling?"

I swallowed. "The way Albert looks at me makes my skin crawl."

She was silent for a few moments. "I see. But you're a grown woman, Mara. You know how to handle yourself and any man who comes along. If you sense he's getting out of hand, end the game. Tell Garrett. You know how possessive he is of you. You're his property."

My eyes widened. "I am not."

"Tell him that. He'll never tolerate another man touching you."

I lifted my brows at her. "Have you forgotten our arrangement?"

"Have you utilized your arrangement?"

I looked back to the pool as Adam broke the water and the instructor praised him.

Victoria snorted. "I didn't think so. Listen to me. I've been there. You think someday he'll get this out of his system, someday he'll realize he can be happy with only you in his bed. And maybe someday he will. But until then, make your own damn happiness."

"I find it a bit disturbing that you're so concerned about my sex life."

Leaning forward, my aunt tapped a manicured nail on the table. "From the day you came into my life, my number one concern has been your happiness. The longer you hold on to hope for a man who will never change, the less happiness you are going to find in this world. A man doesn't give a damn about a woman unless she has her legs open."

An exacerbated sigh left me. "That's not true. My

parents had a wonderful marriage. My father adored my mother."

Victoria frowned in that way she did whenever I brought up my parents. She had never had children, but she'd been a devoted surrogate. She tended to take my memories of life before her as a personal assault, so I didn't mention my parents often. But I did cling to those memories. I'd hoped my marriage would be more like my parents' than like my aunt's, but I'd definitely taken after Victoria in that area—at least in the give-and-take part.

"I've had plenty of lovers," Victoria said, "but I didn't love a single one. And not one of them loved me. I loved *you*. I gave everything I had to you. I still do."

This guilt trip was the price I paid for mentioning life before moving to the mansion.

Aunt Victoria held her hands out. "Look around you. You are here because I gave you the tools to be here. I taught you to be proper. I gave you the best tutoring. Circulated you through the right social circles."

"I know, Aunt Victoria. And I'll be forever grateful for everything you've done for me."

"You are surviving in this life because I learned from my mistakes and taught you better."

She was certainly laying the guilt on thick. "What mistakes?"

"I warned you not to marry for love, didn't I? You didn't listen. You fell head over heels for that man. I don't blame you. Women's hearts are blind. I fell in love once too."

My eyes widened behind my sunglasses. She'd never mentioned loving a man before.

She didn't pause long enough for me to ask. "And the first time he betrayed me, it nearly destroyed me. And you very nearly let Garrett's betrayal destroy you. But look at you now. You put him in his place, and you rose above. You have cemented your role by his side. Now your job is to lift him higher, and in doing so, you'll lift yourself and your son higher."

I frowned. "I have been doing that for six years. King Incorporated is growing every day."

"But I see in your eyes, you want more from him. You want to believe him when he whispers in your ear."

I swallowed as I returned my attention to Adam. I did want to believe Garrett. I wanted him to love me as much as I had convinced myself I loved him.

"Don't," my aunt warned. "Mara, you believe *me*. He's saying the same thing to all those other women. But you do have one thing they don't. His name. That's the only thing you need from him, darling. The only thing you should *want* from him. Keep this marriage in perspective, or you are giving him the power to bring you to your knees. And I don't doubt for a moment he would have you beg before him if he could. Never give him that power. Do you understand?"

I drew a breath, wishing I could defend Garrett against her accusations. Wishing I could say that I'd never be so weak. But I knew better. If six years of marriage to Garrett King had taught me anything, it was to never underestimate him or his ability to manipulate me. "Yes. I understand."

Satisfied, Aunt Victoria leaned back, taking her coffee with her. "As for Albert Carter, he's a horndog, not a sexual predator. He may test your boundaries, but he won't cross any lines."

I exhaled heavily. "So you agree with Garrett. I should flaunt a little for him."

"No, darling. You should flaunt a little for yourself. Who will benefit if Garrett closes those deals? You will, Mara. And when you benefit, so does your son."

I scoffed. My God. She sounded just like Garrett. That was the exact card he had played. *Do it for Adam's future.* I reached for a towel as the so-called benefactor climbed from the pool.

His wet feet slapped against the tiles as he ran to me. "Did you see?"

"I did. You are turning into a little fish, aren't you?" I wrapped the towel around him before he sat next to me.

He turned his bright eyes across the table, seeking Victoria's approval. "Did you see, Auntie?"

"I most certainly did." She lowered her face as she peered at me over her big sunglasses. "Auntie sees everything."

I sighed and pushed a plate of fruit closer to my son.

[3]

I COULDN'T DENY that Albert's beach house was beautiful, but his yacht was even more impressive. At over a hundred and thirty feet, the boat was more like a high-end condo on water.

I sat on the upper covered deck, eating lobster for lunch with Garrett to my right and Albert sitting across from me, pretending I didn't notice how Garrett continually looked away so Albert could focus on me.

A gauzy, white, low-cut sundress covered my bikini, but neither hid much, and Albert had all but thanked me for that. His smile was sly, his dark sunglasses hiding where his eyes were undoubtedly looking every time he spoke to me. Not that he had to be sneaky about it. Garrett made sure to give him plenty of opportunity to stare.

Mara, tell him about this. Mara, tell him about that.

And then he'd conveniently find something to look at out on the water.

Usually the wives were politely quiet so the men could

pretend to bond, but today's lunch was focused on my role at King Inc., yoga classes, swimming, and other uninteresting stories that gave Albert plenty of time to admire what was on display for him.

Garrett had said that he'd break Albert Carter's arm if he touched me, but after lunch, when Albert suggested we move to the lower deck with the lounge chairs and, conveniently, a pool, and held his hand out to me, Garrett didn't hesitate in walking ahead and letting the other man lead me toward the stairs.

I don't know why I was surprised. I'd agreed to this—not only to this unwanted lunch with Albert but to be his distraction. Garrett was sly. He knew how to prod for information. That was one of his many talents. He'd picked up all the subtle cues he'd needed during the gala and over lunch. Now that he knew how easy it was to keep Albert preoccupied, he was going to start putting his plan into action. He was setting the trap that I was slowly leading Albert into.

Still holding Albert's hand, I blushed as I slipped and *accidentally* leaned into him. Looking up, I smiled. "Sorry. These shoes aren't the best for walking on a boat."

"Women's shoes never are." His arm went around my waist, and he gripped low on my hip. "Just lean on me. I won't let you fall."

We made it to the stairs, but Albert didn't remove his hand from my waist. He kept his palm low on my side, as close to my ass cheek as he could get without actually cupping me. I pretended I didn't notice as we awkwardly took the steps.

Garrett was far enough ahead of us now that he couldn't

hear a word said between us, nor did he seem to be interested in trying. He was keeping a steady pace, the wind blowing his dark hair and contrasting white shirt and slacks as he went by the chairs, the pool, and right toward the stern.

"He certainly loves the water," Albert said, keeping me close to his side as we walked closer to the pool.

"He does."

"Does he have a boat?"

"Oh, of course. We don't use it as much as he'd like."

"His choice or yours?"

"Neither, I'm afraid. We're always so busy."

"That's a shame. You're too young to be so focused on work that you miss the joys of life."

"We focus on our son. He's the biggest joy we have."

"Well, I'm glad his meet was canceled so you could join me."

I smiled. "Yes, it's been a lovely day. I'm just sorry Grace decided not to join us."

"She's never been much for the beach. She doesn't like the sand or the constant crashing of the waves." He pulled me closer. "Or young, beautiful women flaunting their scantily clad bodies for all the men."

His laugh rang out, and I smiled my best fake smile at his assessment.

"I must admit," he said as he leaned closer, "I never took you for that kind until the other night."

My heart flipped. So it began. My cheeks heated, and I knew I was blushing, though I guessed he took it as flattery rather than the self-loathing and humiliation and dread at what I had done.

Putting his mouth against my ear, he said, "I wasn't the only one pleasantly surprised by your dress the other night. Every man who attended the art gala has a new appreciation for you."

I put my hand to his chest as I leaned back a bit, but he didn't allow me to put space between his lips and my ear. He just pulled me in even closer.

"Garrett is a very lucky man." His breath was hot and damp against my neck. The dry wine he'd drunk caught on the breeze and mixed with the salt air, filling my nostrils as his bony fingers gripped me tighter. "As much as I enjoy your company, though, you should enjoy the pool while your husband and I catch up."

My stomach clenched tightly, but I turned into his near embrace. "I think I will."

"Good."

He led me to the lounge chairs and stretched out in one while I sat, lifting the hem of my sundress much higher than necessary as I worked on releasing one strappy sandal, then the other, before standing. I acted oblivious to his eyes on me as I lifted my dress over my head and then leaned over the chair, spending far too much time draping the material across the back.

Garrett had determined a full-on thong bikini was too obvious, but the bathing suit he'd chosen for me to wear wasn't much more than that. Three small white triangles and a sliver of material to cover my ass. I took my time pulling the band from my ponytail, arching my back more than necessary so Albert had plenty of time to fully appreciate my full and barely covered breasts as I shook my long hair out.

Finally, I was ready to pull out the lame and overly used seduction of applying sun lotion. I wasn't about to allow the old man to put his hands on my skin, but he didn't seem to mind watching me rub my hands over my body. The silence was heavy and awkward, but I did my best to ignore his blatant staring as I rubbed over my thighs, stomach, and chest.

Garrett arrived just in time. I handed the bottle to him, and he squirted a blob into his hand. I should have known he wasn't there to save me, though. He ran his hand over my back, then around the front, and over my thighs.

"I always get too much," he justified, though the way he was stroking my skin was seductive and clearly not for my benefit.

Albert watched intently as Garrett's hands moved over me, and he smirked when Garrett finally gripped a handful of my ass and delivered a loud smack against the cheek he'd just squeezed.

"Have fun, darling," Garrett said, dismissing me.

I walked to the stairs, slowly easing into the pool under Albert's watchful gaze as Garrett stretched on a chair beside him. I floated on a raft for some time, always aware of the eyes on me as the men talked.

Finally, Garrett called for me to join them for a drink. I did, easing from the water just as I'd eased in, for the benefit of those who were watching.

I sat on the other side of Albert, where I'd undressed, and accepted a glass of champagne. My nipples peaked against the breeze as the water prickled and dried in the sun. I drank, listening to how easy it was for Garrett to pick small bits of information from Albert as he watched me eating berries, licking my fingers, and sipping his alcohol.

The scene was trite—overplayed—so very obvious, but the man was falling for the bait.

By the time I finished my drink and snack, Albert had divulged far more than he should have about an upcoming deal. Standing, I bent, messing with the chair, trying to get it to lie back so I could stretch onto my stomach.

I was having issues with figuring out how to get the chair flat until Albert came to my rescue. He pressed against me, his crotch to my ass, and I nearly yelped with surprise, but he leaned us forward as he grabbed a lever.

"Here," he said as innocently and friendly as his action should have been—*would* have been if he weren't gratuitously grinding his dick against me as he lowered the back. And in front of my husband! Who did nothing! He skimmed his hand along my stomach as he stood upright, and as Garrett had done earlier, Albert took a moment to grip my ass before stepping away.

I didn't react. Outwardly anyway. I hoped that Garrett hadn't noticed, and a quick glance proved he was looking away. Though I suspected that was intentional.

Sighing, I sprawled on my tummy and let the sun warm my back while Garrett continued to subtly pry Albert for information. When he seemed to be getting stonewalled and Albert turned the conversation, I sighed and drew his attention again. I rolled onto my back and pushed myself up, strutting to where the champagne bottle sat in a tub of melting ice. I refilled my glass.

Albert passed when I offered him more, but Garrett held

his glass out. I was pouring his drink when he reached out and ran his hand up my side. I very nearly dropped the expensive bottle when he intentionally brushed his hand over my breast.

I lifted my brows at him as I handed him the glass—a silent warning that he'd gone too far—but he didn't pay any mind. In fact, he tugged the edge of my suit down, not quite exposing my nipple but too damn close.

"I think you may be getting a bit too much sun," he said, running his fingers over my skin. "Perhaps we should go inside."

"We wouldn't want you to burn," Albert agreed.

I wasn't given a chance to put my dress and shoes back on. Garrett grabbed our glasses and the champagne while I gathered my things, then Albert had his hand low on my back as he had when he'd guided me to the pool.

My suit was still damp, so as soon as we entered the cabin, my nipples tightened from the blast of cool air, and I shivered. Albert, ever the hero, pulled me closer and ran his hand up and down my side, lingering as his hand slid up enough to touch the side of my breast.

I smiled my thanks and pulled away. "I just need to get my dress back on."

"Your suit is still wet." Garrett patted the cushion beside him. "Come sit with me until you dry."

Though the sitting area spanned the width of the boat, the oversized couches that lined both walls and the table in between made the space seem uncomfortably intimate. The dark wood walls and tinted windows didn't help.

The material Garrett was lightly rubbing was obviously

meant to resist water—it was on a boat, after all, but I lamely said, "Oh, I don't want to get the couch wet."

Albert nudged me toward the sofa. "It'll dry."

So would my dress, but I didn't argue. I sat close to Garrett, fearing Albert would sit next to me, but he sat directly across from us as Garrett handed me my drink. He put his hand on my knee, and we started talking about an upcoming fundraiser.

I was just starting to relax when Garrett's finger brushed over my bikini bottom. I hadn't even noticed that he'd moved his hand that high, and I assumed it was an accident until he did so again, and a third time. I tightened my thighs enough to let him know that wasn't appropriate.

He didn't take the hint. In fact, his not-so-subtle movements grew a bit more aggressive, and he stroked lower between my legs, causing me to sharply inhale at the surprise.

"More champagne?" Albert asked.

Taking the opportunity, I leaned forward and held my glass out, thanking him when it was full. When I eased back, Garrett draped his arm over my shoulder, and I sighed with relief, glad he took the hint. But then he started rubbing my shoulder, intimately massaging the muscle.

I glanced at Albert. A slight smile was playing on his lips.

Somehow the game had changed, and I'd missed the memo. And I didn't like it. The atmosphere was different now. I no longer felt like the willing bait. I felt like the unwitting prey.

Leaning forward, I set my glass on the table. "Where's the restroom?"

Albert gestured toward a hallway, and I found the tiny room. I reached it before I realized I'd left my bag—and my sundress—on the floor next to the sofa. Goddamn it. That meant I wouldn't be putting my dress back on.

I hated this. Hated every moment of it and was ready for Garrett's game to end, but I had to admit he was right. He was gathering more than enough information to sabotage at least two deals Albert's company was working toward. That would help us kick the feet out from under Carter Enterprises and keep King Inc. growing. Which was what we both needed and wanted.

Taking a breath, bracing myself and promising that I'd find a way to put an end to the afternoon soon, I headed back to where I'd left the men.

"I know how to read my wife, Albert. She's not there yet," Garrett was saying.

I held my breath. Wasn't *where* yet?

"I am not sacrificing those deals to you for nothing, King. Dinner is in less than an hour. She better be ready in time for dessert."

My heart dropped. My stomach rolled. Realization crashed in on me, and I suddenly felt sick. No. No. Garrett wouldn't. He *wouldn't*. He wouldn't prostitute me for a business deal.

"She will be."

The old man's voice was chilling when he said, "If you renege on our deal—"

"I'm not reneging on anything," Garrett said, sounding bored. "Let me go check on her. I'll be right back."

I backtracked as quickly as I could to the restroom. He

opened the door and was met with a vicious glare. "You motherfucker," I seethed.

"Hey." He grabbed my arms before I could push by him.

Where I was headed, I didn't know. We were miles from shore, but I'd be damned if I'd stay there.

"Stop," Garrett insisted.

"You sold me? For information?"

"Shh," he warned as he closed the door. "Of course not."

"I heard him. He expects to fuck me before dessert."

"No. I'd never do that to you."

I widened my eyes at him. "I heard him."

"He caught on to our little game before lunch was even over." He frowned. "We need to work on being subtle. Both of us."

"Garrett."

"While you were swimming, he told me he knew exactly what we were up to and offered a deal. He'd back off his deal for the property on Sanders Avenue—a huge deal, mind you—if I let him have you. I told him no, that would *never* happen."

"Well, he's expecting *something* to happen," I snapped.

"Yes, he is. We...negotiated a little."

I ground my teeth together. "Negotiated?"

"Instead of backing out of the Sanders deal, he is giving me information to undermine two smaller deals. He can't back out of both. That would raise flags with his VP."

"And in exchange?"

Garrett gave me his most innocent smile. "Trust me."

"No."

"Mara. I'd never hurt you or allow you to be hurt. You

just keep doing what you've been doing. Keep teasing him. Taunting him. And let me do the rest."

"What is the rest?"

He pinched my nipple lightly. "You've been driving him crazy with your teasing all day. He'd like to see you go a little crazy, too."

"You *did* sell me."

"No." Putting his hands on my face, he made sure I was looking at him as he said, "If I'd sold you, you'd already be on your knees and full of dick."

I swallowed hard. That almost sounded like a threat.

"Finish the game we started," he whispered. "That's all I'm asking."

"I don't want his hands on me."

He hesitated and then nodded. "Okay. I won't let him touch you."

Taking a breath, I slowly nodded. "Fine. But as soon as dinner is done, I want off this boat. Do you understand me?"

"You will be. He's going to wonder what we've been up to." Then he kissed me hard, sucking my bottom lip, nipping at the flesh as he pushed the material of my top aside and gripped my breast.

When he pulled back, he turned my face to the mirror. My mouth was red from his assault. He tugged my suit back into place, but clearly it'd shifted, and my skin was red from his rough treatment. It looked like we'd just had a quick heavy-petting session.

"That should put his mind at ease, don't you think?"

When we returned to Albert, he looked up and smiled. Suspicion lit in his eyes, but then he looked at my mouth and my suit and smiled. Garrett pulled me back to sit beside him, and the conversation and sipping of champagne continued as I took deep, calming, bracing breaths.

Play the game. Just play the game.

Before the game shifted, I would have smiled at Albert and pushed my cleavage together. So I did. Albert looked. Garrett brushed his finger over my nipple as the older man watched. I moved again, stopping Garrett, forcing him to pull me closer, pretending I didn't know what he was doing. I gave him a disapproving look for Albert's benefit.

I kept my focus on Albert, took my cues from him, and when he glanced at Garrett, as if demanding more of a show, I rolled my head back and ran my fingers through my hair.

"You know, I think you're right," I said. "I think I did get a bit too much sun. That champagne is going right to my head." Nothing sounded more like a sex call to a man than a proclamation of too much alcohol.

Garrett didn't waste a moment. He jumped up and grabbed my legs. "Lie back. I don't want you passing out."

I did as he said, stretching on the couch. "Hand me an ice cube, will you? I just need to cool down a bit."

Within an instant, Albert was on his feet and looming over me with ice bucket at the ready. Garrett dug into the cold water, found a cube, and brushed it over my parted lips. I closed my eyes and made a show of licking the water from my mouth as he traced the cube lower, over my neck and in a path across my chest and between my breasts.

"Better?" Albert asked.

"Mmm. Getting there."

A hand dug into the bucket, and I opened my eyes to find

Garrett pulling his hand from it. I gasped as water dripped over my stomach before Garrett put the cube to my skin. He dragged it in circles around my belly, causing me to wriggle. The ice melted quickly, leaving a trail of water trickling down my waist.

I flicked my eyes up to Albert. He was practically panting as he watched my husband rubbing ice over my body. I gasped and arched my back, pressing my breasts forward as Garrett traced the cube along the waistline of my suit bottom. And then lower.

He pushed my legs apart, and I let him. It was torture, feeling the cold on my skin, but I tolerated him dragging ice up my thigh. The gasps I let out were real, the biting of my lip to stop myself from moaning was real, and when he grazed over my crotch, the surprise that jerked my eyes open was real.

I let a little laugh out, a nervous sound, as I looked up at Albert. The hunger in his eyes was blatant and, even if I didn't want it to, it pleased me. I wasn't a master seductress—if I were, he wouldn't have figured out what we were up to—so seeing the want in his eyes lit a bit of an unexpected spark in me.

Garrett moved cold fingers along my skin. Up my thigh, again brushing over my bikini bottom just as blatantly as before, and I'll be damned if I wasn't getting off from his touch.

"Cooling down?" Garrett asked.

"Mmm. Not exactly."

The ice shifted, and another series of droplets fell on me.

I kept my eyes closed, letting his touch surprise me. I jolted when the ice cooled my lips.

"Open your mouth," he whispered.

I did, and he slipped the ice in, but I quickly realized it wasn't ice. I was sucking his water-covered finger. I wrapped my tongue around it, sucking the liquid away before he pulled it from my mouth and dragged his hand down my body.

He cupped my breast, and I licked my lips, bit them hard, and let a little smile touch my lips as he tweaked my nipple before moving his hand lower. Down my stomach, over my bathing suit bottom, up one thigh, down the other, then deeper between my legs, stroking once, twice, and then back up.

I was lost in the feel of him when footsteps pulled me from his touch.

"Dinner is served, sir," someone called from what seemed to be a million miles away.

"Damn it," Albert cursed, still standing over me with the ice bucket clutched to his chest. His pants had an obvious bulge.

I smiled. "Oh, it's okay," I told him. "I'm much better now."

Garrett helped me sit, and I realized he too had a hard-on. I might not have asked to be put on display, but seeing these two men want me was a thrill. My heart pounded, and I'd swear disappointment at being interrupted settled over me.

If the steward hadn't interrupted, I had no doubt Garrett

would have pushed my legs apart and shoved ice-cold fingers inside me. And I would have let him. I longed for the orgasm I'd been robbed of, and heat crept up and settled in my cheeks at the thought that I'd so willingly let him get me off in front of Albert.

"Darling?" I asked, my voice coming out a bit sultrier than I'd intended. "Will you please help me with my dress? I don't want to eat in my bathing suit."

Garrett focused on finding my dress in the oversized bag I'd packed, and Albert stood there, staring at me, looking like he had been two seconds from ejaculating in his pants.

Garrett helped me stand, and I lifted my arms above my head, letting him know I expected him to dress me.

I stood there, arms up, hard nipples barely covered, staring at Albert as Garrett pressed his body against my back and eased my dress over my head.

He lowered my arms and wrapped his around me, pulling me back as he kissed my neck. "I'm glad you're feeling better."

"Me too," Albert choked out. He set the bucket down and gestured toward the stairs. "Shall we?"

I looked at Garrett and grinned, both of us knowing I'd more than fulfilled his end of the deal. What he didn't know was that I had enjoyed it as much as they had.

[4]

I slid out of the back of the car as my driver held the door
open, then smiled at the doorman as he bowed slightly and
opened one of two panes of glass for me to walk into an air-
conditioned lobby. The old building seemed to be sculpted
completely of black-and-white marble and glass. Behind the
desk, a man in a crisp black uniform stood and, like the doorman, bowed at the waist.

"Mrs. King," he said.

I lifted a brow at him. Aunt Victoria was expecting me,
but I didn't realize everyone else would be as well.

"Welcome. Ms. Richards is waiting for you."

The man led me to an elevator and pushed a button. The
doors almost immediately opened. We stepped inside, and he
pushed another button. The elevator started, rose, and
stopped smoothly. The doors opened with a quiet ding, and
the man handed me a key.

"Suite 2509. To your right."

One thing my aunt had taught me was to never let

anyone see me doubt myself. So instead of questioning the man, I took the key as if I'd been expecting it, tipped him well, and then stepped out into the plush-carpeted hallway. I turned to the right and waited until the elevator doors closed before looking at the gold key in my hand.

At door 2509, I slipped the key into the lock. My footsteps clinked on the marble floor as I walked through the entryway. I was immediately drawn to the floor-to-ceiling windows. Walking into the living area, I bypassed an L-shaped white sofa with a large square table and went straight to take in the view of the city below.

The view was amazing, as I finally spun to look at the rest of the room, I determined the decor was definitely my aunt's.

A long glass table filled the area to the right of the living room, offering space to seat at least ten for dinner. A square chandelier hung over the length of the table, and recessed lighting shone on contemporary artwork hanging on the walls.

Victoria preferred crisp lines and bright whites. She said it felt clean. This room was practically sanitized, leaving no doubt this was her place.

"You're late." Aunt Victoria walked from the open kitchen with two martinis in her hands. "I call this suite the Bird's Nest because of the view. What do you think?"

Looking back out at the city, I smiled. "This is lovely. Are you moving?"

"No, sweetheart. This is for you."

Turning sharply, I creased my brow. *"Me?"*

She held out a glass. "How many men have you had since your agreement with Garrett?"

I focused on accepting the martini instead of admitting I hadn't. But that wasn't what caused my cheeks to heat. I was recalling the night before when I'd sprawled out on Albert's yacht and let him watch my husband all but molest me.

"That's what I thought. Darling—"

"There are aspects of my life that even you aren't privy to."

"I'm not asking for details."

"What are you asking?"

She took a slow drink from her glass, licked her lips, then gave me a sympathetic look. "Sweetheart, where do you think Garrett takes all his whores? Do you think he spends thousands of dollars renting rooms? That'd be a bit dangerous, don't you think? A married man parading in and out of hotels. How long before someone saw him and realized what he was up to? Additional properties, however... The well-to-do have plenty of those, don't they? And if he were questioned visiting a complex like this, he could say he was visiting a friend."

My heart dropped to my stomach. "I-I never..."

"You never thought about it."

"No." Looking at the drink in my hand, I suddenly felt incredibly betrayed by my husband. Yes, I'd opened the door, but I'd never considered how calculated he'd been walking through it. I'd always pushed the thoughts from my mind, never dwelled on the how or when or where. I spent more time pretending I didn't care than thinking about how much I did.

Facing this bitter truth was hard to swallow, and I had to force my throat to work before I could ask, "Is that what this is? A place to bring men?"

"If that's what you want to use it for, yes, a place to bring men. The staff here is paid very well for their discretion. You aren't the only socialite who needs her own life. Nor is Garrett the only man in the world to need his. Let the staff know when you are coming and who, if anyone, you are expecting, and they'll take care of the rest."

"You think Garrett has a place like this?"

"You don't?" She pressed a cool finger to my chin and lifted my face. "I'm not trying to hurt you, Mara. I'm trying to teach you."

"Well, you don't have to. I already know I married a bastard."

She dropped her hand. "My name is on the deed. Should push ever come to shove between you and Garrett, he'll never be able to pin this place on you. And you'll always have somewhere to go, should you need it. Not that I believe you will. You still have a lot to learn, but you are coming into your own so much more quickly than I did. I'm proud of you, darling."

"For having a failed marriage?"

Victoria cupped my cheek. "You haven't failed. You may not be ready to accept reality just yet, but you've not failed. You've compromised. And what is marriage if not compromise? Come. Let me show you the rest of the suite. It's lovely. Just lovely."

I FROWNED AS I SAT IN MY OFFICE AT KING INC. I'D already scoured our personal accounting records, and nothing stood out. I recognized all our assets. None were hidden. But there, in the report I'd requested from the King Inc. accounting department, were two apartments in a building just blocks from the one my aunt had given me.

I'd only known of one of them—the one where the company put visiting business associates. Keeping an apartment was much nicer than putting long-term guests in a hotel. The second, I realized, was likely where Garrett spent so much of his time. Suddenly his affairs felt like the betrayal I'd been denying for so long. They felt more real. More deceptive.

For years, I'd pretended they were flings. Little moments that meant nothing to him. But he had a rendezvous point, a lovers' loft, a place these other women knew about that I hadn't. Somehow that felt like a lie hidden in his half-truth. Somehow that seemed more personal. Even a little vindictive on his part.

This wasn't Garrett getting physical pleasure elsewhere. This was Garrett giving a part of him—of *us*—to someone else. That cut. That hurt.

That was what my aunt had been warning me about.

Sitting back in my chair, I closed the asset report and let the realization sink in. The cuts to my pride that I'd been ignoring for so long started to sting. My heart started to break. I thought once again about what had happened on the yacht—it seemed I couldn't stop thinking about it. Not only had he sold me out, but I'd let him. I gave in. And I'd enjoyed it. I'd let him manipulate me into seducing Albert, and I'd fucking enjoyed it.

For the first time, I felt Garrett's duplicity. Really felt it. And it hurt.

I had humiliated myself.

And he'd let me. He'd convinced me. He'd fucking negotiated for it.

And I let him!

Walking to the bar in the corner, I filled a glass with scotch two fingers deep and took a long drink.

"A little early for that, isn't it?"

I turned, startled by the voice at the door. Jake Decker eyed the glass in my hand. I too looked at the drink for a moment before toasting him and downing what was left in my glass.

"It's five o'clock somewhere, right?"

"Somewhere. But it's barely after noon here. Are you all right, Mara?"

I eased the glass down and nodded. "I'm just wonderful. Obviously." I closed my eyes and sighed before shaking my head. "Sorry. It's been a trying day already, but I will be all right. Thank you."

He came farther into my office and looked at me with soft amber eyes. He had unique-colored eyes. Why hadn't I noticed that before? All the times we'd talked about business deals and he'd taught me about rowing, I'd looked into his eyes, confidently held his gaze. But I'd never noticed the color.

His cologne, something crisp that reminded me of autumn, seemed fitting for him. I could picture him now, his brown hair blowing in the breeze as he called out orders to his team as they sailed across the bay, like ice sliding across glass.

Ice.

I inhaled deeply as Garrett's cold hands moving over me flashed in my mind, but the image quickly faded as Jake's scent filled my senses. He pushed Garrett's betrayal away, replacing it with the image of him gliding across the water.

I'd been looking at this man for years, but right now, when that image overpowered Garrett... That was the first time I'd ever really *seen* Jake.

He was handsome as hell. Brown wavy hair, a long but straight nose, and full lips that he'd brushed across my cheek more times than I could count.

I swallowed and lowered my gaze when he smirked. I'd been staring. I silently cursed myself, though I wasn't sure why—for believing in Garrett, for refusing to see the truth, or for looking so wantonly at Jake. I was angry and bitter and drinking on an empty stomach. None of those presented the right time to notice how attractive a business partner was.

Turning away from him, I refilled my glass.

He closed the distance between us. "You look troubled," he said, sounding genuinely concerned. "Anything I can help with?"

"Not unless you can tell me why I'm such a fool."

His brow creased, and I closed my eyes, giving my head a shake.

"Sorry. That came out without thinking."

"What happened?"

"Nothing."

He took my hand between his and gently tugged until I looked at him. "You're upset. Why?"

He brushed his thumb over the back of my hand, and I very nearly sagged into him. The show of concern, slight as it was, was exactly what I needed—someone to care.

I drew a breath, prepared to tell him what a mess I'd gotten myself into, but before I could speak, Garrett strolled in.

I pulled my hand from Jake's.

"Sorry to intrude," Garrett said, coming toward us.

Jake held my gaze for a second longer before turning to my husband. "You're not intruding. I was just saying hello while I waited for your call to end."

Garrett looked at me, and there was something unsettling in his eyes. "It's ended. If you're ready, we can dive into those reports now," he said to Jake, though he was staring at me. Garrett smiled, and I recognized the venom in his eyes. I'd seen it before he struck associates before. Only this time, it was directed at me. "Let's take this to my office," he said, "so we don't bore my wife."

Jake eyed me for a moment. "It was lovely to see you, Mara."

"You as well."

Jake left, and Garrett moved close. I was expecting him to call me on the tension between Jake and me, but he said, "I just got a call from accounting. You pulled our asset records?"

"Yes."

"Care to tell me why?"

"Because I wanted to."

"What are you looking for, Mara?"

I touched his collar as if to straighten the fold, even though that was unnecessary. He looked impeccable, as always, but staring into his eyes was unsettling, and the biggest mistake one could make with Garrett King was letting him know he'd unnerved them.

"I just like to keep track of where we stand, darling. Nothing to concern yourself about."

He gripped my hand, pulling it from his collar. "The next time you want to keep track of where we stand, let me know, and I'll tell you."

I looked into his eyes again, my resolve restored. "I'm the vice president, Garrett. I'm allowed to review company records."

"We have accountants for that, Mara. Leave it to them, hmm?"

I tugged at his hand before he could turn away. I wasn't usually so forward with him. I usually fell back when he pushed the slightest bit. I didn't want to fall back this time.

"This is my company, too. I have just as much invested in our assets as you do. Don't forget that."

He pulled his hand away. "I haven't."

I watched him leave, then glanced at the fiscal report again. After taking a deep, cleansing breath, I drank down the contents of my glass as I replayed every word my aunt had ever said to me, finally hearing them.

Garrett King was a manipulative, selfish bastard, and I was done pretending I was somehow immune to being used by him.

IF I HAD GIRLFRIENDS, THIS WOULD HAVE BEEN ONE OF those nights where we sat around a table in a bar drinking martinis and bitching about how horrible our lives were.

I didn't have girlfriends.

Women in my social circle were threatened by me. Sure, they smiled and chatted politely when we were attending events, but that was hardly the kind of friendship where I could divulge my problems. No. One word about my agreement with Garrett or all but getting fingered in front of Albert Carter to one of those selfish bitches, and they'd all know before I finished getting the words out.

And since I wasn't in the mood to listen to Aunt Victoria's smug lecturing, I chose to sit in the corner of an upscale bar by myself, pretending it didn't hurt to be drinking alone. Pretending I wasn't so alone.

"There it is again."

I looked up, pulled from my miserable thoughts, and offered Jake as much of a smile as I could manage. "What are you doing here so late?"

"I could ask you the same."

I swallowed and looked at my nearly empty glass. I was there because my husband was out with his wife. How was that for irony? I almost let the words slip, but I didn't. If Jake didn't know what his wife was up to, I wasn't going to be the one to break his heart.

He sat uninvited and leaned on the table. The concern in his eyes was there for all to see as he looked at me.

"You don't have to talk. I'm fine with silence. I'm not fine leaving you sitting here alone when you look so sad."

I managed a slight tilt to my lips. "Do I look sad?"

"You look devastated."

I drew a slow breath as a waiter stopped at the table.

Jake ordered two of whatever I was having, and the waiter darted off to grab dirty martinis.

"Have you ever known the truth about someone and convinced yourself that you were wrong? Or that somehow you were special to them? Knowing deep down that you weren't?"

He lowered his gaze.

I realized right then he was perfectly aware of what Garrett and Megan were up to.

I inhaled again. "I've known for years what he is like. What he does behind my back. I don't know why I've suddenly let it get to me."

"Because Megan doesn't play by the rules. She never has."

"We made love the other night after the gala. She called. He went to her. He left my bed to go to hers." I downed the last of what was in my glass.

"I'm sorry."

"Why? What did you do to be sorry about?"

He looked at me and smirked. "She was telling me how he was much better to her than I could ever be. I told her she should go to him, then. She apparently did."

I laughed softly. "He chose to leave me alone. That's on him, not you."

He leaned back as our fresh drinks were set in front of us. We both took sips, ignoring the awkward silence.

Finally, I asked what had been nagging me since that night. "So you have an agreement? An open marriage?"

"I guess that's what you could call it. Her father invested in my company. I don't need his money now, of course, but I wouldn't be where I am if it hadn't been for her family. I guess I tolerate her out of obligation."

I nodded. "Congratulations on having a realistic outlook. I'm just now pulling my head out of the sand."

"The light of day can be harsh, can't it?"

"Very much so." I took another long drink.

"How many of those have you had?"

I couldn't recall. Too many, I knew, but I didn't care. "Does it matter?"

He smiled slyly. "I guess that depends."

"On?"

"On how shitty you want to feel tomorrow." He waved our waiter over. "Two clean glasses and a pitcher of water, please." Once the man disappeared, Jake leaned on the table again. "It's the dehydration from the alcohol that does you in. We'll get some water in you before sending you home."

I gave him a lazy smile. "That's sweet. Thanks, Jake."

Silence again found us until the waiter returned and filled two water glasses. I swapped my martini for the gentler liquid. "How are the plans going for the new development?"

"Work talk? Really?"

I laughed when he did. "Well, I don't want to talk about how our spouses are probably fucking right now, do you?"

His smile faltered a bit. "No. I don't want to talk about that."

"What else is there for us to discuss?"

He leaned closer. "Have you ever cheated on Garrett?"

My heart rolled over in my chest, and I instantly began to tremble inside, but I didn't hesitate in answering. "No. Have you cheated on Megan?"

"No. But I've considered it. Many times."

"Why haven't you followed through?"

He pondered for a moment. "Because even though part of me loathes her for her lack of morals, I don't blame her. I work long hours. I travel. I drag her to parties and dinners and boring social events to further my career. She has no career. She has nothing."

"That's no excuse to fuck around," I said quietly.

He grinned. "You're an idealist, Mara. I like that about you. I like that you still believe in something beyond making a dollar."

"Do I?" I asked before I could filter my response.

He was clearly as surprised by my answer as I was. But once it was there, it was there, and I was buzzed enough to not care that I shouldn't share.

"I agreed to an open marriage because I wanted financial security, Jake. I don't want my husband cheating on me. It hurts. It breaks my heart. It makes me wonder what my son will think of me when he gets old enough to understand that I turn a blind eye to my husband's betrayals. What kind of example are we setting for Adam? He'll be just like Garrett when he gets married. He'll lie to his wife, cheat on her, and expect her to be okay with it because I pretend that I'm okay with it. I don't want that for him. Or for his future wife."

"You can end it," he said.

I wasn't sure if he meant my marriage or the agreement we had. Either way, I knew I couldn't. I couldn't walk away from Garrett any more than I could force him to keep his dick in his pants. This was a no-win situation of my own making.

I should have walked away six years ago. Now, I didn't have a leg to stand on. I knew of his infidelity. Hell, I'd signed a contract agreeing to it. And I'd agreed I wouldn't divorce him unless one of his affairs came to light. I was stuck, and I'd done it to myself.

I shook my head, instantly regretting it. The martinis were getting to me. Rolling my shoulders, I drew a deep breath. "I'd lose everything. You know I would."

He didn't deny it. Instead, he finished his martini, then gulped down some water. Sighing heavily, he turned the glass one way, then the other. "Can I ask you something?"

"Why not?"

He blushed a bit, and I couldn't help the drunken giggle that slipped from my throat.

"Oh, shit," I said with a moan. "What are you thinking?"

"I'm thinking about you in that damn dress at the art gala. Actually, I haven't stopped thinking about you in that damn dress. What was that about? I've never seen you dress like that before."

I laughed, even though I could feel the heat in my face. "Garrett." I sighed and giggled again. "Okay, so he bought me that dress when we were away for our anniversary last year. I don't have to tell you why."

"My imagination is running wild already."

Another stupid little laugh left me. "Anyway, when I got out of the shower before the gala, he had that dress laid out for me even though I had bought a dress. He convinced me to wear it. He said it was for him. Gave me this whole seduction bit. So even though I hated it, I wore it." My amusement faded as feelings of being used returned. "He was testing Albert."

"Testing Albert?"

"Garrett wants Albert distracted so he can close a few more deals. And he wanted to see if my tits in his face would do the trick."

"Oh, it did. I can tell you that."

I nodded. "Yeah. I know. Believe me, I know."

"It's just business, Mara," he said softly, as if using a soothing tone would take the shame from what I'd been asked.

"I'm quite certain most men wouldn't resort to borderline prostitution of their wives for a business deal."

"You'd be surprised." He sighed. "This is the world we are in. Our hearts, our souls, our bodies, even our spouses are all commodities that can be tossed on the table when the need arises."

"It shouldn't be that way, Jake."

"There's that idealism again." He reached out and tucked a strand of hair behind my ear. "I'm sorry, Mara, but it *is* that way. That's the harsh reality of high-stakes business. Be happy you've made it this long without falling victim to the games."

I looked around the bar. Though it was a work night, the dark space was full. Booths were tucked into walls, almost hidden to ensure the privacy of the occupants. Some were clearly networking, others were cuddled up on dates—maybe some of them were even out with the person they were supposed to be with.

Jake and I sat at a small table in the back, as close to being in the dark as I could get when I sought out a table. At first it was because I didn't want to be seen drinking alone. Now I was glad because I didn't want to be seen drinking with Jake.

And because I wanted to cry, but it seemed that I'd lost the ability years ago. I was so sad inside. Sad not only for me but for every person I'd surrounded myself with who really felt that life was meant to be what Jake was describing. Did they really think we were there just to make a few bucks, no matter the personal cost?

Yes. They did. And I'd just never felt it until now. Until I realized I was one of *them*. I sold myself for money. For security. And had continued to do so all these years.

"Are you okay?" Jake asked.

I swallowed and nodded. "How far do I go with this?"

"With what?"

"With Albert. How far do I go before it's too far? How much of myself do I sacrifice before I've sacrificed too much? Do I sleep with him? Spend weekends away with him? Pretend I care about him? Where's the line, Jake?"

"I guess the line is where you draw it." He took another

drink, glanced around, and then took my hand. I didn't pull away as he looked at me. "You want my advice? Really?"

"Yes."

"You are right. If you walked away from him, he would destroy you. Because he's a businessman. A damn good one, and one who refuses to lose. Stop thinking about Garrett as your husband and start thinking about him as your business partner. He's your partner, Mara. Just in different ways than other business partners. Everything is a deal to him. Your marriage was a deal to him from the day you said *I do*. You are smart and beautiful. You bring a lot to the table. That's why he married you. Not because he loves you—which I believe he does—but because marrying you was a good business decision."

God, he sounded just like Victoria.

"How romantic," I said flatly.

"There's no room for romance in this world, Mara. Love is a lie. Friendships are as fake as most women's breasts."

I laughed at his analogy.

Jake grinned. "Those are some hard truths you need to hear." His smile faded a touch. "I'm sorry you're hurting. I'm sorry my wife has a hand in that. But the truth, Mara, the reality, is that this is your life. This is how your marriage has been and will continue to be. The only thing you can change is how you deal with it."

I sighed as I sat back. My head was spinning, and not just from the alcohol. He was right. Aunt Victoria was right. It was time to stop clinging to hope. I had made myself a very uncomfortable bed. It was time I learned how to lie in it.

[5]

I SMILED as Adam landed at the bottom of the slide with a thud—butt-first right into the dirt. He didn't give the rough ending to the ride a second thought. He simply laughed, jumped up, and ran to the ladder to do it again.

"He's enjoying himself." Michael Redmond, Albert's new VP, sat next to me on the bench. His son headed straight for the same slide Adam had been going down for the last half hour.

"He would do that all day if I let him," I said.

"If he's anything like Will, you should let him. That boy has an unlimited supply of energy."

"Adam does too. It's the age. I think. I *hope*. I can't imagine him being this wound up when he's a teen."

"God help us all, right?"

I glanced at him as he watched Will climbing up right behind Adam. "It's ten a.m. on a Wednesday. Shouldn't you be in a board meeting or something?"

"Shouldn't you?"

"I keep a lighter workload during the day so I can be Mom first. I spend most evenings catching up."

He watched his son go down the slide before looking at me. "I always take Wednesday morning off during the summer to be Dad."

I sat back a bit. Garrett wouldn't dream of taking a day off for family time. That was what weekends were for, he'd told me once when I made the suggestion. Though his weekends were just as full of meetings.

"That's sweet."

A sadness touched his eyes, and his smile faded.

I wanted to comfort him. I didn't have to ask where his mind had gone. His wife had been gone for just a year. I still had moments of unexpected heartache for my loss, and I'd been without my parents much longer than I'd been with them.

Michael sighed and seemed to put his sorrow back in its box. "We only have each other now."

I was tempted to ask about his wife, but I didn't know him well enough to venture so deeply into personal territory. Instead, I looked at the boys again.

"I was thirteen when I lost my parents in a car accident. I have few memories of my childhood without them. It's good that he knows you. That you're there. That's important."

"And you're here for your son. I'm sorry. I don't know his name."

"Adam. The moment I found out I was pregnant, I realized my number-one role would be mother."

"How does Garrett feel coming in second to that guy?"

"Did you resent your son being first in your wife's life? Assuming he was."

He shook his head. "No, I didn't resent him."

"So why would Garrett?"

He didn't answer, and I smirked.

"Oh, the rumor mills have been filling your head already," I said. "That didn't take long. You only joined Carter Enterprises a little over two months ago."

"I need to know my competitors."

"That's good business sense. But what does my marriage have to do with Carter Enterprises?"

"I didn't say that it did, Mrs. King."

"Mara. Please."

He nodded. "Michael."

I turned on the bench enough to fully take in his profile. If I had to guess, I'd pin him down for having Mediterranean heritage. There was a deep, darker tint to his skin tone, and his aquiline nose was softened by strong cheekbones.

He glanced at me. Though his eyes were nearly black, I saw a flash of uncertainty there before he turned his attention away again.

"Crescent City has many lovely parks," I said, "and there are seven days in a week, each day with twenty-four hours. I'm suddenly a bit suspicious that you happen to be at this particular park for a playdate with your son during this particular hour on this particular day. Tell me I'm being paranoid, Michael."

His only response was to watch his son go down the slide.

I leaned forward and blocked his view. "Are you actually

sitting next to me at the park watching our boys play in some misguided attempt to get something to use against my husband?"

He laughed softly. "Of course not."

"Good. Because my relationship with my husband is personal. What we do and how we do it does not concern you or anyone else."

He lowered his face for a moment. No, he wasn't nearly as confident as he was trying to portray. But then he seemed to physically steel himself for what he said next.

"Jake Decker might feel differently about that."

And his arrow hit the target. So everyone *did* know about Garrett's affair with Megan.

I didn't flinch, however. I remained steady. I even smiled. "How would you know what Mr. Decker feels?"

"Albert Carter may be blinded by years of friendship with your husband, Mrs. King—"

"I asked you to call me Mara."

"—but I'm not," he finished as if I hadn't interrupted. "I see what King Inc. and JD Construction are doing. I see how you are trying to corner the market and steal business from Carter Enterprises." He met my gaze. "I'm not going to idly stand by and watch that happen."

"Michael," I said softly, "companies often join forces to take out a weaker competitor. And, like it or not, Carter *is* the weaker competitor. Business is business. Don't take it personally."

"And your husband cheating on you. Do you not take that personally?"

I inhaled slowly but kept my sweet smile firmly in place. "I find your approach distasteful."

He grinned. "My approach."

"You brought up my husband's affair with Megan Decker, I assume, in hopes that I'd be upset enough to confront my husband and demand he end things with that woman. And, by proxy, end our business deal with her husband in an attempt to sabotage *our* attempt at overtaking your company. Am I wrong?"

He didn't respond.

Anger ignited in me. Anger fueled by humiliation at being confronted over Garrett's behavior. My fixed smile fell as I glared at the son of a bitch sitting next to me.

"Did it ever occur to you that had you succeeded, had I not known about my husband and Mrs. Decker, that you could have ended my marriage? You could have torn that little boy's world apart." I pointed toward where Adam was laughing as he chased Will, and Michael's smug grin fell to a look of confusion. "Is ending life as *he* knows it really worth what you would have accomplished? Which would have only been a temporary setback in King Incorporated's intent to overtake the market. And, Mr. Redmond, in case you aren't aware, half a dozen other companies are frothing at the mouth to take Carter out of the game. Everyone wants to get into property development these days, and the business is getting more and more cutthroat, as you have just proven. If you want to save your company, do so by making your company stronger, not by destroying an innocent child's life."

"Mrs. Mara," he called as I stood.

I faced him.

He looked truly ashamed. "I'm sorry. I didn't think."

"You didn't think about the consequences, or you didn't think I'd be strong enough to call you on your bullshit?"

"Both, I guess."

"Typical man."

"Yes. I suppose I am."

I admired his honesty if nothing else, but Garrett had run my tolerance for this kind of behavior thin.

"You aren't the first man to underestimate me, and I doubt you'll be the last, so let me make something perfectly clear to you, Mr. Redmond." Leaning close, I met his gaze, my nose just inches from his, making certain he knew how serious I was. "If you ever come after me on a personal level again, I'll destroy everything you have before you even know I've taken aim at you."

My voice was so cold, I even scared myself a little. Aunt Victoria would be proud.

Standing, I turned toward the boys as Will landed on top of Adam at the bottom of the slide, causing them both to laugh.

"Adam! Time to go!" I gestured for him to come on when he whined in response. Facing Michael, I met his gaze. "It was lovely chatting with you, Mr. Redmond."

Taking Adam's hand, I walked away without looking back.

I tried to wipe my confrontation with Michael Redmond from my mind, but I was pissed as hell that

Megan's idiotic behavior had exposed my little marital secret. He'd cut open a wound that hadn't even begun to heal, and the fact that I had to sit across from the bitch was testing every lesson Aunt Victoria had drilled into my head about social behavior. Add in that Megan hadn't stopped making googly eyes at Garrett since we sat down, and I was a lit fuse waiting to explode.

What a stupid game we were all playing, pretending we didn't know Garrett and Megan were sleeping together. Megan could barely stop herself from crawling over the table and into Garrett's lap. Jake had stopped looking like he cared half a bottle of wine ago. Garrett simply ignored the woman and started talking to Jake and me as if Megan weren't there, which was making her act even more desperate. If she leaned over any more in her attempt to gain Garrett's attention, her tits were going to spill into her pasta.

I have to admit, my composure was slipping as I finished my second—or was it my third?—glass of wine.

I couldn't blame Garrett completely. He wasn't doing anything to encourage her behavior. Other than fucking her behind closed doors. She was the idiot who didn't seem to understand the rules. But she was about to understand that turnabout was fair play.

Pushing my plate back a few inches, I mimicked her position—leaning forward, breasts pushed up, and eyelashes batting. It took a moment, but the first time Jake glanced my way to include me in the conversation, he noticed my equally as impressive cleavage displayed on the table.

He more than noticed. He stuttered a bit before clearing his throat and forcing his gaze back to Garrett.

Just like little Miss Megan, I wasn't giving up that easy. Unlike Megan, I had a valid in to the conversation, and good manners demanded Jake look at me when I was speaking. And he couldn't look at me without his eyes dipping lower.

I smiled innocently as I spoke, lightly running my fingers across my bare chest—casually playing with the heart-shaped pendant dangling low and tracing my exposed cleavage.

It wasn't long before Garrett also noticed and Jake no longer had to split his attention—they were both focused on my tits, and Megan might as well have not even been there. This wasn't typical behavior for me, so Garrett was instantly intrigued. And Jake? Poor Jake had tipped his hand about the night at the art gala. He liked what he saw then, and he was certainly enjoying the view now.

With them both spending more time looking at my chest than each other, I focused on taking deep breaths, innocently brushing my fingertips over peaked nipples and occasionally squeezing my breasts together for an extra boost.

Finally, Megan called for an end to dinner. I rose and gave her a fake smile and a kiss on the cheek, but when it came time to say goodnight to Jake, I rested my hands on his chest, and his fell to my hips.

I stepped much too close for our farewell to be proper, but I just needed to confirm my suspicion. I subtly rubbed my body against his, and he took a sharp breath as his erection connected with my lower stomach. And it was an impressive erection at that.

His fingers tightened on my hips, but he didn't take advantage of the moment to pull me closer to him. No. I was the one who did that. Pressing into him, leaving no doubt that I had felt his reaction to the show I'd put on.

"I'm happy to see you too," I whispered in his ear.

He laughed softly.

I leaned back, smiling sweetly. "Goodnight, Jake."

"Not until she gets done pitching a fit."

I gave him a forced pout. "Sorry."

He chuckled. "It was worth it."

When I finally stepped away from him, his wife was glaring, and my husband was looking bored.

Once settled in the car, I glanced at Garrett. "So much for putting Megan in her place, hmm?"

"The evening started off fine. She had too much wine, that's all. You didn't act any better. What the hell was that?"

"If she gets to shove her tits in your face, I get to shove mine in Jake's."

"That's not like you."

I swallowed at his observation. He was right. That wasn't like me. Nor was nearly coming on a yacht because my husband made a business deal.

"He wants you," Garrett said, pulling me from my thoughts. "He would have eaten dessert off your chest if you'd let him."

"Interesting idea. Maybe next time? You and Megan can fuck during the entrée. I'll take Jake for dessert. We can all have drinks afterward."

He didn't answer, and I didn't let on how much the idea of fucking Jake was starting to appeal to me. Just a few weeks ago, I hadn't ever considered utilizing our marital agreement. Since then, my husband had used my body to close a deal, I'd discovered he had a lover's nest, and I'd gotten my own. It seemed I was dipping my toes in, and the water was warm and inviting.

"This is your last chance to get her under control, Garrett," I warned. "Or I will do it for you. Anyone looking could see what was happening."

He scoffed. "And they couldn't see Jake drooling over the way you were fondling your tits for him?"

I glanced at him, far from chastised by his observation. "I saw Michael Redmond earlier today. He tried to throw your affair with her in my face."

"What?"

"He saw through her at the gala. And anyone in the restaurant tonight likely saw through it too. Do you want to lose everything, Garrett? Over *her*?"

He looked straight ahead, but I could see the muscles of his jaw working. "When did this happen?"

"I saw him at the park with his son."

"And why didn't you tell me?"

"Because I handled it."

"How so?"

"I let him know that his attempt at breaking up our business agreement with Jake by hurting me was in poor taste."

A wry laugh left him. "Poor taste?"

"Do you disagree?"

"I'll kill him."

"Hmm. To defend my honor or your image?"

He finally looked at me again. "No one hurts my wife, Mara. No one."

"Except for you," I responded and turned away.

The rest of the ride was spent in tense silence. We rarely fought, but something I couldn't quite explain was shifting inside me. I was hardening. Perhaps finding out he kept a separate living space from our home hurt more than I realized. Or watching Megan Decker so carelessly want my husband was that painful. Or maybe I had finally accepted that we would never have the marriage I was so determined to have when I'd married him.

Perhaps all of the above.

We didn't speak as we went upstairs. As always, I checked on Adam before entering our bedroom to change. Garrett removed his cufflinks, and I tugged my jewelry free, but neither of us spoke. The ringing of his phone sliced through the quiet like a blade. He tried to keep his voice low, but there was no need. I knew it was Megan. And I knew Garrett would leave.

"I'll sleep in another room," he said on his way to the bedroom door.

I exhaled as I watched his reflection in the mirror leaving me for another. "I think it's time for separate bedrooms. You certainly spend more nights out of our bed than in it these days."

He turned around, caught my gaze in the mirror for several pounding heartbeats, then walked away without a word.

I swallowed the pain, the last bit of hurt I was going to allow him to inflict upon me. Closing my eyes, I took a deep breath before opening my purse and removing my phone. I debated for only a moment before scrolling through my contacts, then for one more moment before dialing.

"Mara King." Jake said my name like he was ordering a drink he knew he shouldn't have. "I'm guessing your call means your other half has disappeared as well."

"Megan's gone?"

"Apparently one of her girlfriends is terribly ill. And Garrett?"

"Oh, I didn't ask for an excuse, and he didn't offer one. I don't care to hear his lies any longer." I closed my eyes and swallowed. There was no going back after I said the words about to leave my mouth. "Pity is, I don't want to be alone. Would you like to meet me for a drink, Jake?"

More silence.

Regret stirred low in my belly, mixing with the fear of rejection.

"Yes," he finally said. "I'd like that. I'd like that very much. Do you have someplace in mind?"

I held my breath, settling my nerves, before rattling off the address of my newly acquired suite.

[6]

I DOWNED one scotch before Jake even arrived and had just refilled my glass when a knock came from the other side of the door. I exhaled slowly, imagined Garrett fucking Megan at that very moment, and straightened my shoulders.

I was done waiting for something I'd never have. I was done being second place in my husband's life, in his bed. I walked to the door, pushing down any sense of regret I had for being where I was and what was likely to happen.

Jake smiled as I opened it. His smile was sweet. Warm like his kind eyes. And it chipped away another bit of regret that was lingering.

"Good evening, Mrs. King," he said in a low, smooth voice that made my nerves dance like water on a hot griddle.

I tilted my head and looked up at him with doe eyes. "Good evening, Mr. Decker. Please come in."

I led him into the living area and poured him a drink. Like I had been the first time I'd visited the penthouse, he was immediately drawn to the floor-to-ceiling windows. I'd drawn the sheer curtains and dimmed the lights, providing a touch of privacy from the outside world, but the lights outside twinkled brightly, mesmerizing him as they had me.

I watched him for a few moments before crossing the room to him, my heels on the tiles the only sound until I stopped beside him.

He accepted the glass I offered. "I admit I was surprised you called."

I was tempted to confess that I had shocked myself, but I didn't want to let him see a bit of insecurity in me. Somehow, I felt he'd think less of me if he knew I was quaking inside.

"How long have you known me, Jake?"

"Five years, I think."

"Long enough to consider me a friend, I hope."

"Sure."

I casually lifted one shoulder and let it drop. "What's so surprising about one friend inviting another for a drink?"

He smiled, and some of the tension seemed to leave his face. "You're right. Of course you're right. Here's to friends having drinks." He clinked his glass to mine and held my gaze as we both took a drink. "Megan wanted to rip your hair out tonight."

"I've wanted to rip her hair out since she started throwing herself at my husband in front of my face."

"How long have they been fucking?"

I drew a breath. "Three months at the most, I'd say. While Garrett enjoys the chase and the win, he quickly tires of the prize. He wants to have his way with her until she bores him. And, in case you haven't noticed, he's getting very bored."

"And when you bore him?"

I chuckled. "I already do. Why do you think he takes all these lovers? But I'm not so easily tossed aside." I moved closer and tilted my head back to look up at him. "I don't want to talk about them."

"Well. This doesn't seem like the right setting for a business chat, and I'm not sure what else we have in common."

"Clearly we need to get to know each other better."

"What would you like to know?"

"Hmm... Have you ever fantasized about me?"

He laughed softly, clearly shocked by my question. "A few times."

I pouted dramatically. "Only a few?"

"Have you ever fantasized about me?"

I didn't want to admit that I'd been too enraptured by my cheating husband until a few days ago to even notice him. I'm sure he was playing the same game. If he'd taken an interest in me before we both got fed up with Megan, I hadn't noticed. I suspected his attraction to me was as new to him as mine was to him.

So instead of being honest, I whispered, "Sometimes all I can think about is the different ways I want you to fuck me."

He exhaled slowly. "I've never cheated on my wife."

Stroking his cheek, I gave him a sympathetic smile. "I don't think it's cheating when they are doing the very same thing at the very same moment, do you?"

Hurt flashed his eyes but was quickly replaced by a kind of determination. "You're a very smart woman, Mara King."

"It's okay if you don't want to do this, Jake. Leave right now, and we'll pretend we were never here."

"I don't want to leave." He covered my hand with his and turned his head to lightly kiss my palm. "The way I was looking at you tonight wasn't just because of Megan. You are easily one of the most beautiful women I know. Tonight isn't the first time I've noticed that. I want to be here. With you. I just need a minute to wrap my head around this."

I didn't blame him. I'd been doing the very same thing when he'd arrived. Lowering my hand, I took his and led him to the white straight-back chairs facing the windows.

"Sit."

He did, and I flipped off the light switch before walking to the window to look over the city. "Beautiful, isn't it?"

"Yes."

"This place was a gift from my aunt. You've met her."

He laughed quietly. "Yes. She's...bold."

"Yes, she is. I went to live with her when I was a teenager. She decided it was up to her to teach me the ways of the world. She still is. She gave me this place when I refused to accept him for what he is. A liar and a cheat who never goes without a piece of ass on the side." I looked at Jake. Though the room was dark, the city lights and the moon illuminated his profile enough for me to see him contemplating my words. "I spent an awful lot of time pretending I wasn't lonely while he was leaving me alone night after night. I'm tired of pretending, Jake. I give and I give, and he takes and he takes, and I'm ready to get something in return."

"What do you want in return, Mara?"

"To feel appreciated. And wanted."

The way he lowered his gaze and looked at his glass

before taking a drink, I suspected I'd hit a nerve. "Do you feel appreciated, Jake? Do you feel wanted?"

"No."

"Do you want to?"

He thought before nodding. "That'd be nice."

I never dropped to my knees for a man—another life lesson from my aunt—but I made an exception for Jake and eased down in front of him. Taking his glass, I set it along with mine on the little table between the chairs. Putting my hands to his knees, I spread his legs enough to make room for me to lean up. Moving my hands to his face, I brushed my thumbs over his cheeks as I looked into his eyes.

Though it was too dark to make out the color now, I remembered the curious amber of them from the day in the office when he'd found me so distraught, the compassion when he'd sat with me in the bar, and the heat that had radiated from them earlier in the night as I teased him from across the table.

"It isn't too late," I whispered. "We can stop this before it starts. Leave. Pretend we were never here. Go home. Go back to empty houses, empty beds. Empty marriages. Or we can take this step, and maybe for a little while, we could feel a little less lonely. I can make you feel like the most cherished man in the world." I brushed my hands through his hair. "All I want in return is to feel like a cherished woman. When we're alone like this, I want to forget the rest of the world exists. I want to be your everything, just for a while, and I'll make you mine. Would you like that, Jake?"

My heart started pounding. My chest tightened. My nerves tingled as he stared at me. I'd never imagined I'd put myself in this position, but really, it was only a matter of time. Garrett had been hurting me for years. I needed to start tending to the wounds before my soul bled out, and if that meant getting what I needed from another man, then it was time to do so. I just hoped that man would be Jake Decker. Otherwise, I'd just made a fool of myself.

Finally, he nodded. "I'd like that very much, Mara."

My heart rolled in my chest. I wasn't sure if it was excitement, relief, or fear. Maybe it was all of them. I had to remind myself to breathe.

"What we do here," I said, "stays here. I'm not in this for bragging rights."

"Nor am I."

"I doubt either of them would care, but even so, this is our secret. Promise me you won't tell them."

He nodded his agreement before leaning forward. He stopped, just a breath from kissing me. Swallowing what was left of my hesitance, I closed the slight gap between us and pressed my mouth to his. He dug his hand into my hair and held me as he deepened the contact. I didn't know where the courage came from, but some part of me seemed to come unleashed as I finally turned the tables on Garrett.

I suddenly felt alive. Sexy. Wanted. And, more importantly, *in control*.

Breaking the kiss, I stared into Jake's eyes as I stood. I took his hand and led him to the bedroom. The walls were the same floor-to-ceiling windows, but these had tinting that dimmed the view but didn't block the lights completely. We would still be able to look down on the city if we wanted to. I didn't. Not this time. This time, I led him to the bed. Stopping before taking the first of two wide steps that led to the king-size bed.

Like the rest of the Bird's Nest, this room was so crisp and clean, it nearly felt sanitized. I'd have to remember to add some softer touches. This was too much like a hotel room for my liking—cold and impersonal. If I was going to take a lover to this bedroom, I'd like it to have a bit more warmth than the white bed, gray walls, and silver accessories had to offer. But this room would do for tonight. It would definitely do.

Turning, I held Jake's gaze as I gripped the zipper on my skin-tight navy-blue dress and eased it down. Moments later, the material was at my feet, leaving me in nothing but a pair of dangerously high nude-colored heels.

His shocked gaze slowly moved over me. Down then back up again.

"Have you been naked under that dress all night?"

I grinned. "One less obstacle to overcome."

He swallowed hard enough for me to hear him. "That's very considerate."

"Hmm. I try." I eased down on the bed, then leaned back and parted my legs, revealing my neatly trimmed self to him. I was trying to find the words to tell him what I wanted, but I didn't have to. He crossed the room and ran his hands over my legs as he dropped to his knees before me.

I liked that. It evened the score. I'd been on my knees just a few minutes ago. Though my reasoning hadn't been quite as satisfying.

He looked at me, laid out before him like a treat. He ran

his hands lightly over my thighs up my stomach, cupped my breasts, and rolled my nipples.

"I nearly climbed across the table tonight. You have no idea how much I wanted to touch you."

I drew a deep breath and let it out slowly. "You have no idea how much I wanted you to touch me." I chuckled as I looked at him. "I was tempted to stretch my leg under the table and press my foot against your dick. Just to see what you'd have done."

"I probably would have come in my pants. My God. Seeing you like this..." He inhaled and ran his hands back down my stomach. "I don't know where to start."

"Put your mouth on me."

He smiled as if I'd given him the permission he'd been wanting. He licked the length of my thigh to my center and inhaled deeply.

"You smell so good," he muttered. "Better than I'd fantasized." He slid his hands under my ass and pulled me closer to the edge of the bed. "Brace yourself, sweetheart. I've been wanting this for a long time. It may be a while before I get enough."

I gasped as he dove into me. He didn't bother warming me up to his assault, he pressed his tongue between my labia and licked a long stroke from hole to clit before gently sinking his teeth into the nub, causing me to gasp and involuntarily jolt.

He tightened his hold on my ass to keep me where he wanted me. The added pressure of him lifting me as he pushed his mouth in was heaven. I moaned a deep and primal sound. Jesus, his mouth felt good on me, warm and soft, but hard at the same time. He licked, nipped, sucked, and moaned in a rhythm that had my body clenching and singing and begging.

He ate me with much more enthusiasm than Garrett ever had. Jake was like a starving man, getting as much of me as he could. His excitement was contagious. I gripped his hair and pushed him down as I started grinding up into him, unable to stop myself. He didn't seem to mind. He actually increased his pace—alternating between dragging his tongue over me and sucking.

"Put your fingers in me," I ordered.

He complied—two, possibly three, fingers pushed inside, pumping as his tongue settled on my clit. He flicked, licked, nipped, flicked again. And bit one more time, just a bit harder.

Then my climax hit. Sweet fucking God, did it hit. I closed my eyes so tightly, I saw stars and clenched my teeth to stop from screaming, but a desperate groan ripped from me anyway.

I had just remembered to breathe when Jake's mouth found mine. I kissed him hard as we both worked to remove his clothing. Finally, he stood naked, and I took in his body. He was gorgeous. All those years of rowing showed in every ripple under his skin.

His muscles were defined, and I licked my lips as I lowered my gaze to the cock standing up, waiting for me. I couldn't wait to feel him inside me, but I needed just another minute of looking at the masterpiece before me.

"I don't know that I could ever get enough of looking at

you. You're perfect," I whispered as he pulled a condom out of his pants pocket.

He grinned at me as he sheathed his cock. "How do you want it?"

Before Garrett, I'd only had one lover, and that was the clumsy and awkward sex of the innocent. Not the hot, steamy sex of a woman finally taking control. This was my moment. My coming of age, in many ways. Standing, I turned and put one knee on the bed as I glanced over my shoulder at him.

"Hard. I want you to fuck me hard."

He exhaled slowly as he situated behind me. Reaching between my legs, I guided him into me. The first few pumps were slow as our bodies introduced themselves to each other. I stretched to accommodate his girth, then he started moving faster. I rubbed my clit as he thrust harder and harder with each move, igniting yet another fire inside me.

Grinding my teeth as my muscles tightened, I did my best not to scream, but fuck, my mind was blowing apart. He felt so damn good as he shoved himself deep inside my body. And part of me, vindictive as it was, couldn't help but feel that every stroke Jake made was a proverbial slap in the face to my husband.

Garrett could have Megan. Dear God, he could have her whenever he wanted as long as I got this in return. I gasped when Jake gripped my hips and shoved his dick so deep it hurt, but the pain and surprise only lasted a moment before pleasure took over again.

"Just like that," I demanded. "Fuck me just like that."

And he did, and that moment of pain hit again, but quickly subsided, over and over, and then I was crying out, and I didn't care if the whole damn building heard. I was finally getting mine. I was finally taking. I was getting fucked hard by a man I had no obligations to beyond this night. Beyond taking the pleasure I wanted and finally getting it was like being set free.

I was free from the chains I'd put on myself when I'd agreed to let Garrett cheat. I was free from the denial that kept me in the dark for so long. I was free from the lies I'd been telling myself.

And freedom felt so fucking sweet.

I tilted my hips, sending Jake's cock deeper into my willing body. *My* willing body. Not Garrett's. Not Mrs. King's. Mara's body. My body. Mine to do with as I pleased. And this...this pleased me like nothing I'd felt before. It wasn't the sex. Not that what Jake was doing didn't feel amazing—it definitely did. But the freedom of being here and taking what I wanted was so much more.

Another orgasm crashed down on me, but this time Jake grunted as he finished with me.

When he finally released his hold on me, I slumped breathlessly onto the bed. He collapsed beside me, panting and sweaty, and then he looked at me and grinned, and I knew this wasn't the last time I'd take out my frustrations on this man.

[7]

I could have sworn the temperature in my office dropped ten degrees when my aunt marched in and closed the door behind her. She wasn't pleased with me. I wasn't sure why, but when she was angry, forget hell's fury. She turned as cold as Antarctica in the dead of winter.

"Are you avoiding me?" she demanded.

I leaned back. "No."

"We haven't had dinner once this week."

I sighed as I relaxed. She wasn't angry. She was hurt. Which was almost as bad, but a little reassurance would soothe her. Pushing myself up, I gestured toward the sitting area of my office and filled two cups of coffee before joining her.

"No, I'm not avoiding you. I've just had a busy week."

She eyed me, not taking the drink I still held for her.

"Take this before it burns my damn hand."

She finally accepted the mug and set it aside. I sat across

from her and sipped my black coffee before I gave in and sighed under the weight of her sapphire blue stare. Though we were distant relatives, we had the same blue eyes, and I imagined if I'd ever seen her natural hair color, it'd match the gold in mine.

We looked similar despite the distance between us, so when she gave me that stern look, I couldn't help but fold. Mostly because I looked just like my mother, and when Victoria seemed so disappointed in me, I saw Mom in her.

Setting my cup aside, I sat back. "Michael Redmond tried to pull some kind of emotional sucker punch on me last week. He let me know that he knows Garrett and Megan are sleeping together." I lifted my hand when her icy eyes narrowed. "I handled it."

"How?"

"I told him that I already knew and I don't care. And then I sucker punched him back by pointing out that had I not known, he could have ended my marriage, which ultimately would have hurt my son more than saved his business. He felt sufficiently guilty."

"I'll have his balls in a jar before the day is out."

I smiled. "No need, Auntie. I've handled it."

"Garrett better do something about that twit before she ruins everything."

I nodded at that. "Yes. He better. And he's been warned."

"And what of your affair with Jake Decker?"

Surprise hit. I usually was able to hide it, as I'd done with Michael, but Victoria threw me. Only for a moment.

"Are the doormen keeping you abreast of my guests?"

She smirked. "I just wanted to know if you'd taken my advice."

Shaking my head, I rolled my eyes. "Don't do that. You said the Bird's Nest was my sanctuary. Let it be that."

After a moment, she nodded curtly. "I won't ask them again now that I know you've taken the leap."

"Taken the leap?"

"Did you have him for tea, darling, or did you screw the man?"

I laughed softly. Screwing wasn't exactly what we'd done. We'd fucked. Hard and fast. And then we sank into the hot tub and talked about our college days like Megan and Garrett didn't exist. We hadn't gone to the same college, but one Ivy League school is the same as the others. Parties, drinking, and high pressure to succeed.

After relaxing and climbing from the hot water, we'd gone to wash the chlorine away. And Jake had lifted me up, wrapped me around him, and we'd fucked again as the hot water beat down on us. It'd been the most glorious night I could ever recall having. Better even than fucking Garrett in the back seat while riding down the streets of Paris.

Jake didn't make me feel used. He didn't make me question his motives. He wanted me. I could see that. And I wanted him. And we took what we wanted, and it was wonderful.

"You're blushing," Victoria said.

The grin on her face was smug, and I pushed myself up.

"I have to get back to work. I have a report to wrap up

before picking Adam up. I promised I'd take him to the park, and I want to do that before it gets too hot."

She sat for a moment longer before standing. "I'm proud of you."

"For getting laid."

"For finally giving as good as you've been getting. You're spitting in their faces. Garrett and Megan—two for the price of one. Good for you, darling." She kissed my cheek. "You just might have what it takes to survive this world after all."

I laughed softly, accepting her compliment, but as she left, my smile fell as I wondered if I wanted to have what it took to survive this world.

"Do you mind?" Michael asked as he stood next to the bench where I was sitting.

I let his question linger as I watched Will run as fast as his little legs could toward the slide.

"Sit," I finally said, and Michael eased down next to me.

"Mrs. King," he said after a moment.

"Mara," I reminded him.

"I'm sorry. About what I said last week. I was out of line."

"Yes, you were."

Like I'd done, he let my words hover for a moment.

"Before Carter Enterprises bought out my company, I was mid-level at best. I'm still learning to play with the big boys. I hit under the belt by dragging your personal business into the game. I'm sorry."

"Apology accepted." I watched Will and Adam intentionally fall and roll as they landed at the end of the slide. "Did my husband confront you?"

"No."

I glanced at him. "Oh. Well, expect him to."

"You told him."

"Only to make a point—and not about you. Megan Decker is not very discreet. She needs to learn, or he needs to cut her loose."

"So...you really did know he was sleeping with her?"

I finally focused on him. Though the sun was beating down, he chose to squint instead of wear sunglasses. I wish he had something to cover his eyes. Something there, the genuine confusion, I suppose, made me want to explain myself to him, but I didn't. I didn't know how to. I couldn't imagine he'd understand. Instead, I focused on the kids.

"I have a lot to learn about this level of society, don't I?" he asked after a few moments.

I nodded. "But your innocence is refreshing. I'm sure that's what Albert liked about you. He's very old school. A handshake is as good as a contract with him. Anyone else, you'd better be damned sure to get a legal and binding signature. Remember that."

He sighed. "I won't be here long. If I don't stop your company from undermining some of our deals, it will become painfully obvious that I don't deserve my job."

"Well, I hope you aren't trying to play on my sympathies. I'm not going to help you."

"I didn't suspect you'd help me. Maybe some pointers on survival, though? I'm clearly out of my element."

I smiled. "You were on the right track last week."

"When I tried to break your heart?"

I nodded. "Yes. Sadly, that kind of brutality is what it takes sometimes."

He shook his head. "I feel horrible about that."

"Don't." I watched the boys run to the swings.

"No. You were right. It was beyond reprehensible to try to hurt you."

I bit my lip for a few moments before looking at him. "When I married Garrett, I was so convinced that our relationship would be different from all those I'd seen before. I believed he loved me. That I was enough for him. It didn't take long to learn differently. Even after he cheated, I held on to the belief that somehow we were better than everyone else. That somehow I was better than all those other wives who watched their husbands slink off into the night because I made Garrett tell me the truth about where he was going. But in reality, I'm not better, Michael."

I looked away from him as memories of my behavior of late tugged at me. "Maybe I'm worse because I can't pretend that I don't know where he goes. But this is what I have. And it was my choice to keep it. The only way you can hurt me by pointing that out is if I let you. I've decided—rather recently, to be honest—not to let anyone hurt me anymore."

Turning when he remained silent, I offered him a smile to try to ease the concern on his face. I don't know why his opinion of me mattered, but I didn't want him looking at me with such sympathy.

"Don't look at me like that. I may not have the undying love and devotion I expected from my husband, but I have security for myself and my son. Garrett will never leave me.

And if he does, I have a contract stating the only thing he's taking is himself. I can live with that."

"Doesn't sound like much of a marriage, Mara."

I shrugged to hide my agreement with his observation. "It's enough."

"Is it?"

I looked at Adam as he and Will laughed and ran in circles chasing each other.

"Yes. It is. For Adam to have both his parents and the security of a stable home. It is definitely worth it." Taking a breath, I focused on Michael again. "Now, not only do you have to be a bit brutal to survive, you need an excellent assistant."

He willingly followed the change of subject. "I think I have that covered."

"Good. Have her get in touch with mine and set up an official playdate for these boys."

He pulled out his phone. "What's your assistant's number?"

I grinned wickedly. "If she's excellent, she'll figure it out." I snagged his phone. "But I will give you my number. I'd love for Will to come over. Does he like to swim?"

"My wife was teaching him before she passed away, but I'm not much of a swimmer, so he isn't that great."

"Oh, that won't do, Michael. It's a safety issue. I have a wonderful instructor who will come to you. I'll put his number in here too. Call him. Tell him I sent you so he makes room for you."

"Cars," he blurted out of nowhere. "Will loves cars. Does Adam?"

"Oh, does he ever. I fear he'll grow up to be a drag racer." I held his phone out. "Thank you."

"For what?"

"Do you know that boy is the center of my world, but I never get to discuss basic parenting with anyone? Other mothers only want to talk about which secondary schools they intend to ship their kids off to and how quickly they can be gone so they can get back to whatever it was they were doing before motherhood disrupted their lives. No one wants to discuss swim lessons or cars or playdates. This is refreshing."

"Well, I'm a single dad now, so anytime you want to give pointers or share instructors, let me know. *Please.* I'm begging. Let me know."

I smiled, relieved the stress between us seemed to have faded. "Wednesday mornings work for me."

I LOOKED UP, SURPRISED WHEN MY BEDROOM DOOR opened. Apparently, Garrett didn't feel he had to knock first. It'd been just four nights since he'd agreed to sleep in the other room, but it was obviously bothering him. He spent more time in my room now than when he'd slept here.

"You're getting dressed," he said.

"Yes."

"Going somewhere?"

"Yes."

"Girls' night?"

I slid my feet into stilettos and ran my hands over the tight-fitting dress. "No. But I think you knew that."

He actually looked a bit hurt. "I'm staying in tonight. I thought we'd have dinner."

"I wish you'd told me sooner. I made plans."

"Cancel them."

Oh, that was cute. Like he'd ever cancel his plans for me. I put my hand to his face as I walked by him, pausing long enough to kiss his cheek. "Let's have breakfast, hmm?"

"We could camp out in front of a movie. We haven't seen *Cars* in about three days."

I chuckled flatly. "Speak for yourself. But you and Adam watch it. You need some father-son time. It'll be good for him. Good night."

Crossing the hall, I laughed at Adam trying to pull his pajama top on.

"Looks like you're stuck."

"Help, Mommy!"

I tugged the hem down and planted a kiss on his head. "I'm going out to see a friend, but Dad's going to get you tucked in."

"Going to see Mr. Redmond? Is Will going?"

"Aw, no, buddy. I'm seeing a different friend. We'll see Will on Wednesday, like always. Be good, okay?" I kissed his head one more time before heading for the door.

"*Michael* Redmond?" Garrett asked suspiciously.

"We've seen him and his son at the park a few times. The boys have become friends."

"Mara—"

I hushed him with another kiss to his cheek. "Breakfast, yes?"

"Sure."

I walked away, but damned if my heart didn't ache. How many nights had I been the one left standing there wishing he'd stay? Now I was leaving. But I'd wanted that long enough, and I had no doubt that the only reason he wasn't out with one of his whores tonight was because Megan Decker was visiting her sister. I knew this because Jake had called earlier in the day asking if I'd like to have *a drink* again.

I'd already ordered dinner for two to be delivered at the Bird's Nest. I wasn't going to cancel the meal *or* the drink. Not even if Garrett wanted to spend family time together. He sure as hell wouldn't make that concession for me.

I pushed thoughts of Garrett from my mind as my driver wove in and out of traffic. I intended to have several actual drinks—I wouldn't be driving myself home. Once at the apartment, I thanked the caterer, who set up an intimate table, complete with candles and a bottle of wine. The scent of grilled fish and steamed vegetables wafted in the air as I looked over the setup. I nodded my approval, thanked the pair who had delivered the meal, and prepped the table before dismissing them with a healthy tip.

I hoped I hadn't overstepped. Jake and I had only met here once, and now I had a candlelit dinner set up. Maybe it was too much. Too far. But we'd agreed to make each other feel cherished. Wanted. And one thing I missed was dates like this.

Whenever Garrett and I had dinner, it was usually business—or at least with business partners. Rarely did we have dinner out that wasn't schmoozing with someone.

No. I wanted this dinner. I wanted this intimacy. And I was taking what I wanted now.

Jake arrived right on time, and the seductive smile he gave didn't disappoint. It was that same warm and inviting grin that drew me in every time.

I held the door for him to come in, and he immediately pulled me against him. His lips were on mine before the door clicked closed.

His heat enveloped me, soaked into my skin, warmed my heart, and soothed my soul. By the time he pulled back, my concerns about the dinner were gone. This was what we had agreed to. What we'd signed up for.

"Dinner is on the table. I hope you don't mind that I ordered for you."

"Do I get dessert?"

I grinned as he leaned in and kissed my neck. "If you're good."

"Oh, I intend to be."

Leading him to the table, I waited for his reaction. He simply smiled and complimented the choices I'd made as he pulled a chair out for me. He filled our glasses, and I cleared my mind.

Garrett had been trying to nudge his way into my thoughts since I'd left him standing bewildered in the hallway. I would not allow myself to feel guilty. He'd been doing this very thing to me for years. I would *not* feel guilty for taking my turn.

Even so, we were halfway through dinner and Jake's one-sided conversation when he put his hand on my arm.

"Mara, if you don't want to be here—"

"I do."

"Are you sure?"

Frowning, I leaned back from my barely touched food. "I'm sorry. I'm breaking my promise."

"What promise?"

"To make you feel like the most cherished man in the world when you're with me. It's just... He asked me to stay home tonight. I can't even begin to tell you how many times I've asked him the same thing. He always left. And I doubt he ever felt as shitty about that as I do right now."

Jake took a moment to look at what was left of his fish before meeting my gaze again.

"Garrett is a player. He'll screw anything that will stand still long enough. But I have no doubt in my mind that he loves you. He smiles when he talks about you. He respects you. But he'll never change."

"I know that."

"If you want to go home to him, I understand. He *is* your husband."

I shook my head. "If I know him, and I *do*, I wasn't even out the door before he found someone to replace Megan for the night."

"You don't believe me," I said when he lifted his brows.

Standing, I grabbed my phone and dialed Adam's nanny. "Leah, I just wanted to check in. Mr. King mentioned watching a movie with Adam. Did they get settled?" I smirked at Jake as I listened to her response. "Oh. He had to go to the office? What a shame. Well, it'll be a few hours before I get home, so be sure to give Adam a hug goodnight for me. Thanks."

"My poor husband got called to the office right after I left. How surprising."

"I stand by my earlier assessment. He does love you."

I set my phone on the table and resumed my seat as I eyed Jake. "Do you love Megan?"

"Yes."

"Yet you're here with me and she's off...where?"

"Probably spending the weekend with one of her lovers."

I nodded. "I'm starting to realize love has nothing to do with what we do when our spouses aren't around. Don't you find that a little sad?"

"I find it a lot sad, actually. I didn't know what I was getting into, I guess."

"Me either. My aunt tried to warn me, but I didn't listen."

"Not everyone is cut out to live like this, Mara."

"Are you?"

"I'm working on it."

I pressed my lips together. "Do you think they went through this too? This kind of guilt before they learned to put it in a box and set it on a shelf."

"I think some people are just naturally able to categorize their feelings. Garrett loves you. He thinks that because you are his wife, you're on a pedestal above all others and that should be enough for you. He doesn't understand that to you, what he's doing isn't just sex. As for Megan, she's selfish. She's always been. It's about her. She thinks fucking Garrett makes her special to him. Where he thinks it's only sex, she thinks it's because he wants her above all others."

"And when she realizes where she really stands with him?"

"Sound the alarms."

My alarm did sound. "Garrett and I have an agreement. If she goes public with their affair, he loses everything. He'll destroy her before he lets that happen."

Jake nodded once, a slow, solemn movement. "I haven't decided how I feel about that yet."

Taking a breath, I let it out slowly. I should be shocked that a man would be willing to let his wife go down in flames. But then again, it was getting more and more difficult to be surprised by anything the people around me did—including myself. "I suppose if he takes her down a peg or two, you and I will both come out ahead."

"I suppose we will."

"I don't want to talk about them anymore," I said. "Did you get enough to eat?"

He shook his head then crooked his finger at me. I answered his beckoning, rising and slowly rounding the table. He spread his legs and then lifted one of mine, setting the tip of my shoe at his crotch.

I watched his face as he brushed his fingers up my calf, along my thigh, and then under my skirt, smirking when he realized that once again, I hadn't bothered with underwear.

He stroked for a moment before slipping his fingers in me. He pushed deep inside, curving them, hitting just the right spot to make me sigh. But then he stopped, pulled back, and held my gaze as he put his fingers in his mouth, tasting me.

"I'll never get enough to eat," he whispered.

He was on his feet and had me pulled against his chest before I could come up with a witty response. His mouth crashed against mine. With one arm around my waist and the other hand gripping my ass, Jake lifted me off the floor just enough that my feet didn't drag as he crossed the room.

At the couch, he set me down and used my hips to turn my back to him, then pushed me forward until I planted my hands on the cushions. He moved my feet apart and dropped to his knees behind me.

I closed my eyes as he kissed his way up my leg, licking behind my knee as he lifted my skirt. Then he buried his face between my legs.

Just like the first time, his enthusiasm was contagious, and it wasn't long before I was moaning and grinding into his mouth.

He licked front to back, back to front, tasting every bit of me.

"Put your fingers in me," I demanded. And he did. Only he gave me more than I bargained for. I cried out as he filled me completely. I'd never been into any kind of anal play and had firm lines with Garrett, but I didn't pull away when Jake crossed the line he hadn't known was there. In fact, I moaned and arched my back, allowing myself to try something new with him.

He wasn't rough, or forceful, or selfish about what he was doing, as I guessed Garrett would be. Jake was giving me pleasure, and for once I put aside my fear and let him. He seemed to have his hands and his mouth all over me all at once, and it wasn't long before it was more than I could handle. I came with a cry, and my legs started to tremble.

He lifted my dress over my head, tossing it aside, and ordered me to get on my knees on the couch. He didn't have to tell me twice. I felt like my legs were about to give out on me. While he stripped and tore a condom packet open, I tried to catch my breath. I'd barely gotten control of my body when he gripped my hips and pulled me back to him, filling me with one stroke.

He gripped me so tightly, the thought crossed my mind that I might be bruised in the morning. But I didn't stop him. I focused on the pressure of his fingertips and the rhythmic stroking as I reached between my legs and rubbed my clit until I once again shattered into a sweaty, breathless heap. Leaning forward, I gripped the back of the couch, holding myself up, panting.

I yelped when Jake gave me a firm slap on the butt cheek. I'd definitely never let Garrett spank me.

"I'm not done with you yet," Jake said in a voice that was strained and demanding.

I breathlessly laughed, mostly because I was surprisingly excited by the tingling in my skin and his unwavering demand for more. He yanked me back to him as he rammed forward. Again, I was surprisingly unoffended by his actions or the spark of pain he'd inflicted. He was acting like he'd die if he didn't have all of me. I liked that. I liked that he needed me so desperately that he was on the edge of losing control.

As his body hit the spot where he'd smacked my ass, the tingling increased and took my breath away.

Shit.

This was something new. Everything he was doing was new. I bit my lip harder, trying to hold on to the sensation, but the sting was fading. I wanted that back. Needed more of that.

I wouldn't beg. Would *not* beg. But then the plea left me before I could stop it.

"Again."

"This?" he asked just before his hand landed on my ass.

I rolled my eyes closed. Bit my lip. Refused to beg. But then I said, "Yes. More. Give me more."

He spanked me again, a bit harder, and I gasped. Dear God, that felt good. Better than good. That felt like being fucked, and I definitely needed to be fucked. I had years' worth of frustrations pent up. Not feeling wanted enough. Not feeling needed enough. Denying myself because I felt too damn guilty to fulfill my own needs.

Pushing myself up, I gripped my breasts, pinching my nipples as Jake moved his hand around my waist and between my legs. I cried out when he rolled his fingers over my clit. Then his hand was in my hair, fisting and pulling my head back.

I would have slapped Garrett if he'd done that. But Jake's gentle pull was the last thing I needed to throw me over the edge. Holy fuck. With all that stimulation—his dick in me, my ass stinging from his palm, my nipples feeling raw from my grip on them, and one of his hands buried between my legs while the other tugged my hair—I came about as hard as I ever had.

I screamed. I actually fucking screamed. Finally, he

released me, and I laughed softly as I fell forward onto the couch. A moment later, he fell beside me, and I looked at him. I didn't doubt for a moment my face was red with embarrassment as he reached up and gently ran his knuckles over my now sensitive ass flesh.

"Well," he said with a smirk, "Mrs. King has a naughty side even she didn't know about."

I laughed and exhaled slowly before leaning over and kissing him. I didn't know how else to thank him for what he'd just done.

[8]

"ADMIT IT, Mara King. You just fell madly in love with me."

I pushed Michael's hand away from my face. "You're being ridiculous."

Undaunted by my resistance, he held his hamburger under my nose again, waving it back and forth. "You can't resist me."

Finally giving in to temptation, I grabbed his hand in both of mine and took a huge bite out of the burger he'd been tormenting me with since we'd sat down in the play area of the fast-food restaurant.

Rain had prevented the boys from playing at the park, so we'd agreed this was a reasonable substitute. Then he started mocking me for ordering a salad and a bottle of water, making me regret the decision to meet here instead of just canceling the Wednesday playdate.

Just because men could let themselves go, that didn't mean women could. I couldn't even imagine the hell Garrett would give me if I couldn't parade in front of Albert Carter for him.

"Oh, my God," I moaned as I chewed a flavorful burst of charbroiled meat, pickles, and about half a dozen high-calorie-count condiments. "That's so good."

"Told you so," Michael sang before also biting into the sandwich. "Want me to get you one?"

"No. Damn it. *No*." I turned my face away when he offered me another bite. "You're the devil, Michael Redmond."

He laughed as he looked across the table at the boys, who were so engrossed in chatter and chicken nuggets they hadn't even noticed their parents teasing each other.

"I worried about him fitting in here," he admitted. "I'm so glad they hit it off."

"He's six. Why wouldn't he fit in?"

"We're new to this level of society, remember? Like you said last week, all the parents here care about is which boarding school their kids will get into. I'm not like them. Neither are you, thank God."

I smiled as I stabbed at my lettuce. "Don't tell them that, please. They haven't noticed yet."

"Speaking of schools, where is Adam going? Maybe I can get Will in there too. Then he won't have to start school without any friends."

I stopped messing with my lunch. "Oh, Michael. Adam was on the waiting list for two years before he got in. Don't worry," I insisted when his eyes bulged. "I'll make some calls. I'll get him in. You're new to town. There's no way you could have known to enroll him early." I nudged him gently. "You may have to pay a little extra enrollment fee. Bribery is not unheard of around here."

"Whatever it takes." His stiff shoulders relaxed a bit. "Thanks, Mara. Seriously. You've saved my parental ass more times in the last few weeks than you realize."

"I can't imagine trying to get settled into a new town, a new high-demand job, and still be a hands-on parent. You're doing great."

"Yeah?"

I nodded to show my conviction. "Yeah."

"So. Would you mind if I asked for another favor?"

I made a show of hesitating before laughing. "Of course. What do you need?"

"I kind of fired my nanny this morning. Will just didn't like her. I thought they'd warm up to each other, but it's been two months, and this morning she got so frustrated with him, she made him cry."

"Oh, no."

"I told her to get out. But...now..."

"Now you need a new nanny."

He nodded. "Immediately. And when I called my assistant, she made it clear that wasn't her job."

I lifted my brows. "So you also need a new assistant."

"I do?"

"Your assistant doesn't tell you what her job is. You tell her. No," I said with a cock of my brow when he started to protest. "*You* tell *her*. Listen, she isn't some underpaid clerk just trying to make ends meet. An assistant to an executive at your level is paid very, very well. Her job is to do whatever it takes so that you can do your job effectively. If that means she helps you find a nanny for your son, then that's what she does. Trust me. She *is* paid to do this. She's pushing you around, testing your boundaries, and you're letting her."

He frowned, and I chuckled. "Where is Will going today?"

"I was going to take him to work with me. Just for today. But by tomorrow…"

"He'll stay with us. He can hang out with Adam and his nanny for the afternoon. As for you, you go in there *today* and tell your assistant that she will line up nanny interviews or you will line up assistant interviews."

He stared at me. "Just like that, huh?"

"Yes. Just like that. And when she has new nanny interviews scheduled, you let me know. I'll weed through them. And I'll put the fear of God into your assistant if need be. Now give me that thing." I grabbed what was left of his burger, shoved it in my mouth, and moaned with appreciation. "I hate you for ordering that."

I SIGHED WHEN GARRETT FROWNED AND SCRATCHED HIS chin. We'd been sitting at the table in the corner of his office for over half an hour as I showed him what I'd spent a good portion of the last few months working on. I'd been observing him long enough to know he was finding the right words to shoot down my proposal.

"This is a good investment," I pressed.

"I just don't see it, Mara."

"The warehouse district is ripe with empty buildings and—"

"Crime and noise and litter. Who is going to want to buy there?"

I couldn't believe he didn't see the same potential I did. "Millennials who think reusing old buildings makes them environmentally conscious. Artists needing large lofts. Rustics looking for something old on the outside but updated on the inside. We could make amazing lofts, Garrett, and the bones are already there in these old buildings."

"You aren't thinking about the investment in the buildings, in rezoning, in making the warehouses viable for resale. This is too much."

"Investing here is a risk, yes, but we can do this. The commute to downtown is fast and easy. We could break these buildings into multiple units and still have larger spaces than what most of the urban living allows. The natural light, the high ceilings... We could make these contemporary without breaking the budget because these buildings—"

He did his damned good-dog pat on the back of my hand. "I know you have a vision, and your research is impeccable, as always, darling. It's too large of a risk."

I sank back in my seat. I knew him. There was no reason to keep pushing. His mind was made up.

He leaned back in his seat too. "I mean, you can present it to the board—"

"And have you shoot me down in front of them? No thanks."

"Mara," he said with a patronizing tone that made me want to reach across the table and punch him. "That happened once a long time ago, and I wasn't shooting you down."

"Bullshit."

I gathered up the papers I'd agonized over—weeks and weeks of research and planning—and tucked them in a folder. "Someone is going to beat us to this, Garrett. And you're going to regret ignoring the fact that I actually do have more to offer you than a place to put your dick."

He grinned. "You also have very nice tits."

"I'm glad you remember what they look like," I said before leaving his office for my own. He called out to me, but I didn't stop. There was no point.

I was not going to push him on this again. As a matter of fact, I was tempted to call a competing company and give my research to them. Maybe they'd run with it and prove me right so I could shove Garrett's nose in someone else's success.

My assistant looked up when I walked by her. "Mrs. King—"

I ignored her and walked into my office, not wanting to hear whatever messages were waiting for me. Dropping into my desk chair, I stared at the folder for a moment before opening the cover and looking over my proposal again. Cursing under my breath, I slammed the file shut and dropped my research into the trash.

I didn't know why I even bothered taking projects to Garrett. I'd been the vice president of the company for the last six years, and he still didn't take me seriously. He didn't take me seriously as a business partner, as a wife, as a mother, as a lover...as a *woman*.

I sat back and looked around my office. This was it. This was all I was ever going to get out of being *Mrs.* Garrett King. A corner office, a fake marriage, a fake vocation, and fake respect. I was never going to have anything real, and as much as my aunt told me that was okay, I didn't agree. I wanted more. I wanted a real relationship. A real career. And someone to have some genuine fucking esteem for me.

I drummed my fingers as I looked at the folder that held my proposal and considered my options. I wasn't giving up on my idea. Not this easily. I'd done the legwork. I knew this was a good idea.

I could do this. I could buy my own properties. Make my own way. I just had to find a way to do it without Garrett finding out, because if he did, there'd be hell to pay.

I grabbed the folder from the trash and tucked it into my bag instead. Yes, it was a risk. But what was life without risks?

[9]

"No."

My mouth dropped as I looked at my aunt. "What do you mean *no*?"

"I mean no."

I looked at my research, my well-planned project, as she slammed the folder closed and pushed it back to me. "Aunt Victoria—"

"I will not allow you to do this, child. Do you know the hell you will pay if Garrett ever finds out you even considered working against him?"

"I am not scared of my husband."

"You should be." Her face softened. "Don't act like you didn't expect this."

"My husband's constant rejection, or yours?" I snapped. I crossed my arms and leaned back, knowing I looked like a petulant child but not caring. I expected Aunt Victoria to support my venture, to even be proud.

"Mara."

"I'm not asking for a handout. I'll pay you back. I just can't invest money in this that Garrett can trace, and I don't have a dime to my name that he can't."

She nodded. "He keeps a close eye on you. I know that. Which is exactly why you can't do this, darling. You cannot compete against him without him finding out. And once he does, he will make you suffer for what he is sure to see as betrayal. I know you want more than what he gives you, but, child... You have to learn to accept the limitations of your gender."

I widened my eyes at her. "*What?*"

"You want more than society—forget Garrett—*society* is ready to give you. You always have. You've always pushed and demanded more than the world was ready to allow. I know your parents filled your head full of big dreams, and I hate to be the one to always pull you back to reality, but this is the way the world works. You have a beautiful home. Financial security. A husband who allows a certain amount of freedom. An aunt who thinks the world of you. A beautiful, healthy child. Let that be enough." She pushed the folder to me. "If you want this, find a way to convince your husband to give it to you. You'll be amazed what a woman can get a man to do if she applies herself."

I scoffed. "Not as amazed as you'd think." Taking my folder, I pushed myself up and debated for a moment before looking down at her. "He's consuming me. Parts of me that I never thought he could touch. If I don't do something to hang on to the person I want to be, I will become the person *he* wants me to be. I don't want to be that person, Victoria. I don't want to be the type of wife who whores herself out for the betterment of her husband's career. My parents taught me better than that, and I'm not turning my back on them without a fight. You don't have to support me. You don't have to agree with me. But know that I will do whatever I have to do to stop Garrett King from killing what little bit of them remains inside of me."

I HAD SPENT FAR TOO MUCH TIME THINKING OF THAT last night with Jake. Every moment I was alone, my mind wandered back to our frenzied sex. I'd lost my mind while he was fucking me. Part of me was humiliated. But the other part of me... Well, I couldn't deny how I got wet every time I remembered the sting his hand left on my ass.

However, seeing him across the large open living room of Betty Samuels Tuscan-inspired home made me wonder if I'd ever be able to look him in the eye again. Then he saw me. His eyes met mine, and I froze. A good kind of frozen. The kind of frozen that made my breath catch and my heart pound. The kind of frozen that made the most intimate parts of my body clench with anticipation.

He smiled slightly, and warmth spread through me. Laughter drew me back to the group I was standing with. Another evening, another social gathering I could have done without. This time, a birthday party for a socialite I couldn't care less about. But all the have-to-be-seens were present, and that meant the Kings were as well. Well, one of them anyway.

I continued scanning the room, looking for Garrett. He'd

excused himself without telling me where he was off to. At first, I assumed he was going to chat up a business associate, but he rarely did that without me. I was the one who whispered in his ear all he needed to know to make small talk. His disappearance made me a bit uneasy.

I skimmed the room again. This time, my gaze caught on Albert. He smiled and toasted me.

This was the first time I'd seen him since on the yacht. I refused to let him see how humiliated I was. Instead, I smiled and toasted him as well. But I couldn't deny that my stomach had tightened and my heart picked up its pace at the recollection of lying in front of him as my husband touched me in my most intimate places with only a skimpy bikini to stop him from being skin-on-skin. And I knew Albert was thinking of that moment as well by the heat in his eyes as he started.

My cheeks heated as I looked away. But that all faded away when Jake started toward me, and I swear I saw that now-familiar hunger in his eyes.

Oh, dear God. Don't let anyone see him look at me like that.

The desire on his face was obvious—at least to me.

I did my best to ignore him, fearing he was going to pull me into one of those hot kisses that made my legs go weak, but he didn't pay me any mind as he continued on without stopping to talk to me. My relief was short-lived, however.

As he slid between me and whoever was behind me, he pressed his body to mine much more than was necessary, muttering a lame, "Excuse me, Mrs. King," as he brushed his hand over my ass, briefly cupping my cheek.

I glanced back and nodded slightly. "You're excused, Mr. Decker."

He finished his intentional but subtle assault on my backside and came to stand next to me. "And where is Mr. King? I could have sworn I saw him earlier."

"You did." I smiled. "I'm afraid we bored him to tears and he disappeared. I was about to go look for him."

He held his arm out to me like a true gentleman. "Ladies, if you don't mind. I'll escort Mrs. King to find her husband. I, too, have been bored to tears and need his assistance."

The women laughed at his charm, and I slid my arm through his. His heat instantly surrounded me. That damn cologne of his beckoned me to bury my face in his neck and inhale as he pulled me against him. I could almost feel him deep inside my body, and I swear I moaned.

"I want to see you tonight," he said quietly as we weaved through the crowd.

"You do?"

He put his hand over mine and lightly ran his thumb over my skin. "Desperately."

My heart sped up, and my insides warmed. I tried not to smirk, but I'm not sure I succeeded. "How desperately?"

"It's taking all my strength not to leave with you right now."

I stopped and pulled from him, making a show of looking around. "How long are you staying at this horrible party?"

"I'm leaving now. You?"

"I plan to leave as soon as I find Garrett. I can't stand faking one more laugh."

He lowered his voice. "Would you rather scream?"

I inhaled and looked the other way as images of what we had done once again pushed into the forefront of my mind. "Behave yourself, Mr. Decker. If anyone catches on to our little game, it will be over."

He put a bit more distance between us. "Sorry. I just can't stop thinking about last time."

I breathed slowly, deliberately, to stop the sultry smile that wanted to spread across my lips. "That was...enlightening."

"Not the first word that comes to mind."

I couldn't seem to stop my tongue from darting out and running over my lips. "I'll let you know when I'm on my way."

Jake smiled and lifted his arm and waved. "Garrett. Here. We've been looking for you."

Garrett stumbled toward us, and my smile fell. He was drunk. And disheveled. "Have you, Jake? And here I was afraid I was interrupting something after the way you've been looking at my wife all evening."

"Shut your mouth," I warned him quietly as I glanced around. If anyone heard him, they didn't respond.

"Sorry, darling," he whispered dramatically.

I closed my eyes as the smell of another woman's sex hit my nostrils. Wherever he'd been, he'd had his face buried in some whore's nether region.

"Jesus, Garrett. Your breath smells like an STD. Drink this." I handed him my champagne.

He swished before swallowing.

I looked at Jake pleadingly. "Help me get him out of here."

Jake put his arm around Garrett's shoulders and, thankfully, pulled him into a conversation about baseball as they headed for the door. They looked like two slightly inebriated men, bonding over the kind of scoring that had nothing to do with our sex lives. The male bonding continued while we waited for our cars to be brought to us.

As Jake poured Garrett into the back seat, he frowned at me. "Will I see you later?"

"I don't know." I gestured toward my drunk husband. "Let me handle this, and I'll text you."

He nodded his understanding, and I felt like a jerk.

"I want to see you," I whispered. "Desperately."

He smiled as I tossed his response back at him. "I know. But we'll have more nights if this one doesn't work out."

I walked around the other side of the car and climbed in next to Garrett. "Are you fucking kidding me with this?" I asked before the car had even left the curb. "What were you thinking?"

"Well, if you have to ask."

"If you'd gotten caught—"

"I didn't."

"I would crucify you. Do you hear me? I would absolutely *crucify* you. You would lose everything, Garrett."

His playful smirk fell. "I've had a bit too much to drink, I'm afraid. I wasn't thinking." He leaned close to me. "Are we going home?"

"Yes. We're going home."

"Good."

Pulling me close, he put a kiss to my head, and I wanted to retch. I pushed him away. "Don't."

"Mara."

"I can smell her pussy on you. It's making me sick."

He smirked. "Hearing you say pussy is making me hot."

I shook my head. Not because I was surprised he'd have sex with some random person at a party, but because he had acted so carelessly.

"What is wrong with you?"

Slouching a bit, he ran his hand over his face and let out a long breath. "Nothing."

"Oh, no. There is definitely something. It's not like you to be so stupid, Garrett. Are you trying to get caught betraying me? Because if you are, save us both the trouble of a humiliating divorce and just walk out now."

"I didn't mean to..."

"To what? Have sex at Betty Samuels's party?"

He looked at me, and the sadness in his eyes took me by surprise. "I didn't mean to push you too far." Slinking into the seat, he let his head fall back and closed his eyes. "I knew the moment you decided to take advantage of our agreement. The night I left you to see Megan. I left your bed, and I went to her. And I pushed you too far." He gripped my hand and looked at me with that same pathetic look. "I only went to tell her that I'd never leave you for her. I didn't have sex with her that night, Mara. I swear."

"That doesn't matter." I looked out the window and inhaled as I debated my response. "There was no one moment that pushed me too far, Garrett. There were hundreds of them." I focused on him again, taking in his drunken appearance. "They all came together and crashed down on me. That's all. But this... What is this? You feeling sorry for yourself because I stopped sitting at home pretending I didn't mind being alone night after night?"

"I love you."

"And I love you. But I won't fight for your affection or your appreciation or anything else. I'm your wife. I shouldn't have to. I'll find someone else to give me those things if you aren't willing. Just as you have done for the last six years. I'm sorry if you can't handle that. But this is what you wanted. This is how you wanted our marriage to be."

"I know." His voice was surprisingly thick with emotion. Or was it the slur of alcohol?

Either way, it tugged at my heart, and I had to fist my hands to stop from soothing him.

He'd made our bed, and for far too long I'd slept in it alone. I would not allow him to make me feel guilty for doing the same damn thing he'd done for years. If he wanted to throw a tantrum and fuck some bimbo at a party, risking everything we'd built together, that was his business. I knew better. I was smarter than that.

He could have his fit. I would have everything else when he broke our agreement.

But then he put his head on my shoulder and took my hand. "I'm sorry, Mara. I'm so sorry."

Sighing, I tilted my head and rested my cheek to the top of his head. "I know."

"Stay with me tonight," he said quietly. "Don't go to him. Not tonight."

I looked back out the window. By the time we got home he was snoring softly, his head still on my shoulder. I gently woke him, but our driver had to get him out of the car and onto his feet.

"Shall I help you inside, Mrs. King?" the driver asked as I slid under Garrett's arm to support him.

"No, thank you. I've got this. Tomas," I called when he started for the driver's door. "Your discretion will be greatly appreciated."

"As always, ma'am."

I walked Garrett into the house, stumbling our way upstairs and into my bedroom—simply because it was the closest and I couldn't support his weight much longer. I nearly dropped him on the bed. He curled onto his side, pulled a pillow under his head, and was snoring again before I could even stand up straight.

I watched him for several moments, my emotions in a blender violently mixing my love for him, my guilt, my anger, years of loneliness, and everything else I had been ignoring for so long, until all I had left was a mess that I couldn't quite identify.

Reaching down, I stroked my hand through his hair, hesitating when I noticed that it was far more salt than pepper now than I seemed to recall. When had that happened? Taking in his face, I noticed that he had aged somehow. And I'd missed it. All this time I was so angry at him for neglecting me, but I hadn't noticed that he had been changing right before my eyes.

"You stupid bastard," I whispered, blaming him for my inability to see what should have been obvious.

Walking into the bathroom, I yanked two cleansing towelettes from my makeup drawer, because I'd be damned if he'd sleep next to me with remnants of some whore on him, and wiped his face, particularly around his mouth. After tossing the wipes into the trash, I eased out of my dress and heels and into a nightgown and readied myself for sleep.

Sitting on my side of the bed, I plugged in my phone and then glanced back at my sleeping husband before texting my lover and letting him know he was on his own for the evening. He responded that he understood, but I figured he was as disappointed as me.

Instead of meeting up with Jake, losing myself in his passion, I curled onto my side and watched Garrett sleep.

I JOLTED WHEN SOMEONE RESTED A HAND ON MY shoulder. Jerking my head up, I sighed and forced a smile that I didn't really feel. I was still trying to sort out what had happened the night before and why I felt like it was all my fault.

"Hey, Michael."

"Fancy meeting you here on a Saturday morning."

I hadn't planned to bring Adam to the park, but I had to get away before Garrett woke up and tried to make amends. I didn't like feeling off-kilter, and he had knocked me completely off balance with his behavior the night before. Since when did he act out in jealousy? Since when did he pout? Or ask for something from me that wasn't sexual?

Garrett had always gotten off on other men wanting me. I guess me actually letting one act on that was more than he could handle. Now he knew how I'd been feeling all these years. But, as usual, I suspected I was the only one who felt guilty about the pain inflicted.

"Mara? You okay?"

"Yeah. Sure." I didn't even sound convincing to my own ears, so I tried to be more convincing with a forced smile. "I'm fine."

"You're a terrible liar."

I looked to where Adam and Will were playing by their favorite slide. "How's the nanny search going?"

"Oh, you'd be so proud." Michael sat next to me.

I looked at him and creased my brow. "Elaborate, please."

"I scared my executive into helping me."

"And how did you manage this amazing feat?"

"I told her that if she didn't comply with my demands, Mara King was going to pay her a visit. She whipped right into shape."

I lifted my brows in surprise, then laughed. "For future reference, that tact also works on in-laws, pets, *and* party planners."

Michael chuckled. "You know that was fifty-fifty there. You were either going to laugh or slap me. It was quite a risk. I'm glad it worked out in my favor."

"You do live dangerously."

"Gotta get my kicks somewhere."

"Glad to see you feel comfortable enough to get those kicks at my expense." I looked back to the boys.

"You were right. I was letting her push me around. I made it clear she could do what I told her, or she could clear out her desk. She put a pile of résumés on my desk before she left last night."

"When do you want to go through them?"

"I can probably take it from here."

I leaned over to nudge him with my elbow. "I'm sure you can, but indulge me."

He repeated the gesture. "Okay. How does now sound?"

"*Now?*"

"Sure. The boys can play while I pretend I don't notice how you are slowly taking over all my parenting decisions." He stood and held his hand out to help me up. "Come on. Follow me in your car so you have means of escape should you need it."

I debated for only a moment before slapping my palm into his and letting him pull me to my feet. He whistled, and Will immediately looked at his dad. Michael gestured for him to come on.

"You, too, Adam," Michael said. "Let's go."

I pulled my hand from his as the boys raced toward us. I ruffled Adam's hair as he crashed into me. "Mr. Redmond invited us over to his house. What do you think?"

The kids immediately started rambling—Adam with excitement and Will going over all the toys they could play with.

I looked at Michael. "I think he's on board with this plan."

I got Adam situated in my Escalade and stuck close as I followed Michael's Jeep Cherokee through the neighborhood before turning up a winding road and parking in front of one of the smaller houses in the area—but that didn't mean the house was small by any means.

We walked into a gloriously modern foyer with a high

ceiling and tall windows. The boys immediately ran up the wide staircase, talking so fast I couldn't understand anything they were saying. I looked at Michael and laughed. He gestured for me to go deeper into the house.

"Coffee?" he asked.

"Please. Just for future reference, I don't say no to coffee. You *never* have to ask."

"Good to know." He led me to the kitchen and went to work on making two cups.

I sat on one of the stools at the counter and took in the décor. "How long have you been here?"

"Uh, we moved in right after I was hired at Carter Enterprises. So...two...almost three months."

"Just long enough to put ceramic cocks on the wall."

He very nearly dropped the cups he was getting from the cabinet as he turned to face me. I pointed to the line of plaques touting brightly colored poultry and chuckled.

He joined in my quiet laughter. "Those came with the house. I'm not really a ceramic cock kind of guy."

"Well, that's too bad. There's nothing a girl likes more than a nice ceramic cock."

Michael smirked as he glanced at me. "Does that go for the good girls or just the ones like you?"

I laughed as he focused on putting grounds into the filter.

"I always have sensed an air of mischief about you but never really thought you'd be the dick-joke type. You just showed your hand, Mrs. King." He crossed his arms and leaned against the counter, watching me as the coffee brewed.

"Oh, come on, even the best girls like a good dick joke now and then."

He lifted his brows at me. "Give me a break. You're mischievous as hell, aren't you?"

I simply grinned.

He leaned forward, putting his forearms on the island that separated us. His dark eyes twinkled. "Tell me one mischievous thing you've done."

"No."

"Come on. You tell me yours, and I'll tell you mine."

I shook my head.

"Fine. I'll go first." He rolled his eyes to the side as he thought. "Oh, got one. Once, in high school, this football player kept bullying my friend who was crazy insane smart with chemistry. So we decided we were going to soak his jock strap in this formula that would give him serious jock itch."

I widened my eyes. "You didn't."

He nodded. "We broke into the locker room after school, and I jimmied his locker open. Halfway through the next home game, he couldn't stop digging at his junk. By Monday morning, everyone was talking about how he had crabs. His girlfriend dumped him, and someone painted a crab on his locker. My buddy got his vengeance."

I gawked at him for a minute before throwing my head back and laughing. "Oh, my God, Michael! That's horrible."

"No, it's not. It didn't stop the jerk from picking on my friend, but he spent the rest of his high school days known as Lice Dick."

I laughed again. "That's horrible *and* wonderful at the same time."

"Your turn."

I drew a breath and shook my head. "I, uh...I don't have any stories like that."

"Yes you do. Come on."

I shrugged. "I really don't."

"You and your best friends never got in trouble?"

"I, um, I was the outcast."

"So was I, but I still found someone to get into trouble with."

"No. I was really an outcast. My parents...died when I was young, and I was sent to live with my mother's first cousin twice removed or some other crazy family tree bullshit. I just call her my aunt for sanity's sake. I'd never met her and was completely intimidated by my new lifestyle, so I did my best to be invisible. It kind of became a way of life for me. I never wanted to make waves and be noticed, you know? All the other girls at the private schools were training to be trophy wives. I wanted to run a business like my parents had done when I was a kid. Even though my aunt didn't approve, she did her best to support me. Part of that was throwing a huge graduation party. I met Garrett. He hired me that day and...well... The rest is history, I guess."

He stared at me for a moment. "And now? You don't have friends to get into mischief with now?"

I drew a breath and held it, then let it out as I shook my head. "The other mothers at Adam's school aren't the mischievous type."

"Friends, Mara. You have friends, don't you?"

I laughed slightly then lied. "Sure. I mean...nobody to soak jock straps with, but I have friends."

"Have you ever TP-ed a house?"

"No."

"Coated someone's car in shaving cream?"

"No."

"Left a shit bomb on someone's porch?"

I widened my eyes at him. "Oh, my God, Michael. *No.*"

"Me either." He let a slow grin curve his lips. "But if you ever decide to do those things, let me know. I'm definitely the mischievous type."

I laughed. "Coffee's done."

He turned away and filled the mugs, and I looked down at the wedding ring on my hand.

I'd always felt like I'd missed out on life in a lot of ways. My parents had pounded it into my head that I had to work hard, study hard, and take life seriously if I were going to have a better life than they'd had. Even after a better life had been handed to me, I hadn't been able to take the gift for granted.

Even if Garrett had wanted a traditional marriage, I would have wanted to work. I would have wanted to make my way at King Inc. That was the only thing my parents ever asked of me. I wouldn't disappoint them by taking the easy way out. So, yes, I'd sacrificed fitting in and having friends and learning how to make those deeper connections with people because I had no idea *how to* connect with the people who lived in the world I'd been dumped in. The girl from the city slums had nothing in common with the girls from the mansions on the hills. I still didn't.

"Hey," Michael said gently, pulling me from my thoughts.

I blinked as I realized a cup of coffee had been set in front of me.

"Mara, I didn't mean to upset you."

"You didn't."

"I think you'd disagree if you could see the frown on your face."

I shook my head. "No. It's not that. It's just..." Exhaling, I blinked away the fog from my mind. "Aren't we supposed to be looking at nanny résumés?"

He put his hand on mine. "If I said something—"

"Do you want to hear something stupid?" I blurted out.

He was clearly surprised at my interruption. "Sure."

"Everything my parents wanted me to be conflicted with everything my aunt wanted. I spent so much of my life trying to figure out how to balance those two sets of expectations that I never learned how to...how to be me, you know? My best friend would probably love to cause mischief because my best friend, my *only* friend, is a six-year-old boy who sleeps with toy cars and would live at the park if I let him."

He opened his mouth, but nothing came out.

I closed my eyes and shook my head. "I just said all that out loud, didn't I?"

"You did."

"I'm sorry."

"Don't be."

"No, I just..." I exhaled and slid off the stool. "I've had a shitty few days, and... Thanks for the coffee. I'm going to get Adam and go home and never see you again."

"Mara," he called as I started for the kitchen door. He grabbed my arm and pulled me to a stop before I could step into the hallway. "After my wife died, I shut everyone out. Everyone. And they let me. The reason I sold my company to Carter and agreed to work for him is because I realized that old saying is true—you really do see who your friends are when you're down and out. You know what I learned? *My* only friend is a six-year-old kid who loves cars and hates pudding. What kind of kid hates pudding?"

I wanted to throw my arms around his neck and thank him for not mocking me. Instead, I shrugged. "You should probably take him back. Clearly he's broken."

He offered me a sweet smile. "You're the only person I socialize with outside of work who doesn't wet the bed at least once a week. Wait... You don't wet the bed, do you?"

"Not regularly, no."

"Good. That's good. I'd recommend seeing a doctor if you did."

I stared at him for a moment and then giggled. "That sounds like something my dad would have said." I blinked rapidly when I felt the surprise sting of tears fill my eyes. "I'm sorry. I don't think about them often, but they've been on my mind a lot lately."

"It never gets better, huh? I hate to think of Will missing his mother like that for the rest of his life."

"It does get better. It never fully goes away, but it does get better."

"He has nightmares. Bad ones. Sometimes he sits up crying for an hour before I can get him calmed down enough to go back to bed."

"I'm sorry."

He leaned against the doorjamb. "I thought moving here

would be a good idea. We could kind of have a clean slate, you know? Hasn't worked out that way. I think I just stressed him out more."

"Maybe he and Adam should spend more time together. They seem to really get along."

He smiled again. "That'd be great. Will talks about him all the time."

"So does Adam."

We both looked at my purse when the phone rang. The music let me know it was Garrett calling.

"You going to get that?" Michael asked.

I shook my head. "No. How about those résumés?"

He ran his hand over his dark hair. "Yeah. I, uh, realized on the way over here that I'd left those on my desk at the office. I meant to bring them home."

"Oh, I see."

"You see? What do you see?"

"You don't want my help."

"I do. Trust me, I do. I honestly forgot them, and by the time I realized it, we were halfway here."

"That's fine. Um. I'll just grab Adam, and we'll go."

"No. Stay. Please. Let them play for a while." He gestured to the island. "Stay for coffee and more incredibly awkward conversation."

I lowered my face and shook my head. "We have a lot of these awkward conversations, don't we?"

"Yeah. I'm sorry about that. I feel like those are usually my fault."

"Oh, I think I get a little blame there." Sitting on the stool, I reclaimed my cup and sighed as he rounded the countertop to where he'd been standing before. Meeting his gaze, I smiled. "First one to think of something non-awkward to talk about gets a cookie."

"Frogs," he blurted out.

"Frogs?"

"I used to feel about frogs the way our boys do about cars. So, therefore, I know a lot about frogs."

I held my breath for a moment. "Okay. Tell me about frogs."

I WASN'T SURPRISED WHEN GARRETT MET ME AND ADAM in the foyer when we got home. It was nearly dinnertime. He'd called countless times. I'd ignored them all.

He opened his arms, and Adam jumped into them. "Hey, buddy."

"Daddy, you won't believe how cool Will's room is."

Garrett plastered a smile on his face, but his eyes filled with suspicion as he looked at me. "Oh, yeah?" He indulged a few minutes of excited rambling before putting Adam down. "Go wash up. Dinner's almost ready."

The boy dashed off, and Garrett shoved his hands in his pockets before looking at me. "Hey."

"Hi." I set my purse on the table in the foyer and tilted my head. "How are you feeling?"

"Like the world's biggest asshole. I'm sorry about last night."

I shrugged slightly. "It's over."

"Mara, I..."

"Garrett. It's done."

He crossed the room and put his hands on my face. "I'm not humbled often. Let me do this."

I nodded for him to continue.

"I crossed a line. And not just last night. I knew Megan was getting out of hand, that she was incapable of being discreet. I thought if I ignored her, she'd go away. I had no idea how my behavior must have cut at you. Last night, seeing the way Jake was looking at you, and knowing that you'd probably go to him after the party finally gave me a taste of what you must have been feeling lately, and I acted like a petulant child."

I inhaled slowly as anger boiled low in my gut. "*Lately?* Garrett, you've been having these affairs for six years."

"But this one is different. This one is personal. We can't get away from her. From *them*. We're partners on this takeover. We need them. Listen, I'm going to end things with Megan. She won't like it, but I don't care." He stroked his thumbs over my cheeks. "And you'll end things with Jake."

"No," I said without hesitation. "I won't."

He leaned back as if I'd slapped him. "What do you mean you won't?"

"Megan may not understand the rules, but Jake does. He can be discreet."

"He was looking at you like he wanted to eat you alive last night."

"Maybe he does," I whispered. "And he wasn't the only one. Albert Carter hasn't exactly forgotten the show I put on for him."

He lowered his gaze, and I saw in his eyes that he hadn't

either, but he turned the topic back to Jake. "Muddying the waters with our business partner is a bad idea."

I pulled his hands from my face. "For me. Right? That's what you're saying. It's a bad idea for *me* to muddy the waters. But it was okay for you."

"No. It was a bad idea for me, too. Look how Megan has behaved. Like I owe her something."

"That's on you, Garrett. Jake isn't stupid."

"Are you sure about that? Because it was pretty obvious to me what was on his mind last night."

"Is that why you got drunk and fucked some whore at Betty's party?"

He ran his hand over his hair as he exhaled. "Come with me." He took my hand and led me into the study. Like the other rooms in our home, the acoustics of the high ceiling echoed our shoes on the tile and the click of the door as he closed it behind me. The sunset shining through the arched windows was a rainbow of orange and yellow, turning the bindings that lined the bookshelves into an interesting array of earth tones. Any other time, I may have pulled him across the room for a better look, but this evening, I turned my back to nature's show and crossed my arms.

"When you came home to me that night after I'd told you I'd had an affair, you offered me the best of both worlds, and I jumped at the chance. I could have the woman I loved—my beautiful wife—and any woman who came along? What man wouldn't take that? And like most men, I didn't consider the consequences. For six years, you've been happy taking care of Adam and our home and me. You've been an integral part of the business. I thought we had this thing figured out. This sudden change in you—"

"This change wasn't sudden, Garrett. That's what you aren't understanding. There was nothing sudden about my decision to take a lover. This has been building since the day I learned you'd betrayed me. I just..." I scoffed as I looked at the five-carat diamond that dominated my left hand before holding it up to him. "This meant something to me. Our vows meant something. I never thought a man like you would want someone like me. I was so different from the women who were chosen by men of power. But you married *me*. You chose *me*. I just wish you'd told me before I accepted that I was never going to be enough for you."

"Mara, it's not like that."

"Stop. You're never going to be the husband I want, Garrett. The husband you pretended to be until that stupid assistant of yours came running to rub your affair in my face. I gave you that agreement for one reason and one reason only —to make certain my son has the life he deserves. Even so, part of me, the part that so wanted to be your wife, held out for you. I kept thinking one day you'd realize what you have right here in front of you. But you never will, and I can't keep waiting around for you to see how good our lives could be. And I'm not going to keep trying to be a loyal wife to the husband that *you'll* never be. You wanted a business arrangement for a marriage. You've got one. But don't you ever negotiate sex on my behalf again. Do you understand me?"

I started to step around him, but he put his hand to my hip and turned me, pressing my back against the door.

"I'm sorry," he said gently.

"For what? Fucking some whore at Betty's party? Fucking every whore you've stumbled across since the day we met? Destroying my hopes for our future? Breaking my heart into so many pieces it will never be whole again? Or for throwing me at Albert Carter in exchange for a little information? I loved you," I whispered. "I loved you so much."

"And now?"

I shook my head. "I don't know."

Garrett stared at me, clearly surprised. "What do you mean you don't know?"

I tried to dislodge myself from where he had me cornered, but he blocked my escape. With a sigh, I leaned against the door and closed my eyes for a moment. When I looked at him, I found him staring at me with what appeared to be genuine concern in his eyes.

"I love you, okay? I still love you. I'll always love you, but..." I lowered my face, and a tear escaped. I ignored it. "Not like I did when we got married. Not that wild, endless, unyielding love. Now I don't trust you not to hurt me or betray me. Or throw me at some business associate to close a deal. You call me your queen, but you treat me like a prostitute that you could replace on a whim."

"Don't say that. You mean the world to me, Mara. I would never hurt you."

I scoffed and looked away.

Garrett put his hand to my chin and turned my face back to him. "You are the heart of our family. Of our home. I could never hold another woman in as high regard as I hold you. Believe that. Never forget that. You are my wife. The mother of my son. No one will ever be as precious to me as you." He dropped his hand to my hip. "I haven't been showing you what you mean to me. That's why you turned to Jake."

"No. Garrett—"

"I'm going to do better."

"That's not what I'm asking."

Smiling, he kissed the corner of my mouth. "Because you never ask for anything. Another thing I respect about you." He brushed his lips over mine. "I've taken you for granted. Again. That's a bad habit I'm trying to break. Be patient with me, darling. I'm a work in progress."

I turned my face away, and he moved his kiss to my neck.

Putting my hands to his chest, I pushed him away. "Stop. Garrett, stop it."

He finally leaned back.

"You think fucking me in the study is going to make this better?"

"I was just trying to..." He exhaled heavily and raked his hand through his hair. "Tell me what to do."

I shoved him back another step. "Leave me alone," I said before opening the door and slipping out. I rushed up the stairs to my room and headed straight for the bathroom.

I undressed while the oversized tub filled and then sank into the hot water. I needed to clear my head. My mind was so confused these days. Every time I thought I had a handle on my life, my emotions nosedived and I started questioning every decision I'd ever made.

Sinking into the water, I tried to clear my head of all the problems bouncing around it. I needed to focus on something other than Garrett and Jake and Albert and my aunt's fucked-up advice. Sighing, I cupped my hand and lifted it out of the water. I turned my hand over, watching the water trickle back into the tub. Then I smiled.

Frogs don't need to drink water, Michael had told me. They absorb it through their skin. His eyes had sparked with something she hadn't seen in him before. I'd seen his eyes fill with shame at his attempt at being a corporate barracuda. I'd seen sorrow when he thought of his wife. Pride when he spoke of Will. I'd seen kindness and sympathy when he tried to understand my disaster of a marriage. I'd even seen a real spark of mischief.

But when he'd talked about frogs, he'd gotten so animated, so full of life, I couldn't help but laugh at him. His eyes lit and his smile spread, showing that his front teeth were just the slightest bit crooked. Not enough that most parents would have put their kids through the hell of braces, but it was rare to see a single imperfection on people in my world—even a slightly crooked tooth—that I'd caught myself staring at his mouth a good part of the afternoon.

He was adorable. So completely adorable. Like a kid in a candy store.

"Do you know…" That phrase left his mouth a hundred times, and I hadn't known any of the useless facts he'd tossed my way. I knew now. I knew more than I ever needed to. And I smiled as I slid deeper into the water and remembered every single one.

[10]

WALKING into Carter Enterprises was a bit like stepping back in time. Albert Carter's father, way back in the day, had modeled the business in the most contemporary and expensive tastes. And it seemed the offices hadn't been updated since. Which, for a property development company, was a death knell and a major reason Carter Enterprises was fading into oblivion.

The building held a certain charm and an air of innocence, but that wasn't going to appeal to the newer market. I'd actually tried to discuss that with Albert's wife once, and she rebuffed me, assuring me that Albert knew what he was doing and that the 1950s charm of the building reflected the old-fashioned values Carter Enterprises banked on to do business.

I'd hoped to avoid Albert Carter as I walked into the dated offices, but I wasn't so lucky. He looked at me, much as he had at the party the other night—hunger barely hidden behind a smirk.

"Mrs. King," he said smoothly as I headed for the elevator.

I drew a breath to brace myself. "Mr. Carter."

"To what do I owe the pleasure?"

I smiled sweetly. "Actually, I'm here to see Mr. Redmond. He's struggling to hire a nanny, and I offered my assistance."

"How kind of you." The elevator doors slid open, and we stepped inside. The tension in the air was palpable. "I'd love to have you and Garrett on the yacht again soon," he said as soon as the doors closed.

"Oh, we're so busy, Albert."

"You're never too busy to enjoy life, Mara. And I know you enjoyed the last visit. We all did."

I smiled. "Until the heat and champagne got to my head, I'm afraid. I very nearly ruined the day."

"Nonsense. I'm just glad Garrett was able to...make you feel better."

The memory flashed through my mind, and I had no doubt it was going through Albert's as well. I jolted when the doors opened and he put his hand to the small of my back to lead me out into the lobby.

Michael came to a stop as he saw us, and an uncertain smile curved his lips.

"Morning, Michael," Albert said casually. "Good luck with the nanny search, kids."

"Thanks, Albert," I said.

He leaned down and kissed my cheek lightly. "Always a pleasure, Mara."

He walked away, and Michael took a moment to look at me before gesturing toward his office.

"You're early."

"It's called manners, Michael. You should always be early. Never late."

He nodded. "Another thing I need to work on."

We walked by his assistant, and she didn't even look up. I started to stop, to ask for coffee, but he grabbed my arm and pulled me into his office. He closed the door and went straight to the coffee pot.

"Someone once told me that you never say no to coffee."

I smirked as I set my bag in a chair. "If I were a frog, I'd just soak in it all day."

He laughed as he carried two cups to the sitting area in his office and opened a file. "Okay, then." He rubbed his hands together.

"Give me the file." I opened the surprisingly thin stack of papers and creased my brow at the first haphazardly organized résumé. There was nothing professional about it. "No." I tossed it aside and moved on to the next one. "No. And no."

Michael frowned as he picked up the papers. "You're not even reading these."

"I don't have to. Not only is the formatting a mess, but these people don't have enough experience."

"Nobody has enough experience until someone gives them a job to gain experience."

I tossed aside another nanny application. "Do you want that experience to come at the price of your son?"

He didn't respond.

I glanced at him and saw that he'd accepted my point. "Where did your assistant find these people?"

"I don't know. I didn't ask."

"Call her in."

"What?"

I gathered the résumés and tapped them into a neat pile. Reaching for his phone, I pushed the button.

I had to push it twice more before a snippy voice came through the intercom.

"Yes?"

I held my breath for a moment before letting it out slowly. "Stacey, this is Mrs. King. Come in here for a moment, please."

"What are you doing?" Michael asked.

"Completely overstepping my boundaries. Just sit back, keep your mouth shut, and let me handle this." I stood, papers in hand, facing the door so I was prepared when his snarky assistant entered.

The woman came in, head tilted and jaw set, clearly not appreciating the interruption to whatever she'd been doing.

I held up the papers. "Which agency sent you these applicants?"

She creased her brow. "Does it matter?"

Anger lit in me at being so easily dismissed. "Yes. It matters. Where did you find the applicants to assist Mr. Redmond in effectively and safely raising his child?"

"Online."

"Where online?"

She narrowed her eyes. "I posted an ad."

"*Where?* A professional childcare site?"

"Does it matter?"

My fury came to life, and I pointed at the door. "Get out."

"What?"

I closed the distance between us. "If you don't care enough to do this job, I will find someone who does."

"You're not my boss."

"Are you sure about that?" I asked with a cocked brow.

Stacey looked from me to Michael and back. "Mr. Carter wouldn't allow you—"

"Oh, sweet girl, you have no idea what Albert Carter would allow me to do." I stared her down as she seemed to accept that I wasn't the pushover Michael had been. "Do you want this job?"

"Y-Yes."

"Then act like it. Do you honestly believe a man in Mr. Redmond's position would hire a nanny off some random website?"

"N-No."

I tilted my head. "Excuse me?"

"No, ma'am."

"Why didn't you contact a nanny agency? Surely you are smart enough to know that is proper protocol."

"I-I'll call them now."

"I didn't ask you to do it now, I asked why you didn't do that in the first place. You've been absolutely worthless since Mr. Redmond started. Why? You didn't get to this level acting like this toward your previous employer. Why are you giving Mr. Redmond such a fit?"

She stared me down, but after a moment seemed to sense

her defiance wasn't going to get her anywhere with me. "I...I was close to Mr. Banner."

"The previous vice president?" I clarified.

Stacey nodded, and I softened my approach. She wasn't simply a disgruntled employee. She'd been taught a very harsh lesson and was still angry.

"I suppose he told you that when he left, you'd be going with him."

"That's what he said."

"Was this a professional or a personal promise?"

She hesitated, taking a moment to glance at Michael. "Personal."

"Listen to me," I said gently. "Men have always used women and tossed us aside like we are nothing. They always have, and they always will. Until we get smart enough to no longer be used. He lied to you. He deceived you to get what he wanted. You're angry. I understand that. But acting like a bitch to Mr. Redmond isn't going to do a damn thing other than get you fired. Do you think Mr. Banner will care if you lose your job?"

"No."

"No. He won't care. Nor will I or Mr. Redmond or Mr. Carter. I'll have a perfectly competent and proficient replacement here within the hour. This company won't miss a beat without you, but I suspect your life will be somewhat disrupted without this company. If you want this job, *do* this job. If you don't, leave. This childcare situation is a great hindrance on your boss. It is distracting him from work he should be doing. It is your job to make his life easier. I want you to schedule an hour tomorrow for Mr. Redmond and me to review another set of nanny résumés—*real* nanny résumés. If you don't have at least three professionally prepared and independently vetted candidates for us to review, don't bother coming to work. Do you understand me?"

She again glanced at Michael, but she nodded as she answered, "Yes, Mrs. King."

"Good. Find a time that works for Mr. Redmond, and let me know when to be here. And, Stacey," I called before the woman left. "Men *never* leave their wives for their assistants. Don't fall for that line again."

She scoffed. "Trust me. I won't."

Once Stacey closed the door, I turned and smiled sweetly. "If that doesn't straighten her out, you really must fire her, Michael."

"I don't completely understand all of what just happened here, but uh...did...uh...did you insinuate that we're..."

"Lovers? Yes."

"You also may have insinuated that you and Albert..."

"Are *close*? I did. Will she rush to the watercooler to tell anyone who will listen? Probably. But people presume all kinds of things, so...whatever." I crossed my arms in front of me. "Now. About those swim lessons for Will. I hear you still haven't called the instructor I recommended. Do you plan to?"

Michael raised his hands in surrender. "I'll do whatever you say, just don't throw your wrath my way. I'm thoroughly terrified of you now."

I grinned. "Good. I like it that way."

"Do you?"

"Of course. I prefer my men quivering and begging for mercy."

He chuckled. "I sensed that about you from day one. Since we aren't going to be going through résumés, want to talk about something else while you finish your coffee?"

I lifted my brows, and he nodded toward the sitting area. I dropped into a chair and sighed.

"Why do I get the feeling you don't want to talk about frogs again?"

"Something's off with you. I could tell the first time we talked—really talked. And when I saw you step off the elevator this morning, you seemed upset. I've tried not to push, but now I'm pushing."

"I'm fine."

"You're not."

"I am."

He put his hands on his hips and dipped his head down. "Mara."

I sighed at his demanding stare. It was very similar to the one I gave Adam when he didn't obey the first time I said something.

"I'm just... I have a lot going on."

"Garrett?"

I darted my gaze to him, and he shrugged.

"Just a guess."

"I don't think I should discuss my marriage with you."

"You've already told me of your agreement with your husband. You've admitted Adam is your only friend. And you just inadvertently started a rumor that we're having an affair. I think we've reached the point where you can talk to me about pretty much anything."

I laughed softly and then shook my head. "It isn't Garrett. I mean...not directly. It's me. I'm changing. I'm... evolving into something I swore I'd never become."

"A sloth?"

I creased my brow and then chuckled as I shoved his shoulder. "You ask me to talk to you, then you mock me."

"I'm not mocking." His smile softened. "I'm not. I'm sorry. I just hate seeing you look so sad, and I see it far too often."

Lowering my face, I drew a breath. "I told you before, I thought our marriage was different than the others. I acted like what I didn't know couldn't hurt me. But it did." I swallowed and lifted my gaze to him. "It hurt me more than I ever realized."

"Now you're realizing it?"

I nodded.

"So get out."

"I can't." I blinked as tears started to form in my eyes.

"I know you care about him—"

"I can't, Michael." I leaned back in the chair and rolled my head back, laughing at my own stupidity. "Let's talk about something else."

"What if we pinky swear?"

I looked at him again, creasing my brow. "What?"

He held his hand out, lifting his little finger. "Whatever is said in this room won't ever leave this room. Pinky swear."

"Michael."

"I know you didn't have a lot of friends growing up,

Mara, but even you have to know how unbreakable a pinky swear is." He pushed is finger toward me again. "I'll never tell another soul. I swear. Not even my non-pudding-eating, bed-wetting best friend."

I laughed as I wrapped my pinky around his and we shook. Dropping my hand, I took a deep breath and decided that of all the insane things I'd done in the last few weeks, talking to Michael was probably the least crazy.

"In my attempt to control him and his affairs, I had an agreement drawn up. A contract. Allowing him to have his affairs under certain rules. One of them is that he cannot divorce me without walking away from everything, including Adam. He agreed. On one condition..."

"The same rules applied to you?"

"The same rules apply to me. I can screw around. I can have as many lovers as I want. But I can't leave him without losing my son."

"Do you want to leave him? Because if you do..."

I lowered my head.

He grabbed my hands, and I looked at him. "If you do, I'm quite confident an agreement like this could be challenged in court."

"Oh, the spectacle that would make. We'd both be ruined, Michael. And everyone would know. Adam would know."

"He's six."

"He won't be forever. Can you imagine the things he'd hear about his parents when he turned into a teenager? I can't do that. Besides, I'm not there yet. I'm not ready to leave him. I just... I don't like what I'm becoming. I don't like how reckless I've been behaving, and when I think of every stupid thing I've done, they always tie back to him."

"He's your husband, Mara. Most things in your life do tie back to him. Can you tell me what you've done that you're so upset about?"

Images flashed through my mind. Stretched out on Albert's yacht. Bent over the bed in my suite. Aunt Victoria rejecting my request for an investment so I could build my own company. Humiliation hit me hard. I couldn't imagine there'd ever be a way to make Michael understand those things.

Pushing myself up, I walked to his window and watched dark clouds rolling in, quickly blocking out the sunlight. The scene seemed fitting.

"I can feel something shifting inside," I said. "Something that makes me justify things in my mind that I shouldn't be able to justify."

"Like your husband's infidelity?"

I thought for a moment before nodding. As the sky outside darkened, his reflection became clear. He looked concerned. Genuinely concerned. Jake had given me that same sad look when he'd caught me downing scotch in my office before noon.

Turning, I offered Michael a soft smile. "Call me tomorrow. Let me know when you're ready to look at the new résumés."

He stepped in my way as I headed for the door. "Wait. You can't leave when you're still so upset."

"I made these choices, Michael. Now I'm paying the

price. I'll be okay. I just need to... I need to readjust my outlook. That's all."

"You shouldn't have to learn to accept your husband cheating on you. You can find a way out, Mara. I'll help."

"That's sweet, but I learned to accept his shortcomings a long time ago. It's mine that I have to come to terms with now. I'll see you tomorrow."

[11]

I jolted at the feel of something brushing over my thigh and had to blink several times before I noticed Garrett sitting on the edge of my bed. I moaned in misery at being pulled from a deep sleep.

"What are you doing?"

"Waking up my wife."

It was too early for his games. My mind wasn't clear enough to be on my toes.

"Well, don't."

"I need you to get up, darling. We're going to have guests."

I pushed his hand away when his palm crept up my thigh.

"Garrett. Leave me alone."

"Albert and Jake are coming for breakfast. Albert asked if you'd be joining us. Of course, I was coy about it. Told him you'd prefer to sleep in. But I got the hint. He wants to see you." He tugged the sheet away despite my attempt to cling to it. "I thought I'd suggest we have our meeting outside—the weather's so wonderful, you know—and then, oh, look, there's my beautiful wife climbing out of the pool." He ran his finger through the crease between my breasts. "Soaking wet and in a tiny bathing suit. He has such good memories of the last time he saw you in a bikini."

I narrowed my eyes at him. "Did you negotiate another deal with him?"

"No." He pinched my nipple, and I gasped and glared at him from the stab of unexpected pain. He narrowed his eyes too, but I was certain he looked far more menacing than I did. "But a little goodwill goes a long way. Don't you think?" He eased his hold and eased the pain with a few gentle strokes before leaning down and putting a gentle kiss where he'd pinched. "I had the nanny take Adam to the park. I want all your attention on that old geezer. He'll be here any minute, so get up and get changed."

He pushed himself up and left, and I lay there letting the fury sink in. The son of a bitch. For all his sweet words and promises of how much I meant to him, it was becoming more and more clear that I was just another piece of meat for him to drag around. And now he was showing me off for *goodwill*.

I scoffed. He wanted a show for Albert's benefit? Oh, he'd get one.

Marching from my room, wrapping myself in a pink satin robe as I went, I stormed down the back stairs and through the kitchen to the patio. Outside, I smiled and nodded at the gardeners who were obviously surprised by my appearance. I didn't parade around the house undressed. Ever.

At the pool, I carelessly discarded my robe and dove

naked into the cool water. I swam every morning without fail, so routine kicked in, and I started doing laps. I only managed to finish three before Garrett guided Albert and Jake to the seating area.

"Darling," Garrett called and waved at me. "Come say hello."

I swam to the edge and grinned sheepishly. "I'm not really in a state to greet guests. I *really* wish you'd told me you were expecting company."

"Nonsense." He waved again. "Don't be shy. Come have breakfast with us."

"Garrett..."

"Mara," he said more firmly. He lifted his brows at me. "Come. Now."

"Okay." I swam to the stairs and smirked as I stood. The men froze. Albert's eyes widened and went straight to my bare tits, then lower, while Garrett's jaw muscles tightened. Jake, on the other hand, lifted his brows appreciatively and smiled brightly, clearly amused.

"I'm so sorry, gentlemen. I meant it when I said I wasn't expecting company." I didn't flinch—didn't falter—as the three men stared at me. I simply strolled to where I'd left my robe, bent to pick it up, and slid my arms into the sleeves.

The pale material clung to my wet skin as I pulled the front closed and tied the sash around my waist. I didn't look down to see if the waterlogged satin had turned sheer. The way Albert stared at my tits and licked his lips confirmed the robe wasn't doing a damn thing to offer me an ounce of modesty.

Holding my head up, shoulders back like the fucking lady I was, I walked to the old man and kissed his cheek.

"Please forgive my appearance." I looked at my husband and batted my eyes. "Shame on you. You know my morning routine."

"N-N-No need to apologize, Mara," Albert stuttered out, still looking at my chest. "Accidents happen." His face was flush, and the tenting of his slacks confirmed that he indeed appreciated my *goodwill*.

I kissed Jake's cheek.

"Scoundrel," he whispered.

I winked at him as I leaned back, then took a seat at the table.

Albert sat across from me, Garrett to his right, and Jake to his left.

One of the servers came out, carrying a tray of coffee cups and an urn and nearly tripped. She made a beeline for me and bent down.

"Mrs. King—"

I grinned at Albert as I lifted my hand to hush her.

"But, Mrs. King—"

"Serve the coffee and leave us, Rosa," I ordered.

Garrett sat back, looking disgruntled.

Jake cleared his throat, looking amused as hell.

Albert stared, looking like he could climb over the table and bury his face in my chest any second.

Rosa trembled as she filled the mugs. She looked at me from across the table as she filled Albert's cup and widened her eyes as she gestured toward my chest.

I ignored her. I smiled at Albert and lifted my mug to my

lips, sipping the hot brew. "What brings you by this morning?"

"Uh. Um." He gestured lamely.

"Garrett," I said, reminding him of my husband's name.

"Garrett extended the invitation."

I put my hand on my husband's and smiled sweetly. "He's so full of goodwill, isn't he? Always thinking of others. One of the many things I love about him. He's so generous. Always sharing what's his."

Jake choked on the coffee in his mouth, but I pretended I didn't notice. I returned my focus to the man nearly drooling across the table.

"It was wonderful to see you gentlemen this morning, but I should put some clothes on." I stood, and, as gentlemen do, they stood, but none of them completely. I grinned, imagining they all had raging hard-ons.

I walked into the house, dismissing yet another housekeeper who attempted to warn me of my appearance and went straight upstairs to shower away the chlorine. After slipping into a sundress, I stood in front of the mirror, dragging a brush through my hair as I cursed my husband.

With my hair neatly brushed and my makeup perfectly done, I headed downstairs. I didn't know how long Garrett's breakfast would last, but I wasn't going to sit around waiting for the inevitable confrontation. In fact, it was probably best if we both had time to simmer down before I gave in to temptation to cut Garrett's heart out with a letter opener.

I headed to the kitchen where I knew Tomas would be sitting, likely sampling whatever the cook was making for lunch.

"Tomas, can you give me a ride?"

"Of course, Mrs. King." He brushed his hands free of breadcrumbs and jumped to his feet. He grabbed his uniform jacket and shoved his arms in it, then pulled the keys from the pocket as we walked to the car. He opened the back door to our town car, and I slid in.

I was officially done being the good wife. I needed to take control—*real* control—of my life.

The office was nearly empty since it was the weekend, but I smiled and nodded at the few King Inc. employees I spotted. In my office, I dug my warehouse-improvement proposal from the desk drawer and debated for a moment. I could do it. I could find a way to be free of Garrett without losing my son and my lifestyle. I just had to make my way on my own.

Just like Michael said, there had to be a way out of this mess. I had the plan. I just needed the backing. If I couldn't count on the only family I had—Aunt Victoria—to help me, and I didn't have a single friend I could count on, I'd just have to find another way.

And thanks to Garrett's promises and goodwill toward a dirty old man, I knew just how to get the money I needed without my husband ever finding out. If what Garrett said was true, I could wrap Albert around my finger and twist him to do my bidding. And, per Victoria's advice, I wasn't above using my body for my own personal gain—I just wasn't about to use it for Garrett.

Carrying my proposal back to the car, I directed Tomas to take me to the Carter Estate. I wasn't quite sure how to approach Albert, but I was confident by the time I left, I'd have the investment needed to make my vision for the warehouse district a reality.

My heart was in my throat by the time Tomas stopped the car in front of Albert's house. When he opened the door to help me out, I clung to his hand a bit longer than necessary, bracing myself for what I was about to do.

"Ma'am?" he asked, his voice tight. "Are you okay?"

I flashed a fake smile. "Yes. I may be a while."

"I'll be here when you're ready."

"Thank you," I said, somewhat breathlessly.

I protested when Garrett wanted me to tease Albert, but here I was walking into the lion's den to—what? How far was I willing to go? What was I willing to give to get a check from him? To get an investment?

The door opened and I smiled at the man who answered. "Would you let Mr. Carter know Mara King is here to see him, please?"

The man nodded, and I was shown into the living area of the Carters' sprawling estate. Though I was offered tea, I asked for scotch, which was promptly brought to me. While I didn't think Albert had as much money as Garrett and I had gained, his money was old, and his wealth showed in his home, which had belonged to his father, and his father before that. Built-in bookshelves lined the walls. Most were filled with books that probably hadn't been opened since they'd been deliberately placed, but some shelves had photos or awards prominently displayed.

I stopped perusing the images when I found one that had to have been a young Albert, dressed in knee knockers, a suit jacket, and a little cap. He looked as serious then as he did now. He'd never been overly handsome, even in the photo frame next to the little boy where Albert was standing next to a much younger version of his wife.

I swallowed what was left in my glass, closed my eyes, and prepared myself to give him whatever he wanted.

"Mara," Albert said, coming into the room.

I turned and put a sweet smile on my face. "Hello, Albert."

"I'm surprised to see you here." He glanced around as if confirming I was there alone before closing the doors, ensuring our privacy and making my hands tremble even more.

"I wanted to apologize for this morning."

He lowered his gaze, likely unintentionally, to my chest. I was covered now, but there was enough cleavage to give him something to admire.

"Don't think a thing about it," he said.

"I don't think either of us has to pretend we don't know what that was about."

He drew a breath and squared his shoulders. "Honesty from a woman. That's refreshing."

I chuckled. "I could say the same about men. If you choose to be honest with me, that is."

"Garrett wants something else from me and is sacrificing you to get it."

"He said this morning was just a little goodwill. Of course, he only asked that I flaunt around in a bikini again. I suppose I took it a step too far."

He smiled. "I can't say I minded. You are incredible to

look at. I confess to having a difficult time focusing on anything else since this morning."

A slow smile curved my lips. Garrett was right. I had this man in the palm of my hand. I bit my lip in that naïve way that seemed to tempt all men.

"Good."

"You're a darling, Mara. You really are. I adore you in so many ways. I've always had a great amount of respect for you. I was surprised by your behavior on the yacht, and more so this morning. I didn't take you for the type to play these games. As much as I have enjoyed the benefits of watching, I admit I'm a bit disappointed. I only asked what I did of you because I never imagined you'd agree."

I barely heard the last sentence. I was stuck on the part of him being disappointed in me. That stung for some reason. I didn't care what Albert thought of me. Not really. So the slap of his words took me by surprise.

"It was for naught," he said. "I want you to know that."

"Excuse me?"

"The two deals I *sabotaged* for Garrett were deals that had already gone south. They weren't coming to fruition anyway."

Anger coiled low in my stomach. I was so tired of feeling used and manipulated. I scoffed and shook my head as I realized how much a pawn I'd become in this game. I hadn't even noticed, adding to my conviction to finally take control of my life.

"I was testing him," Albert said. "Seeing how far he'd go to get what he wanted. He failed you, Mara. He didn't hesitate in giving me what I wanted in exchange for a little information."

I stood straighter. "No. He didn't. He told me what you wanted, Albert. And that he'd never let you sleep with me."

"Sleep with you?" Seeing his yellowed teeth as he smirked made my stomach turn. "My dear girl. I'm nearly eighty-two years old and have a heart condition. I don't think I'd survive sleeping with a woman as young as yourself. Not that it wouldn't be a joy to try. All I wanted was to see him pleasure you. I was hoping to watch you...peak, but we were so rudely interrupted. Perhaps next time, hmm?"

My humiliation came crashing down. And my anger.

Garrett had lied to me again. He'd said he'd *negotiated* what I gave him. That he'd drawn a line in the sand of what Albert had asked. That bastard.

"I'm not sure what game he is playing with you, but I didn't ask for anything this morning. I was pleasantly surprised by your appearance, though." He smiled. "I certainly won't be turning down any breakfast invitations at the King mansion soon."

I laughed softly despite my fury. "Garrett came to me this morning. Said you were coming over and that I should show our goodwill. He doesn't appreciate that you're a bit more focused on your business these days. He thought a little cleavage would give you something else to focus on. I'm not his hooker, so I...showed him, I guess you could say."

He chuckled. "You showed us all, sweetheart."

I wanted to lower my gaze as a tinge of humiliation touched me, but I'd be damned if these men were going to make me feel ashamed.

Albert tilted his head. "You aren't here simply to confess that the incident this morning was intentional. What do you want, Mara?"

I turned my back on him and paced across the Oriental rug sprawled in front of a desk that looked original to the house. The reds and blues were faded and didn't match the rest of the décor, seeming to confirm the age. The rug wasn't there for aesthetics as much as sentimental reasons. It was probably one of the first major purchases of Albert's great-grandfather as he built the family fortune. A reminder that the family had humble beginnings.

After taking a moment to gather my thoughts, I faced him. "For years, I've convinced myself that I am more to my husband than a means to an end. Every time I think I've leveled the playing field or earned an ounce of his respect, he pats me on the head and tosses me a piece of jewelry or a vacation. Or he does something like he did this morning to show just how little he really does think of me. I'm sick of lying to myself. I'm sick of pretending that I'm more than a pretty face with half a brain that Garrett King enjoys flaunting around town. The only time Garrett pays attention to me is when he needs me for something."

"And Jake?"

I was shocked by his question but didn't let it show. "What about Jake?"

"Are you sleeping with him?"

Damn. There really were no secrets in this city. "Yes."

"Does Garrett know?"

"Of course he does."

"And he allows it?"

I chuckled flatly. "Allows it? Have you not noticed no woman goes untouched when my husband is near? Listen, you may have been testing his willingness to trade me for secrets, but *he* was testing *me*. It's only a matter of time before he pushes further, trades more. I'm nothing more than a whore to him. And unless I take back control of my life, I never will be."

"I'm guessing that's why you're here."

"I have what it takes to run a company and succeed. I have vision and drive. What I don't have is my own company."

"You want my company?"

"Eventually. Yes."

He lifted a bushy brow.

"King Incorporated is about to swallow Carter Enterprises whole."

He laughed softly. "Mara. I'm this close to closing a deal—"

"We contracted the Sanders Avenue property yesterday."

His eyes bulged. "That's impossible."

"No. That's business," I said. "You slipped. Something you said on the yacht tipped Garrett off to what he needed to undermine you."

"I don't believe you."

"You don't have to believe me, Albert. All you have to do is know that when the call comes in, I have what you need to save our company. Call me when you're ready to hear my offer. Oh, and Albert, I do hope you enjoyed the show this morning. It's the last one you're going to get."

I walked out feeling far more empowered than I had in years.

[12]

GARRETT HADN'T QUITE FORGIVEN me for the stunt with Albert. I don't know why I cared, but whenever he gave me the cold shoulder, I felt the need to make amends. Even when I was right. And I was definitely right that he'd crossed the line by offering me up for *goodwill* with Albert. Especially after learning the truth about the *negotiation* that happened on the yacht.

Even so, after over a day of him avoiding me, I—as always —made the first move to reconciliation. Strutting toward his office, I inhaled a calming breath but didn't slow my stride when I found Megan Decker standing there, glaring down at Garrett's stupid assistant.

Megan turned her nasty look to me and smirked as if to say *sorry, not sorry* that she'd been busted meeting Garrett at his office. She had no reason to be outside his office unless she was there for totally inappropriate reasons. Megan had no part in Jake's business, and therefore, no reason to be there other than to seduce my husband.

Rather than showing the slightest sign of anger, I smiled pleasantly at her. "Hello, darling." I gave the obligatory kiss on her cheek. "Did you have an appointment with Garrett?"

"Uh, lunch." She increased her smirk. "We're having lunch."

"Well, I'll do my best to be quick. I just need to chat with him for a moment." I looked back at Garrett's assistant. "Does he know Mrs. Decker is here?"

"Not yet, *Mrs*. King." Sweet that the girl had some sense of loyalty, but it was likely more to herself than me. She wasn't any better at hiding her affair with my husband than Megan, but she couldn't very well piss on Garrett's leg and claim him. The best she could do was remind Megan the man was married.

"Don't bother. I'll let him know." I walked into Garrett's office without being announced and closed the door behind me.

As the president of the company, he had the best office in the building. The corner windows looked out over the city, much like at the Bird's Nest. He could look down on the world anytime he wanted—just the way he liked it. The clicking of my heels echoed around the large room as I walked toward his oversized mahogany desk.

Garrett met my gaze as he leaned back in his chair, looking like a disapproving father.

I stuck my lip out in a pout. "Oh, sweetheart. Really? You're still not over yesterday?"

"Your behavior—"

I stopped in front of his desk and put my palms to the

surface as I met his gaze, grinning when he momentarily looked down my blouse at the lacy bra I wore beneath.

"Which part, Garrett? The part where I strutted naked to show your goodwill, or the part where I implied you wouldn't mind sharing me?"

His face tensed even further, and I *tsk-ed* as I walked around his desk. Pushing his papers aside, I hopped up and tugged my tight skirt high enough to spread my legs and plant a heel-covered foot on either side of him. As expected, his gaze instantly dropped to catch a glimpse of my panties.

"I warned you not to treat me like a whore," I said.

"You certainly acted like one."

"No more than you had me act on Albert's yacht." I brushed my fingertips over his cheeks. "I think we're even now, don't you?"

"Hardly."

I ran my hand over his tie, down to where it ended in his crotch. "Hmm. And how would you like me to make it up to you?"

Garrett smirked like he'd somehow won, and that little bit of hate in my heart for him grew. I didn't let it show. Instead, I cupped his balls. His cock sprang to life, and I grinned before kissing him deeply.

I didn't owe him make-up sex. If anything, he owed me. But screw those two bitches on the other side of the door for thinking they could have what was mine. Garrett King was an asshole in ways I was just beginning to realize. But he was *my* asshole, and every now and then, I needed to remind his side dishes of that.

He broke free from my kiss. "You think a quick fuck is going to make it up to me?"

I smiled when he ran his hand over my panties. "It's a start."

"A start?" He tugged at my underwear, and I lifted my hips enough to let him remove them.

He closed his eyes and inhaled my scent. The hope in his eyes was unmistakable. He never turned down office sex. Which was why I assumed Megan had shown up here. But I got to him first. And the asshole was *my* husband. I would drain him before she got the chance.

Reaching between my legs, I grabbed his hand and pushed two of his fingers deep between my legs, then sucked them into my mouth, cleaning them of my juices. I didn't do this type of thing, so the thrill in his eyes grew tenfold. I had him. Hook, line, and fucking sinker.

"Holy shit," he breathed. Fisting his still wet fingers into my hair, he pulled me to him and kissed me hard. With his ego thoroughly placated, he stood and released his belt. His slacks fell a moment later. I dug a condom from my purse and slid it over him as he pulled me from the desk. Turning me over, he pushed me forward and shoved his dick in me.

I sighed, but not from pleasure. That was my foreplay? That was my warming up? He must be more frustrated with me than I realized. My enjoyment usually meant a bit more to him than that.

"You feel so fucking good like this," he panted as he fucked me.

"Oh, God," I cried much more loudly than necessary. "Oh, yes!"

The risk of getting caught was always something that plucked the strings of his desires. My high volume increased the odds. As I intended, he responded with enthusiasm, increasing his own volume as he grunted like a caveman claiming me. The sound of our bodies slapping together echoed through his office. He may have known how to exploit my emotions, but I knew just as much when it came to manipulating him sexually.

"Say it," I begged. "Tell me what I need to hear." I tightened my vaginal walls around him as he pumped, milking him. "Say it."

"You're my queen."

"Louder," I demanded and worked my body over his.

"You're my queen. I love you. I love you so fucking much." He fell forward as he cried out, finishing, and my sense of satisfaction grew. That satisfaction wasn't sexual, though. It was a petty kind of pleasure knowing Megan wouldn't get what she wanted from my husband.

I laughed between pants. "Oops, I think we got a little loud."

"I don't care." Pulling from me, he turned me and held my face as he kissed me deeply. "Jesus, it's been too long since you've come to me like this."

I gave him a little pout. "I'm sorry about yesterday."

He stroked my hair and put his forehead to mine. "No, I'm the one who is sorry, Mara. You're right. You're not a piece of property to be used."

"No, I'm not. And I don't appreciate how cheap you made me feel. Promise me you won't do it again." I cupped his balls and squeezed lightly as I gave him a stern look. "Promise."

He laughed lightly. "I promise."

I smirked as he focused on pulling his pants up enough to walk to his private bathroom. Running warm water, we quickly cleaned up.

"I want a family dinner tonight," I said as we stood by his desk—him fixing the mess of papers while I reapplied a wine-colored coat to my lips. "Be home by six, please."

He nodded. "I'll do my best."

I smiled and planted a kiss on his lips. "Oh," I said innocently and wiped at the lip print, leaving enough to be easily discerned. "I forgot to tell you. Megan Decker is outside. Apparently she's expecting to have you for lunch."

He lifted his brows, looking shocked as he realized what I'd just done.

"Hope she likes sloppy seconds," I said and winked at him.

I walked out of his office, knowing I looked amiss but didn't care. "He's all yours," I sang to Megan, whose face was so red, I feared her head might explode as I strolled by her.

I was practically walking on air as I got back to my office.

I'd just sat down when my cell phone rang. Albert's name showed on my Caller ID, and my heart flipped in my chest. I knew why he was calling. He'd learned the truth of my warning. King Inc. had stolen the Sanders Avenue deal from under him.

"Hello?"

"Your husband is a son of a bitch," Albert seethed into my ear.

"Yes, I'm aware."

"My company is ruined. I can't bounce back from this. The only thing I can do is sell out. To that bastard."

"No, Albert. The only thing you can do is make a deal with me."

The line was thick with silence. "Somehow this doesn't feel any less like working with the devil than the alternative."

"Meet me. Hear what I have to say. If you don't like it, sell out to Garrett. Lose your company. Lose your family legacy. He'd love that."

A heavy sigh filled the line. "Fine. Tell me what you have in mind."

"I will." I rattled off the address to one of the warehouses I intended to buy with instructions to meet me there in an hour. Alone.

He arrived in fifty minutes. I looked over my shoulder at the sound of footsteps entering the open space of the mostly empty warehouse.

"You're early."

"Good business," Albert said, and I smiled.

I always said that too.

Turning, I held my arms out. "What do you think?"

He exhaled. "I think this better be a secret meeting place and not your plan to save my business."

I chuckled and put my hand through the crook of his arm. "Come with me." Pulling him through the open space, I walked him up a rusted flight of stairs to the upper level and to a wall of windows. "Now, what do you think?"

He stared out at the city skyline. "This view would be magnificent at night."

"Yes, it would." I steered him to the other side of the warehouse and up another flight of stairs to a door that led to the roof. "Picture this as a courtyard with a community garden, chairs, and an outdoor eating space. You could see the fireworks on the Fourth of July without leaving home. All the festivals downtown are within walking distance. No high-priced parking. No fighting traffic."

He looked around. "This building needs a lot of work."

"Mostly cosmetic. We can have walls erected to separate the warehouse into multiple lofts, but *most* of the work will be cosmetic. And that will be easy. Part of the charm will be the commercial undertones of the structure. They'll be paying for it to *be* a warehouse without it *being* a warehouse."

He laughed. "That's something my wife would say. You women have your own language."

"Trust me. I'm making sense."

"If you say so." He looked around again. "Do you have plans on how to break this space up?"

My smile spread so wide my cheeks ached. "You know I do. Come see."

He followed me to an old metal table where I rolled out a floor plan of the existing structure to break down my vision of how the space would be utilized.

Albert made a few suggestions, but for the most part agreed with my ideas.

"Okay. Now, what about the location?" he asked. "And I don't mean how long it takes to get here from downtown. I'm talking about the isolation. The lack of security. How are you going to convince people to buy in this area if they are afraid of being robbed while carrying in groceries?"

"I'm working on that," I said, trying to keep the reality of that particular hurdle from tainting my excitement. "But overall…" I smiled up at him. "This is good. This is an untapped area for residential development. Garrett doesn't see it. He thinks it's too high-risk. What do you think?"

He shoved his hands in his pockets and looked around again.

If he was anything like my husband, he was working on his spiel to let me down easy.

"Albert, here's the deal. You're out of options. Garrett is going to overtake this market. You have one last chance to take a stand for your company. For your family's business. You have nothing to lose by trusting me."

"But what do you have to gain?"

He faced me, and that natural suspicion had returned to his eyes.

Tucking my papers into a file, I tapped it on the table a few times.

"In the last few months, I've started pushing back against my husband. Trying to become the vice president he's never let me be. In doing so, I've come to a realization. I'm not immune to the heartless business side of Garrett King. His expectations of my role in this marriage are changing, as you witnessed firsthand. I have to push back or I'll be doing more than walking around naked to appease his business associates. He'll have me on my back whenever the need arises. I refuse to be his prostitute, but I can't walk away without losing everything. I have to build a safety net for myself and my son so when I can leave I have the means to support us."

"And how does helping me help you?"

I took a breath before speaking. "I'll save Carter Enterprises. I can do it. This warehouse district is only part of my plans. This is just the surface of what I can do. I know property development inside and out. I've helped Garrett build King Inc. into the monster that it has become. I will work behind the scenes, and I will save your company. In exchange, I want controlling interest of Carter Enterprises when you die. Grace is significantly younger than you. She'll be around for some years, God willing. It will appear as though she's running the company, but I want to be pulling the strings. Silently. No one can know I'm running the company because Garrett would come at us with both barrels. This must be a secret acquisition, but I want the majority of Carter Enterprises in my name. I have to start protecting myself now."

He nodded as if he'd been expecting my proposition. He moved around again, looking from the windows to the high ceilings.

"When I hired Michael Redmond, I had high hopes for his ability to help us bounce back. He's too green. He's too kind. He doesn't have the cutthroat attitude I need to stop my company from sinking." He looked at me. "Clearly you do. You'd honestly work against your husband?"

"To save myself? Yes, I would. I can't start a company of my own and expect it to succeed. But I can pull Carter Enterprises back onto its feet. I can restore your company, Albert. Keep your family legacy alive."

He laughed softly. "This is what they call being stuck between a rock and a hard place, isn't it? Either way I look at it, my company is going to end up in the hands of a King."

I nodded. "Yes. But this King doesn't want to destroy your company. Garrett does. If Garrett wins, Albert, Carter Enterprises ceases to exist. I'll protect it."

He sighed. "Give me a few days to get the paperwork in order."

I exhaled with relief as I nodded again, trying to hide my excitement.

"I'll call you. When I do, Mara, I want a comprehensive plan. I won't sign a damn thing until you convince me this will work."

I smiled then. "Of course." Extending my hand out, I waited for him to take it. "You won't regret this, Albert."

"No. I expect I won't. You, however, better know if Garrett ever finds out how manipulative you can be, you will."

I watched Albert leave before returning to the wall of windows I'd shown him earlier. The sky was darkening. Rain would start soon in the west, but the east was still sunny. The contrast of dark and light seemed like a mirror of the war that was raging inside me.

I was about to commit the ultimate betrayal in Garrett's eyes. If he ever found out, there would be hell to pay, and I'd have no one to blame but myself.

[13]

I smiled my thanks to Jake's assistant when the woman opened the door to his office and stepped aside for me to enter. Much like Garrett's office, Jake's was far larger than needed, but where Garrett's style was contemporary, Jake's was more rustic. Raw wood planks covered the walls and flowed effortlessly into a wall of shelves, creating a homey feel that was all Jake.

His desk was offset, angled in a corner, leaving room for not one but two sitting areas. The second, set away from his desk, had a couch that gave me naughty ideas. But I wasn't there for sex. Not today, anyway. Perhaps another time.

Jake didn't look up until the door closed and I was approaching his desk.

"I was expecting a phone call, not a personal visit," he said.

"Well, when a man sends me a huge bouquet of lilies, I like to thank him in person. How'd you know my favorite flower?"

He tossed his pen down. "My assistant asked your assistant, of course."

I rolled my eyes. "Of course." Sitting across from him, I dropped my oversized purse on the floor and sat back with an expectant lift of my brow.

"What?" he asked after a moment.

"Why did I get flowers, Jake?"

He didn't answer, but shame touched his eyes.

I frowned at him. "You felt guilty for the pool incident."

"I should have told Garrett it was a bad idea to use you like that. I'm sorry."

"As you should be."

He leaned back, and a slow smirk curved his lips. "But that's not why you're here, is it? Dare I ask?"

I giggled. "It's a business matter. I'm debating if I can trust you."

"We fuck three times a week, Mara. I'm fairly confident we've crossed the trust bridge."

"Yes. You'd think so. But sex and business are two different beasts, aren't they?" Decision made, I pulled an envelope out of my purse and handed it to him, watching as he removed and read the contract.

"This is a confidentiality agreement," he said.

"Sign it."

He hesitated for just a moment before he scribbled his name at the bottom and handed the document back to me. I tucked the agreement away, then pulled a folder from my bag.

"I'm working on a project. Something separate from King Incorporated. Something Garrett knows nothing about.

Something he has no hand in. For years, I've built him up, and he treats me like a burden."

He paused as he skimmed the name at the top of the proposal. "You're working with Albert Carter."

"Yes. I convinced him to join me in this new venture. No nipple flashing necessary. As soon as I present him with a sound plan, we'll be good to go."

"And what is your plan?"

"I trust you, Jake. I trusted you before we became intimate, but I especially trust you now. We both have secrets that could be detrimental to our lives if exposed. So...you have nothing to lose by helping me and everything to gain."

"That doesn't explain what you need. Beyond my confidentiality."

"Nothing happens in the property development business in this town that Garrett doesn't know about. I can't build a company from the ground up, but I can pull the strings behind an existing business without my husband finding out. With us closing on the Sanders Avenue deal, Albert was left with no option but to sell out to Garrett."

"Which is what we've been working for," Jake pointed out.

"Until I was whored out to make a business deal," I countered. I knew my tone was sharp. I intended it to be.

"Holy shit," he said with a moan as he rolled his head back and then exhaled. Finally looking at me, he shook his head. "You're going to go into business against your husband?"

"Not exactly. I've been telling him for months that the warehouse district is ripe for upscale residential. He doesn't believe me. He says no one will buy there. So I'm going to."

"I happen to agree with him."

"Because, like Garrett, you have no vision."

He sighed, ignoring my sarcastic response. "Mara, he'll destroy you if he finds out."

"So I have to make sure he doesn't find out."

"Honey, don't do this. I know you're angry—"

"I'm done being angry, Jake. I've spent the last six years being treated like a second-class citizen in my own marriage. Being placated because keeping me happy is easier than accepting that I am his equal. That's not enough anymore. It never was, to be honest. I deserve more, and I'm going to take it. With or without your help. I need a solid plan to take to Albert. I've done the research, I've run the numbers, but I need someone to verify my estimates on the construction side. That's all I'm asking, Jake. Just take a look and verify what I've done is right so Albert doesn't have a reason to reject my plan."

He chuckled when I batted my eyes at him. "You are a world of trouble, lady."

"But I'm so much fun," I whispered.

"I'll look this over and—"

"No. That proposal doesn't leave my sight, and no copies will be made. Take ten minutes and look it over now."

When he didn't budge, I grabbed for my proposal, but he lifted the papers out of my reach and pushed himself to stand. Walking around the desk, he took my hand and pulled me out of the chair and into his arms.

He brushed his nose against mine before whispering, "You haven't accepted my apology."

I tilted my head as if considering my options. "Are you going to help me?"

"I'm going to review this proposal of yours and make sure Albert isn't using you the way your husband did. Less the nudity. If I'm convinced this is solid and he isn't trying to manipulate you...then, yes, I'll help you."

I smiled. "Then you're forgiven."

He leaned down and placed a tender kiss on my lips. "Thank you."

I couldn't resist running my hand through his hair and kissing him again, more deeply this time. "You're welcome."

With my hand in his, he led me to the round table in the corner of his office. Sitting next to me, he opened my proposal. I went over the information with him, line by line and page by page, taking notes and debating the areas where I was confident. Far more than ten minutes went by, and Jake made several suggestions on the construction costs and plans that made my plan even stronger in the end.

Before we were done, he ran his hand over my hair. "Are you sure about this? Are you prepared for his wrath if he discovers what you are up to?"

"I'm not nearly as frightened of him as his business associates are."

"You should be. You have a hell of a lot more to lose. If this gets ugly, do you think he'll just divorce you and walk away? He'll destroy Carter Enterprises, take your son, and leave you with nothing."

The thought had tried to sneak up on me several times,

but I'd pushed it down. "Our marital contract covers infidelity, not competing businesses."

"That won't stop him from trying." Grabbing my hand, he pulled me into his lap, wrapping one arm around my waist and cupping my cheek with the other. "You're leaving yourself vulnerable by letting Albert Carter in on this. He could turn on you."

"I trust him."

"Why?"

"Because when I threw myself at him, he turned me down."

Jake chuckled. "That's the test for honor now? Refusing to have sex with you."

I nodded. "Yes."

"What does that say about me?"

"Oh, well, I trust you because you *are* having sex with me."

He creased his brow. "I'll never understand women."

I smiled. "Don't even try."

Putting his mouth to mine, he let his tongue slide between my lips as he pulled me closer. "Can I see you tonight?"

"That depends."

"On?"

"It's been a few days. Have you been thinking of me?"

He buried his face in my neck. "I'm always thinking of you."

"Do you know what I'm thinking about?" Reaching between us, I stroked the front of his slacks. "You bending me over that couch in the corner and smacking my ass." I moved in to give him a hot kiss, but the intercom on his desk beeped, and I stopped.

His assistant's voice surrounded them. "Your wife is here to see you, sir."

I widened my eyes with exaggerated surprise. "Oh, Mr. Decker. Caught with your lover *and* an erection. Whatever will you do?"

He pulled me to him for a brief but heated kiss. "Like I said, you're a world of trouble."

He easily lifted me to my feet, then turned me around. Pushing me forward, he raised my skirt without a bit of resistance from me. With my ass exposed, he brought his hand to my cheek, making me gasp at the sting. Running his hand over the skin, he eased the pain but then smacked again.

I jolted when I felt his other hand slip between my thighs, stroking as he placed a trail of light kisses over the area that was surely red from his hand. I moaned my appreciation for what he was doing, which resulted in him pulling away.

I looked over my shoulder and gave him a forced pout. "Tease."

"Preview of tonight's events," he corrected as he slid my skirt back into place.

As he walked to his desk and explained through the speaker that he'd be available in just a moment, I gathered my proposal and tucked the folder back into my purse. Meeting him in the middle of his office, I slid my arms around his neck and gave him the sensual kiss I'd been intending before we had been interrupted.

"How awkward is it going to be for *my* husband's

mistress to see *her* husband's mistress leaving his office and looking so amiss?"

"There isn't a thing amiss about you. You look perfect."

Smirking at him, I pulled my shirt loose on one side and mussed my hair. He opened his mouth to protest as I lifted my skirt, but when I slid my panties down, he seemed to lose his ability to speak.

"This may seem odd," I said as I tugged the lace over my shoes, "but it's a little inside joke between Megan and me. She'll love it."

"Somehow I doubt that."

I tugged my skirt down, but not quite enough to hide the tops of my stockings. "You know, I've been walking around without panties so much lately, it's almost like I should just stop wearing them."

"Mara," he warned with a smile.

"Mmm, I love how you make my name sound so dirty." I left him standing there looking half amused and half dreading what was going to happen next. Reaching the door, I turned and winked at him one last time before opening it.

As I walked out, I made a show of holding up my underwear and dropping them into my purse as I said, "Megan, we have got to stop meeting like this." I pushed my skirt down and ran my hand over my hair before walking over and giving her the obligatory fake cheek kiss.

Leaning back, I smiled at the bitch, whose eyes were barely slits and her face red with fury.

"He's all yours. What's left of him, anyway." I wiped the corner of my mouth before walking away.

I saved and closed the document I was working on when Garrett walked into my office. He closed the door behind him and headed right for my desk. His set jaw and clipped pace made my heart do a flip, fearing for a second that Jake had ratted me out already. But no, he wouldn't do that. I could trust him. I was certain of that.

"What is it?" I asked when he sat on the edge of my desk.

He snatched the card out of my flowers. "Jake is sending you gifts now?"

"Jake is feeling a bit guilty about going along with your plan to use me without consulting me first."

"I apologized, Mara."

I grabbed the card from his hand. "So did he."

"Megan said you were at his office today."

"I wanted to personally thank him for the flowers. They're beautiful."

"And how, exactly, did you thank him?"

I smirked. "Do I ask about your extramarital activities?"

He stared at me for a moment before standing and running his hand through his dark hair. Walking to the window, he looked out. I didn't have the great view here that I did at the Bird's Nest, but I didn't mind. If I stood in the corner, I could peer down the street and see a park carved out in the midst of all the cement.

That's where he stood now, in the corner, looking toward the green. "Did you fuck him today?"

He actually sounded hurt, and that struck a nerve.

"You've been having affairs and sending other women

flowers for six years. I never demanded answers from you. Why do you think you can demand answers from me?"

His response was to stare me down until I actually felt a little bit guilty.

I sighed and pushed myself up. Walking to him, I leaned my hips on the windowsill and crossed my arms. "No. But I did agree to meet him tonight."

He met my gaze and then smiled. "What time? I'll cancel my plans and join you."

"Hmm. That's considerate of you, but I think I'll have to decline."

He caressed my face, brushing his thumb over my lip before trailing down to my cleavage. He smiled as he stroked over my erect nipple.

"Let us show you how sorry we are."

I leaned back. "Somehow, I suspect I'll be the one doing all the showing."

He pulled me back to him. "And from what I saw the other day, you don't mind nearly as much as you proclaim."

I leaned back again, avoiding his attempt to nuzzle my neck. "Exactly what are you getting at, Garrett? Hmm? What are you asking?"

He gripped my hips, bringing my groin to his. "I don't have to tell you it's been driving me crazy since you took Jake as a lover."

I sighed heavily. "Garrett, this is a two-way street—"

"I know that. That's not what I'm saying."

"So what are you saying?"

A little grin tugged at his lips, and he dipped his head down. Here we go. The manipulation was beginning.

"I want to see you."

My heart tripped, and I creased my brow.

"With him," he said softly. He pulled me even closer. "I've always wondered what it'd be like to have someone watch us. I got a taste of that on the yacht."

My cheeks instantly heated.

He cupped my face, brushing his thumb over my face. "I never thought you'd be into that, but you were, Mara. I saw it. I saw you. You liked what was happening."

I didn't notice that I'd parted my lips, breathing a bit more shallow, until he ran the pad of his thumb over my mouth.

"Imagine it," he whispered as he dragged his hands down my back and cupped my ass. "Jake's hands on you, touching you in all the ways you like. His mouth on you."

I let my eyes drift shut, recalling the way my skirt rubbed against his palm print on my bare ass as I walked to the elevator. I wanted to turn around and kick his wife out of his office so I could fuck him blind. I was bottling up that desire for when I saw him later tonight. The bottle was so full, the cork was about to pop.

The image Garrett was stirring was making it hard to breathe.

"Knowing I'm sitting right there, watching him pleasure you. Watching him give you everything you want." He bit my lip, and I nearly whimpered. "Tell me you want this as much as I do. I'll give you anything to let this happen."

I met his gaze but didn't have the words to voice what I wanted. Because what I'd always wanted—a real marriage and his unrelenting love—was never going to happen, and I wasn't even sure I wanted that anymore. I'd always wanted more than one child. But not now. Not with him.

I could buy myself jewelry and cars and flowers. I could take vacations whenever I wanted. For the first time, I realized he didn't have a damn thing I wanted—other than financial security, and I was working on a plan to gain that on my own.

He pulled me against him, gratuitously grinding his hard cock against me. "I mean it. I'll give you anything you want."

I chuckled with an intentionally sultry undertone. "Do you watch your lovers fuck other men?"

"Didn't you just tell me you don't ask about my activities?"

He kissed my neck again, nipping at my flesh, and I realized his excitement was my answer. He most likely did. Probably with more than one man. Garrett seemed to be the kind that would enjoy going out on a yacht with five or six buddies and one woman. They'd probably all stand around taking turns with her—passing her around, filling every hole in her body, doing whatever they wanted until they were all spent.

I closed my eyes as a surprisingly vivid image of myself sprawled on the sofa on Albert's yacht surrounded by horny men filled my mind and took my breath away. I tried to push the thought down, tried to be horrified that I'd be turned on by such a vision, but I had to bite my lip and roll my eyes shut to stop myself from moaning.

"You're getting hot thinking about it. Aren't you?" Garrett breathed in my ear.

"Actually," I lied, "I'm getting hot thinking about the long list of things I'm going to ask you for while you're trying to convince me to let you share me with Jake."

He groped my ass and bit my neck again. "Name it, and it's yours." Turning me from the window, he pinned me to the wall with his body. "I know you want this as much as I do. I can see the fire in your eyes thinking about it."

I stroked my hand over his hair as he kissed me again. Pulling back, resting my head against the wall, I sighed. "And what will you be doing while Jake is tasting me, Garrett? Are you just going to sit and watch him bury his head between my legs?"

His breath quivered as he exhaled. "What do you want me to do?"

"Seems like you're the one with experience in this area. You tell me."

He dug his fingers into my thighs as he dragged his hands up my legs, lifting my skirt as Jake had done not too long ago.

"I would touch you if you wanted. Kiss you." He slid his tongue in my mouth, then returned his focus to my neck.

"And what would you be doing when he shoves his dick in me? Hmm? Where will you be when he's between my legs, fucking me so hard, I'm screaming."

He groaned as he ground against me. "Jesus. Do you feel what you're doing to me?"

I lifted one leg and wrapped it around his as he pressed himself against me again. "I do. But I want to know what *you're* going to do to *me*."

"Whatever you want," he whispered.

"You're giving me control?"

"Yes."

Fisting his hair, I pulled his head back and made him look me in the eye. "Say it."

"You're in control. Whatever you want."

Lowering my leg, I hesitated before pushing him down. He didn't resist. He eased to his knees before me, pushed my underwear down, and dove in. I felt powerful in that moment, like I actually had some control over Garrett for a change.

He wanted something from me, and he was there, sucking my clit to get it. He always knew what to do and how to do it, so when he shoved his fingers in me, stroking deep inside as he flicked his tongue over me, I fisted his hair and came hard. He took several more moments to lick me clean. When he finally stood, we were both breathless.

I swallowed and attempted to push down my words, but then said, "I'll talk to Jake tonight. We'll see how I feel about things then." I gently pushed him back when he started to speak—undoubtedly to let me know he and Jake had already discussed the matter. "Go. I have work to do."

The moment he was gone, I felt regret creeping in. One of these days, I was going to learn how to resist him. I suspected today was not that day.

Though I knew Jake preferred to take me from behind, I had managed to get him on his back and straddled his hips as I rode him as his hand repeatedly crashed down on my ass. I didn't doubt for a moment my backside was covered in red handprints. I didn't mind either.

In fact, the stinging, as he alternated between gripping and stroking my cheeks and slapping them, was driving me to the brink of insanity. Pinching my nipples, I threw my head back and cried out as Jake drove himself deep inside me. We came together before I collapsed onto his chest, and he wrapped his arms around me.

He laughed softly as he brushed his hand over my ass. "That was supposed to be punishment."

"Oh, it was awful." I buried my face in his neck. "Please don't ever do that again."

We laughed as I leaned back.

He brushed my hair from my face. "Megan gave me hell after you left my office."

"She flaunted my affair with my husband first. It's not my fault I'm better at being a bitch than she is."

"I'm not saying she doesn't deserve it—"

I sighed. "But you want me to be nicer?"

"Just a touch."

I sighed and sat back, still straddling his hips. "Do you know why she was so upset?"

"Because you made it look like we'd just got done screwing."

"Because when she showed up at Garrett's office for a nooner the other day, I got to him first. I fucked him on his desk for the explicit reason of draining him before she could. She wasn't very happy about that. I'm sure the idea that I'd once again beaten her to a stiff cock didn't sit well."

Jake stared at me, clearly processing what I'd said, before gently but firmly lifting me off his hips and pushing me aside. He rolled from the bed and walked into the bathroom. I stared at the door until I heard the shower start. Crawling from the bed, I followed him.

I opened the door and watched the trail of water wash down his toned chest. Stepping in, I traced the path it'd taken until he looked at me.

"I'm sorry," I said softly. "But it's true. There is no other reason she'd be there. And there's no other reason that you would be here. This is where we are, Jake. This is what we're doing, and the reason we're doing this is because they did it first. Childish as that may sound, you know it's true."

"I know. I'm not angry with you. She deserves to have this thrown in her face for the way she throws Garrett in yours. I just..."

"Didn't think your marriage would take this turn? Trust me, I know."

"She's been having affairs for a long time. I just pretended she wasn't. I don't know why this one is getting to me."

"Because she is flaunting."

He grinned. "Well, she's going to have to step up her game if she's going to compete with Mara King in that department."

"Unfortunately, I've been playing this game an awful long time. I have far more practice than most women."

Pulling me with him, he stepped back and let the warm water run over me. We took turns washing each other and enjoying the warmth before turning off the water. As we dried with fluffy towels, I debated if I even wanted to broach the subject of Garrett's request as I'd promised I would.

Jake rested his hands on my shoulders as I slid my underwear into place. He put a kiss to the back of my head. "You're a million miles away. What's on your mind?"

Turning to face him, I met his gaze. "Garrett has it in his head that I want him to watch me have sex with you."

His nod was subtle. "Yes. He asked if I'd be willing to do that."

I wasn't surprised. Truth be told, I'd be surprised if Garrett hadn't found a way to suggest this long before Jake and I even started sleeping together.

"Would you?"

"Would *you?*"

I laughed softly at his evasion. Walking away from him, I grabbed my bra and had the material secured behind my back before facing him again.

"I'm not opposed to what he's asking. But part of me feels like I'd be rewarding him for his bad behavior. He doesn't deserve to get what he wants from me. I have to wonder..."

"What?" he pressed when I let my words fade.

"Is this another way for him to remind me of my place? Because I can't imagine he wants this *only* for my pleasure. I'm sure any number of his whores would do this for him. And I don't care how he spins it. I know this is for him. I don't know if I should be flattered or furious."

"I can't answer that for you. But I can tell you that he keeps you on a higher pedestal than I think you realize. Those other women—they are his toys, Mara. Not you. He doesn't show it well, but he does hold you in high regard."

"Wanting to share my body is holding me in high regard?"

He chuckled. "Listen. Here's the thing about men. We think with our dicks. Garrett's dick is just very ambitious."

I laughed. "Yeah. I'm aware."

He brushed his hand over my wet hair as he held my gaze. "I don't think he sees this as a way to degrade you. He thinks you'll enjoy it."

"So he wants to please me?"

"Something like that, yes."

I closed the distance between us and wrapped my arms around his neck. "Do you want to please me, Jake?"

"In every way possible." Hugging me around my waist, he pulled my body to his. "But I don't want you to do anything you aren't comfortable with."

"What if I want this?" she asked softly. "Just *not* with him."

Jake hesitated before rolling his head back and laughing. "Jesus, you're such a handful."

I raked my fingers through his hair and tilted his face back to mine. "My hesitancy isn't the sex. I have no doubt that would be amazing. But I do doubt that he's doing this for his wife to explore her sexuality. I don't trust that he wants this to bring us closer, or bring me satisfaction, or any other reason that you entrust your fantasies with your partner. I don't want to give him permission to use me. Not like this."

"Do you know how fucked up it is that you trust me to do this but not your husband?"

"Yes. And that says so much about my marriage. It makes me a little sad."

Pulling me with him, he sat on the bed and tugged me down. I straddled his hips, as I'd done while having sex with him, but the panties I'd taunted his wife with earlier in the day now provided a barrier between our bodies.

Cupping my ass instead of spanking it, he met my gaze. "Are you trying to push every last button that man has? First, a competing business, and then living out his sexual fantasy without him?"

"Maybe."

"And maybe you're asking to get hurt."

I traced my finger along his jaw. "Well, we did discover I have a taste for pain."

"There comes a point when pain stops being pleasurable. You may want to learn how to recognize that line before crossing it."

I inhaled a slow breath. "You keep implying that I should fear my husband."

"Not fear, Mara. Just recognize that he isn't afraid to push back. I have a feeling his push could be harder than you're anticipating."

"You're worried about me?" I asked softly. "That's so sweet."

He pulled my chest to his and kissed my neck. "We've become friends over the years. I care about you."

I hugged him back. "I care about you too."

"So stop pissing off my wife," he said with playful scolding as he pushed me away from him.

I grinned. "She makes it so easy." Leaning in, I gave him a tender, lingering kiss. "Do you want to share me with him?"

"That's not up to me—"

"Hey." I tilted my head and lifted my brows. "I asked a yes or no question, Mr. Decker."

"If you decide you want to do this—"

I put my fingers to his lips. "Would it please you if I allowed him to watch us? Nod for yes, shake for no."

He held my gaze for a moment before nodding once. Gently grasping my wrist, he pulled my hand from his face. "Only if you want that. If you do, I won't let him degrade or humiliate you. I'll be sure he knows how lucky he is to have you and how special what we are sharing is. But listen," he said, holding my gaze. "This is your choice. If you don't want to do this, we don't do this. If you want to stop, we stop. No hard feelings. I promise."

I ran my fingers through his brown hair as I considered his words. "The first time I feel like a fuck doll instead of a goddess, it all comes to an end. Understand?"

"Yes."

I contemplated one more moment before nodding my agreement. "Okay. But I don't want to be fucked and tossed aside. I want to be seduced. I want to be romanced. I want to believe that this means something to both of you. And when I give it to you, I want to be treated like a goddamned lady."

He grinned. "Yes, ma'am."

[14]

ALBERT CLOSED the file I handed him and leaned back in his dark leather high-back chair lined with gold studs. His office at Carter Enterprises was old-fashioned. Everything about Albert was old-fashioned. It was almost as if he was stuck in the past, refusing to let go of his father and grandfather's influence on the company. This was the very thing holding him and the company back.

"Very impressive," he finally said.

"You seem surprised."

"I'm not. I always knew you were more than just Garrett's trophy wife. I'm sorry he doesn't."

Perched on the edge of an equally outdated chair, I clutched my hands so tightly, my knuckles were beginning to ache, but I kept my face and my voice unwavering with my stress.

"Do we have a deal, Albert? Are you prepared to let me implement this and save Carter Enterprises?"

"And only for the small price of willing you controlling

interest in my company?" He drew a breath before nodding and presenting a file of his own. "I'd suggest you have your attorney review these before we make it final."

I tried to offer him a pleased but controlled smile, but I knew the depth of my excitement was showing as I accepted the papers. "Thank you. Sincerely. Not many people are willing to go against Garrett King."

"I've just been waiting for the right opportunity. But I have to ask... Are you absolutely sure about this?"

"I am."

"You'll be successful, I've no doubt. You are the brains behind King Inc. Everyone knows that. Garrett's always been too spoiled to put his heart into the business the way you have. If you aren't driving the King business, their growth will start to slow down. Are you going to compete with yourself and let King Incorporated start to falter?"

I smiled. "Oh, Albert. I sincerely appreciate your trust in me and your discretion. But I'm not prepared to discuss King Incorporated business with you. *Yet.*"

He chuckled softly. "Can't blame me for trying."

Gathering my things, I stood and accepted the kiss he put to my cheek after walking around his desk.

"I'd invite you to lunch," he said, "but I'm meeting with my vice president to discuss sabotaging your husband's latest attempt to undermine one of my deals."

I slid my arm through his as he walked me to the door. "I do love when you talk dirty, Albert."

He joined in my laughter and patted my hand—the action seemed far less condescending coming from him than it ever had coming from Garrett. He opened the office door and escorted me out into the area where his secretary sat anxiously looking up at a man.

"Ah, Michael," I said.

Michael turned, clearly surprised at my presence in Albert's office.

I did my best not to laugh, but Michael was utterly adorable as he stood there not understanding what was going on. I could actually see his mind working to make two plus two equal four.

"Well, I will leave you gentlemen to your sabotaging." I kissed Albert's cheek. "I'll see you soon, Michael." I walked by him, and he finally blinked.

"Uh, excuse me for one moment, Albert," he finally managed to spit out. "I just need to confirm...uh, swim lessons...for the boys."

I smiled as Michael guided me away from Albert's office. "That sounded absolutely awkward. *Uh. Swim lessons. Uh. For the boys.*" I laughed. "What is wrong with you?"

He clearly wasn't amused by my joke. "What are you doing here?"

"I had some business with Albert."

He pulled me to a stop just outside the elevators. "What kind of business?"

My smile faded. "Personal."

"Personal?"

"Yes. Personal. Meaning I'm not discussing it with you."

"You might as well. He'll tell me."

I tilted my head, not appreciating the suspicion in his eyes. I thought we were beyond this. "No. He won't. It's *personal.*"

He raked his hand through his dark hair and took a deep breath. "We may be friends outside the office, but I swear to God, Mara, if you are manipulating that man, I'll take you down."

"Oh, you will?"

"Guaranteed."

I smirked. "I like it when you're feisty, but *I* guarantee that if I were manipulating that man, there wouldn't be a damn thing you could do about it."

"Mara—"

"For your information, *friend*, Albert Carter is perfectly capable of taking care of himself. As am I." The elevator doors opened, and someone stepped out. I took the opportunity to enter the small space. "Enjoy your lunch. Oh, and Michael, if it's the McCullough deal that you and Albert are discussing, you're a bit late, I'm afraid. I pushed that through this morning over coffee and crêpes at that new restaurant on Fifth Avenue. Have you been there yet? It's wonderful."

His mouth sagged, letting me know that was exactly what they were planning to discuss. I smiled innocently as the doors slid shut, effectively ending the conversation.

I chuckled when my aunt cocked a brow at me. Not much got by Victoria Richards, and I was quite sure I was being scrutinized.

"Out with it, Auntie."

Pushing her plate away, my aunt lifted her brow even higher. "You are far too pleased with yourself these days."

"How so?"

"I'm as close to you as a mother, and a mother knows when her child is up to something. And you, my child, are up to mischief."

I laughed softly. "Mischief?"

"What have you done, Mara?"

I took a deep breath as I contemplated spilling my guts about my deal with Albert, but I wasn't quite ready to share.

"I don't want to jinx it. I'll tell you all about it when it's time."

"And when will that be?"

"Soon. I promise."

She leaned across the table and said in a loud whisper, "Tell me you didn't go forward with that stupid plan of yours to cross Garrett."

I hushed her as I looked around, making sure no one could hear. Reaching across the table, I covered my aunt's hand. "I was thinking we should take Adam on a trip before summer ends. Where should we go?"

She frowned at me and shook her head as she sat back. "I suppose he'll enjoy anyplace so long as he can take his cars."

"So where would you like to go?"

"Someplace quiet. This city is getting too loud. You can't escape the hustle and bustle and—" She stopped speaking when my cell phone rang. "See?"

I smiled when I saw Michael's name on the screen. I'd so enjoyed spatting with him that morning that I'd practically been giddy waiting for him to call. I wasn't sure if he'd try to chastise me again or apologize for being out of line. Which, really, he wasn't.

He knew King Incorporated was undermining Carter Enterprises. Seeing me with Albert had to have been suspicious, and he'd been hired to protect the company. Even so, I'd learned very quickly that confrontation wasn't his first choice for solving problems, so jumping down my throat this morning had probably left him feeling a bit guilty.

"I'm sorry. I need just a moment." I stepped from the table and put the phone to my ear as I weaved my way out to the near-empty sidewalk outside the upscale café. "Calling to threaten me again?"

"No." His deep voice came through the phone like a security blanket—soft, warm, and comforting. He was definitely calling to make amends. "I'm sorry about this morning. Albert explained that you were there for a charity event and your meeting had nothing to do with Carter Enterprises."

I chuckled, mostly because I hadn't expected Albert to outright lie. "So you believe your boss but not your new best friend? I'd say our friendship is off to a rocky start, wouldn't you?"

"You can't blame me for jumping to the wrong conclusion."

"I can't. And I don't. I'm just giving you a hard time."

"Let me make it up to you. You and Adam come over for dinner tonight. He can crash at our house—give you an evening of peace and quiet."

"I don't know, Michael. You were awfully vicious this morning."

"Please," he said after scoffing. "I've seen you be harder on the pizza delivery guy."

I laughed. "Fine. We'll be over around six?"

"Six is perfect."

"Michael," I called before he could hang up.

"Yeah?"

"No S'mores."

"Party pooper."

Ending the call, I walked back to the table and reclaimed my seat. I stopped putting my phone back in my purse when I noticed my aunt watching me.

"What?"

"Was that him?"

"Who?"

"This man who is just a friend."

I scoffed. "He *is* just a friend."

Victoria shook her head. "Oh, Mara."

"What?"

"If your smile spreads any wider, your face will crack. And your eyes. Sparkling." She nodded when I opened my mouth to protest. "Just like the last time I saw you talking to him. And that's just on the phone. I can only imagine how you act when you see this friend in person."

I sighed. "It's not like that."

Victoria frowned. "If you say so. But let me give you a little piece of advice."

"Don't fall in love?"

"Do not fall in love with this man—whoever he is. Love is a trap, Mara. And it never ends well for the woman who falls into it."

"I wouldn't dream of falling in love, Auntie."

"I think that was worse than S'mores," I said as I dropped my spoon into the now-empty bowl.

Tonight's feast at the Redmond home had consisted of burgers and ice cream sundaes. I wanted to stop at one scoop of vanilla, but at the boys' encouragement, Michael added a large scoop of chocolate to my dish, then topped it with whipped cream, nuts, and chocolate sauce.

The kids had practically swallowed their ice cream whole before running off to start arranging their toys and blankets inside the tent Michael and I had set up for them while the burgers cooked on the grill.

"Possibly." Michael pushed his bowl aside. He looked at me and laughed quietly, then reached across the table and dragged his thumb across my lip.

The move was unexpected and nothing about it was particularly sexy, but his touch made sparks dance along my skin, and I took a quick breath in surprise.

My gaze locked on his, and I wondered if he'd felt the unexpected chemistry too. If he had, he hid it better.

He dropped his hand and laughed. "Maybe less whipped cream next time. I guess I got a little carried away."

Standing, I gathered the dishes. "I think I'll drop these in the kitchen and take off. You guys don't need me hanging around spoiling your fun." I didn't give him a chance to argue. "Hey, boys!"

They poked their heads out of the zippered door to look at me.

"I'm leaving. I'll see you in the morning."

"Bye, Mom!" Adam yelled and then disappeared inside the canvas.

"Bye, Mrs. King!" And then Will was gone too.

"Good luck to you," I said to Michael. "I think you'll need it after you let them eat so much ice cream." I headed inside and set the dirty bowls in the sink, trying to convince myself I'd imagined that brief moment that had passed between us.

It was Victoria's fault for saying I was sparkling after talking to Michael. Of course I was. He was my friend. He made me laugh. Few people managed to do that these days. We were friends. Of course he made me *sparkle*. That was all there was to it.

I was digging in my purse for my car keys when Michael's footsteps echoed from the hallway.

"I'm sorry," he said as I pulled my keys from my bag.

I glanced up and tried to look confused as if I hadn't felt his touch all the way down to my soul.

"For what?"

"Mara." He kept his tone gentle but firm as he walked toward me. He stopped by the bottom of the stairs, keeping plenty of distance between us. "We've been spending a lot of time together lately. It's natural that at some point our minds would trick us into thinking there is something more to it than there actually is."

I smirked as I dropped the straps of my purse over my shoulder. "Wow, Michael. That is the worst rejection a man has ever given me." Standing upright, I crossed to him, determined to prove there was nothing to what had just happened. "You wiped my face clean because I was a mess."

"Yes," he said with a warm smile, "you are. You are an unbelievable mess. A walking disaster, really."

I shoved him gently. "Hey."

He laughed, but as soon as his gaze met mine, his smile softened. "I am sorry about this morning. I overreacted."

I lifted my chin, deliberately looking down my nose at him. "Damn straight you did. Don't do it again, you jerk."

"Not a chance."

"I'll see you in the morning."

"Good night."

I left, closing the door behind me, but as soon as I did, I leaned against the solid oak and closed my eyes as I reminded myself of what I'd insisted to my aunt—Michael is *just* a friend.

"WHAT ARE YOU THINKING ABOUT?"

I turned from the city lights toward Jake stretched naked beside me in the hot tub at the Bird's Nest.

Michael. I was thinking about Michael. His crooked smile. His loud laugh. His willingness to get down in the dirt and play with the boys. The man was like a scoutmaster— this goes here, that goes there, hammer this—as he taught me how to pitch a tent.

The boys had helped for about five minutes before growing bored and deciding they had to gather sticks for a fire. I watched them run off before offering my assistance.

Michael hadn't needed it, but he'd accepted my help and was only slightly mocking my inexperience with camping. He couldn't believe we'd never taken Adam out sleeping in a tent before. Even in the backyard. My idea of camping was a fully functional cabin in the woods—the woods being a slightly more rural area than Crescent City but definitely not in a forest.

Michael told me about his camping adventures as a kid. He'd had so much fun growing up, I envied him. He reminded me of my father. I'd thought that more than once. My father loved to tell me stories and teach me things. No, we'd never gone camping. But no doubt he would have taken me if I had ever thought to ask.

He was that type of dad. The type that wanted to teach me everything he could about any little thing I showed interest in. Sadly, he died before I ever had too much interest in anything that wasn't dolls or pop music.

Pushing thoughts of Michael away, I smiled at Jake and skimmed my hands over the hot water.

"What were you like as a kid?"

He laughed as he leaned back on the edge. "Uh. Nerdy."

I grinned. "Elaborate."

He found my hand under the water and pulled me closer. "I've always liked building and construction and math and all those things. I started building forts when I was ten."

"I bet the other boys thought that was cool."

"Maybe." He rested his hands on my legs as I settled between his. "And you? What were you like as a child?"

I drew a breath. "Sad and lonely."

"Because you lost your parents?" he asked after a moment.

I nodded rather than telling him that I didn't know if I'd ever fit in anywhere. My parents were wonderful, my mother caring, and my father attentive, but outside our little home, I always felt like a misfit.

"Are you still sad and lonely?" His voice was still as tender, and I couldn't help but be honest.

I nodded again.

He turned and lifted me so I was sitting on his thigh as he looked up at me. Cupping my head, he pulled me in for a kiss. Usually the passion took over, but this time, his mouth was gentle, and his tongue teasing instead of demanding.

"I don't want you to feel that way when you're with me," he whispered. "I want you to feel happy and wanted when you're with me."

I smiled as I ran my hands up his chest. "I do."

He brushed back a wayward strand of hair that had stuck to my lips and shook his head slightly. "You seem sad tonight. Are you worried about going against Garrett?"

Going against Garrett had been the furthest thing from my mind. After leaving Michael's, I'd called Jake and asked him to meet me. Though neither of us are attorneys, between the two of us, we are more than capable of dismantling a contract. We went through Albert's successor acquisitions plan that would leave me the majority stakeholder in his company upon his death. His wife would step in as the face of the company, but I would be pulling the strings.

And no one would be the wiser, as they'd work together to create a ghost company owned by another ghost company for me to hide behind. It would take years for Garrett to realize Grace Carter wasn't the brains of the operation, and years beyond that to uncover who really was. But by then,

Adam would be grown and I wouldn't have to worry about losing custody of my son if I walked away from Garrett.

So, no, I wasn't worried. "I guess I'm more upset than I realized that I have to go against him. I shouldn't have to lie to my husband to feel secure."

He trailed a line of kisses from my temple to my jaw. "No, you shouldn't. If he finds out, Mara—"

"He won't. Unless you tell him."

He ran his hand over my thigh. "I have no reason to betray you."

"Then don't."

"I wouldn't." he almost sounded hurt and I drew a breath.

Stroking his face, I smiled. "I'm sorry. I know you wouldn't." I returned his trail of kisses, starting at his lips and moving over his jaw as his hand moved higher between my legs. I moaned at the feel of his thumb brushing over my clit. "Let's take this inside," I whispered.

He had me on my feet and out of the hot tub in seconds. We grabbed towels on the way in, but neither of us were dry when we fell into the bed.

[15]

I stood unnoticed as Michael stomped through the living room, arms up, hunched over, and roaring like a monster. The boys held up imaginary guns shooting at him, but he was relentless. In three quick steps, he scooped Will up and tossed him mercilessly onto the black leather sofa.

"Die!" Adam screamed and made machine gun noises. He tossed an imaginary grenade followed by his impression of an explosion.

Monster Michael roared and stumbled back.

"Civilian," Will screamed, pointing at me. "There's a civilian on the battlefield."

The monster turned and raised his hands at me.

I pulled out a fake weapon. "A civilian with a bazooka."

"Yeah!" the boys cheered.

The monster pouted and emitted a pathetic grunt that made me laugh.

"Get him, guys!" I coaxed.

More cheers filled the room as the boys tackled Michael, taking him down.

I stood over the heap and nodded proudly. "My work here is done."

Adam rolled over. "Do I have to leave? We haven't had breakfast yet."

"You can't have breakfast at home?"

"Chef is making chocolate-chip pancakes," Will informed me.

I tilted my head and frowned at Michael. "Do you ever eat a well-balanced meal?"

"Not if I can help it," he deadpanned. "Head to the dining room, guys. I bet breakfast is just about ready."

"Can I stay, Mom?"

I held out my hands, one to Will and one to Adam, and pulled the kids up. "Make it fast."

They high-fived each other before disappearing. Looking down at Michael, I laughed. "Did you have fun on your sleepover?"

"I don't know about the kids, but I had a blast."

Grabbing his hands, I pulled him to his feet as I'd done with the boys. "How hyper is he going to be for the rest of the day?"

"We stayed up pretty late. He's gotta crash at some point. How was your evening?"

A twinge of guilt struck me as I thought about my time with Jake the night before. I had no reason to feel like I was betraying Michael, but I couldn't deny that I did.

"Quieter than yours."

"Good. Hungry?"

"For chocolate chip pancakes?"

"Naturally."

"No."

"Which obviously means *yes, but society tells me I shouldn't, so I'll deny myself until my good friend Michael convinces me otherwise.*"

"How do you get all that from a simple no?"

"My wife taught me to speak woman-ese."

I laughed. "I don't think you're fluent."

He gestured for me to go first, but when his hand fell to the center of my back, my heart did a funny little flip, and I silently cursed myself. Trying to ignore the feeling, I searched for some kind of small talk to engage in, but I couldn't seem to think of anything but my need to confess my sins and beg for forgiveness. I'd spent the night with a man who wasn't my husband. And wasn't Michael. For some reason, I was suddenly ashamed of that. So I didn't say anything.

At least not until I walked into the dining room and caught my son squirting chocolate sauce on his breakfast.

"*Adam!*"

"They're chocolate-chip pancakes, Mom. I can't put maple syrup on chocolate chips. That'd be nasty."

I turned to gawk at the leader of this dietary catastrophe.

Michael simply shrugged. "I agree. Chocolate syrup is definitely the way to go."

I drew a breath, but he pushed me toward the table.

"Sit. Eat. Adam, squirt some of that sauce on Mom's pancakes."

"No." I gave him a stern look, and his face sagged with

disappointment. I sighed, fully aware that I was letting him play me. "Fine, just a little."

He immediately squeezed the bottle over my plate.

"Enough," I insisted seconds later, followed by another disapproving look flashed in Michael's direction.

He smiled brightly. "Just admit this is the best breakfast you've had in a long time."

"You are a terrible influence on my child," I said quietly.

"You're a stick in the mud," he responded in the same soft tone.

I widened my eyes and gasped dramatically.

Michael laughed. "It's true."

Digging my pointer finger into the syrup oozing over my pancakes, I coated the tip and dragged it down Michael's nose. The boys laughed as I stuck my tongue out at him. Before I had a chance to process what was happening, Michael grabbed one of the pancakes off my plate and smashed it into my face.

The kids hooted and laughed harder as my mouth fell open, shocked at what Michael had just done. Warm, mashed chunks of pancake stuck to the goop of chocolate on my cheek. Reaching up, I wiped it away and looked at my hand, confirming he really *had* just done that.

I was not about to let that stand. Michael and I both reached for the bottle of chocolate sauce at the same time. With both of us squeezing, the sauce squirted high and landed on our arms, making me squeal and Michael laugh as the boys continued their shouts of amusement. The harder I squeezed, the harder it was to hold on to the bottle.

"No," I cried when I nearly lost my grip. Jumping to my

feet, I grabbed the sauce with both hands, but Michael wasn't so easily beaten.

He rose as well and used his larger size to try to push me aside. Bumping into me, he yanked the bottle. I shouldered him back as our slippery hands wrestled for the win. After a few moments, and clearly at a stalemate, Michael directed the bottle opening at the boys and squeezed.

"Yeah!" Will yelled before practically diving with his mouth wide open.

Adam followed suit, and Michael aimed the bottle at him. By the time he was done, the boys had chocolate covered chins, the bottle was spitting out the last of the sauce, and the table was a gooey chocolate-covered mess.

So much for breakfast.

Still laughing, I gave up my hold on the bottle. It was empty now anyway. Looking at my hands, I shook my head. I needed another shower. A glimpse toward the boys let me know they did as well. Michael grinned as he licked his finger clean, clearly pleased with himself.

"And you call me trouble," I said flatly.

He chuckled. "Boys, go wash your faces while Mrs. King cleans up this mess."

"Excuse me?"

"You started it."

I drew a breath to argue, but he swiped a still-chocolate-covered finger over my nose, reminding me that I did, indeed, fire the first shot.

"Don't even try to deny it. Just clean up your mess."

Glaring at him, I dragged my hand across the table,

covering my palm in chocolate, then held it up, silently threatening to smear it on him.

"Hey, let's not get crazy," he warned.

"Do it," Will yelled.

"Yeah, Mom, get him," Adam encouraged.

I smirked at Michael, then subtly nodded toward the kids. In a spontaneous burst, we rushed around the table and tackled Adam and Will, swiping the chocolate on their faces instead of each other. The boys screamed until Michael called for the fun to end and sent them upstairs to wash.

"And don't touch anything," I warned. I looked at my hands when they were gone. "I can't believe we just did that."

"Oh, believe it. That's how we roll around here."

"This is a normal breakfast at your house?"

"Every day."

I tilted my head and shook it, letting him know I wasn't buying his tale.

"Okay. Not *every* day. Or ever. But..."

"But nothing. My God, look at this mess." I giggled. "Go get some rags. We can't leave this for your staff to clean up."

While he went to get something to clean up the table, I did what I could by scooping the excess chocolate onto my plate. He returned and dropped several cloths on the table, then handed me one.

"Wipe your nose," he instructed.

"Better?" I asked after swiping the damp, warm cloth over my hands and face.

He held my gaze a second or two longer than necessary, then nodded. "Better."

I cleaned the table while he cleared the plates and carried them to the kitchen. I followed a few minutes later, trying to hold in my laughter as he explained to the chef that the bottle was faulty and exploded all over the pancakes.

I washed my hands and followed Michael as he headed upstairs to check on the kids. "A faulty bottle of chocolate sauce?"

"It could happen."

We walked into Will's room, but he grabbed my arm and pulled me to a stop, pressing his finger to his lips in a warning for me to be quiet as the boys' voices filtered out over the sound of water running.

"She never laughs like that," Adam said.

I stopped and scrunched up my face at Michael as if to say that wasn't true.

"My dad didn't used to," Will said, "but ever since my mom died, he's not so mad all the time. He actually hangs out with me now."

"My dad would have freaked out if he saw the mess we made."

At that, I nodded and widened my eyes to let Michael know how much truth was in Adam's statement, and he grinned.

"Dad says we have to enjoy the time we have," Will said. "Whatever that means."

"It means you can die anytime, so you should be happy while you can."

"Well, I don't think my dad's been very happy since my mom died. He pretends, but I think he's still sad."

"I don't think my dad has been happy ever."

My heart sank a bit. I didn't know Adam saw Garrett that way. I didn't want him to see Garrett that way. I had wonderful memories of my parents—laughter and hugs and time together. Adam should have that, too. I'd have to work on that, work on making more family time and memories for him to hold on to once Garrett and I were gone.

"All he does is work," Adam continued, "and when he's at home, all he does is work. He kind of sucks, and he makes my mom really sad."

Lowering my face, I drew a breath.

"Does she cry?" Will asked. "My dad cried sometimes after my mom died, but he doesn't anymore."

"No," Adam said, "she just gets quiet and tries to act like she doesn't care, but she does."

I glanced at Michael, hating the sympathy in his eyes. Having heard enough, I pulled from him and called, "You guys getting cleaned up?"

"Almost done," Adam answered.

I grabbed Adam's overnight bag, then focused on shuffling through it to make sure all his clothes were inside. "Where's your toothbrush, Adam?"

"Got it." He ran up and stuffed the tubular carrier into his bag. "Can we finish our pancakes?"

"Sorry, buddy." I ruffled his hair. "Aunt Victoria is coming over for brunch. I need to get home."

He rolled his head back and moaned. "*Mom, I'm hungry now.*"

"Chef was cooking up a fresh batch," Michael said. "You guys run down and grab one real quick while we finish getting your stuff together."

"I have everything," I offered, but the kids had already disappeared. I focused on zipping Adam's car-themed bag until Michael put his hands on mine. Finally meeting his gaze, I scoffed at the sympathy still blatant in his eyes. "Don't look at me like that."

"He sees more than you realize."

"He doesn't understand."

"That his father is hurting his mother? Actually, Mara, it sounded like he understands that pretty well."

I gawked at him. "Don't judge my marriage."

"I don't give a shit about your marriage. I care about you and Adam. Your son can see how much you're hurting. Maybe he doesn't know Garrett's screwing around on you yet, but how much longer before he figures out his father is a liar and a cheat? How are you going to explain that to him?"

I widened my eyes at him. "How dare you?"

He stepped in front of me before I could head for the door. "How dare *you*?"

Anger ignited in me and mixed with some of that shame I'd felt earlier. Why did Michael stir all these feelings up inside me? I didn't owe him anything—least of all an explanation.

"You do not get to tell me how to raise my child."

"You're right. You raise him any way you want. But when he loses all respect for you, don't look any farther than the bathroom mirror when you're trying to figure out how that happened."

My stomach knotted, and rage burned my chest. I wanted to scream, tell him to go fuck himself. But I couldn't. Because he was right. I knew he was right. I'd known all along that someday my son would realize where his father was going, that someday he'd start to think that was okay. I even feared he'd treat his future wife with the same disrespect.

I just hadn't considered how that would impact how Adam saw me.

My soul died a little as I let the realization sink in that he probably would lose respect for me too. He would see me as less. As his father did. The idea nearly gutted me. I lowered my face and gasped—somehow I'd forgotten to breathe.

"Oh, shit," Michael said quietly. He put his hands on my arms. "Don't do that. Don't cry. I didn't mean—"

"Shut up. Just shut the fuck up." Sniffling, I stepped around him. I made it to the bedroom door before stopping. Turning, I swallowed hard and forced myself to face him. "I was pregnant the first time I found out Garrett had cheated on me. Some little whore came waltzing up to me at the office to let me know she'd just screwed my husband on his desk. I confronted him. He confessed. I left him because, by God, no man was going to treat *me* like that. No, see, I had a prenuptial agreement. He'd have to give me a hefty payment, so I would walk out. I would show him. Right? Divorce his ass and raise his child on my own. Yeah. That'd really put him in his place, wouldn't it? Except, as my aunt pointed out, the only person I was hurting by leaving, was my child. Garrett would replace me without a second thought. He'd have a new wife in no time. I was the one who would be out of a job that I loved, a home that I'd made, and knowing Garrett, he'd take me to court for custody of our child out of spite. He could out-lawyer me any day, drag the proceedings out until I didn't have a dime. Then what? How would I raise my son then? If I ever even got to see him again. So, I went back, and Garrett and I came to an agreement."

"You sold your dignity to the devil."

I smirked. "Maybe I did. But what I got in exchange is worth it. Adam will never want for anything. And my life hasn't been so terrible, Michael. Sure, my husband treats me more like a prize than a person, but...what the hell?" I gestured at my thin, tall body, clad in skinny jeans and a tight-fitting blouse. "Maybe I am. But if he decides to leave me for one of his girls or one of them goes public, I get every-thing. And I do mean *everything*."

"And that's okay with you?"

"Yes. Because my son will never have to struggle to survive."

"But he'll believe that a wife is nothing more than what Garrett has made you, Mara—something to be tolerated without an ounce of consideration for how she feels. Did you hear him? You're hurting, and he sees that."

"I just need to try harder."

"No." Michael put his hands on my face. "No. *Garrett* needs to try harder."

I lowered my face and sniffed again. And then Michael pulled me in for a hug, and my face was buried in his chest. He stroked his hand over my hair, and I damn near fell apart. I'd been pushing the pain and humiliation down for so long. Having him acknowledge it seemed to give my pain a life I didn't want it to have. I wanted to cry, but instead I laughed.

He pulled back and looked at me like I was losing my mind.

"You smell like a goddamned hot-fudge sundae," I whispered.

He smiled and tucked a strand of hair behind my ear.

Pulling his hand from my face, I nodded. "You're right. I need to find a way to make things right before Adam starts to believe women are just—"

"Sexual objects."

"Yeah. And I will. Thank you for making me see that."

"And what about you?"

I creased my brow. "What about me?"

"The sadness Adam sees in your eyes. I see it, too." He took my hand in his and squeezed it lightly. "When you think no one is looking at you, in between faking smiles and pretending this is the life you want, sadness seeps into your eyes."

"You aren't exactly a barrel of laughs all the time either."

"My wife died. I can't do anything about my sorrow. You can."

I drew a breath. "I have to go. Thanks for...whatever this was."

"For being a friend," he said.

I laughed softly. "Great. We just turned into *The Golden Girls*."

[16]

I frowned at my aunt as soon as we sat at the table for brunch. My big hat shaded my face, but I tilted back enough to glare at her under the brim.

"You planted seeds in my head."

"What seeds?"

"About my friend."

"I didn't plant anything, darling." She stabbed at a strawberry. "I just made an observation. What happened?"

I rolled my eyes and glanced to where Adam was getting ready to do a cannonball into the pool. "You know I'd noticed that he was handsome before, but I didn't give it a second thought. Then you go warning me not to fall for him, and all of a sudden, he's like forbidden fruit. He touched me last night—just an innocent touch—and I swear to God my toes curled."

Victoria smirked.

"No. Don't do that, Aunt Victoria. This isn't funny. This isn't someone I can get involved with."

"Why the hell not? You have an agreement—"

"Mom! Watch!"

I sat back and observed Adam's poor attempt at diving. When he broke the surface, I gave him a thumbs up.

"Nice try, buddy! Keep practicing!" Returning my attention to my aunt, I shook my head. "This man, this *friend*, just so happens to be the new VP at Carter Enterprises."

"Oh, darling." Her tone was absolutely conspiratorial. "Sleeping with the enemy?"

"I'm *not* sleeping with him."

"You just said he made your toes curl."

"I didn't say I acted on it. Could you stop focusing on my sex life? It's a little creepy."

Victoria laughed, and I sighed.

"I don't know why I try to talk to you."

"Mara, stop taking life so seriously. Look around you. What do you have to be concerned about? You've got everything, including a marriage with an open door. If you're attracted to this man, take him."

"Not every relationship fits within the confines I set with Garrett."

"So he wants more than a roll in the hay?"

I shook my head. "He doesn't see me that way. His son and Adam are friends. So we're friends. Nothing more."

"That's a lie. I saw your face light up when you spoke to him."

"Because he's funny."

"And handsome."

"That's beside the point." I pushed my plate away, not really hungry. I hated that Michael's words had gotten to me, but they most certainly had. And not just about how Adam would view me when he got old enough to understand his parents' marriage, but I had to wonder if that's how Michael saw me.

What had he said? I'd sold my dignity. Did he really think that? That I had no sense of honor because I came to an agreement with my husband instead of leaving him? I never cared much about what anyone else thought of me because I believed what I'd done was right. But the idea that Michael thought less of me stung.

"You're falling for him," Victoria accused, pulling me from my thoughts.

I gaped at her. "I am *not*. Stop saying that. He is just a friend. A real friend. The kind you don't come across often in these social circles. He..."

"What?"

I glanced around, making sure we were alone. "When I went to pick up Adam this morning, we overheard Adam and Will talking about us. Not together. Not like that. Adam was telling Will how Garrett's never home, and he knows how sad that makes me even though I try to hide it. He said Garrett sucks as a dad. And Michael... Michael knows about one of Garrett's affairs. He just pointed out that someday Adam is going to catch on, and then what? I'm practically raising him on my own, and he's already starting to resent his dad. What happens when he realizes the reason Garrett is never around is because I gave him a free pass to ditch us? He's going to resent me too."

Aunt Victoria frowned and contemplated for several long seconds before answering. "Mara, eventually he is going to grow up, and as well as you raise him, he is going to turn into a man. You know how men are."

"I shouldn't be the one to put it in his head that treating women like whores is acceptable."

"Garrett doesn't treat you like a whore."

I scoffed. "Are you sure about that?"

Victoria pushed her own plate away, and her frown deepened. "What's happened? You used to be happy with this life."

I looked to where Adam was kicking, making the biggest splashes his little legs could make.

"No. I just hid my misery better. I just accepted a role I made for myself for so long that I forgot I cut out this role for a reason. Not just for Adam but because I wanted to be a powerhouse at King Incorporated."

"You've done so much for that company."

I pressed my lips together. "So much that Garrett is given credit for. Even the people who see that I make contributions give all the credit to Garrett at the end of the day if not outright congratulating him on my ideas. They congratulate him on his *wife's* ideas, as if that makes them his. I stayed in this marriage to be his equal, but I'm nothing more than his shadow. I can't lie to myself about that any longer. And I can't keep pretending that's enough for me."

Again, my aunt was silent for a long stretch. "What are you saying? Are you going to leave him?"

I nodded toward my son "Not until he's old enough that Garrett can't take him from me. You know I took a lover."

"Yes." Her voice was strained, but I didn't question why.

"I didn't do that for me. I did it out of spite because his

wife is sleeping with Garrett and she was flaunting. She pissed me off. I took this man into my bed out of spite. That's not the kind of person I want to be, but somehow... He opened my eyes to something I had ignored for far too long. I *do* deserve to be treated better than Garrett treats me. He sure puts on a good show when other people are around, but when it's the two of us, he has no use for me unless I'm naked."

"Darling, he's a man."

I jerked my face to her. "Stop using that as an excuse. My father wasn't like this."

"You were a child. You don't know what he was like."

"I know he loved my mother," I snapped, furious that she'd dare to counter my memory. "I saw it. I saw how he treated her. With love and respect."

Victoria's frown softened and she shook her head. "Mara, this is why you take lovers."

"To think more highly of me than my own husband?" I swallowed when my voice cracked. Never in the last six years had I felt such discontent with my life than I had in the hours since I left Michael's house.

"Yes. Sweetheart, you always had this idealism that I knew was going to break your heart someday. I've tried to make you see reason, but you just want more than—"

"Than I deserve?"

My aunt sighed. "More than any one man can ever give you. You want love? You lose this. Because the men who can give you this aren't in marriage for love. You want this? Give up love and make the best life you can with what you have. Garrett is a louse. But so is every other man out there in his own way. At least Garrett gives you a home and security. And freedom, Mara. Not many husbands would be okay with you having another man."

I sighed miserably as I sat back.

She reached across the table and took my hand. "Darling, I know you want it all. I understand. I used to want it all too. But you have to let go of that. Let Garrett steer the ship. Let him take the credit. What does that matter? At the end of the day, you have enough money to take on the world. Nobody said you had to take your husband along with you when you do."

I looked at Aunt Victoria and debated telling her of my plan to work with Albert. But then I remembered the woman who raised me wouldn't understand. Victoria was content with the money and the facade. And she was right, I had always wanted more. I refused to believe I couldn't have it. Maybe I couldn't now—not today, but if I restored the success of Carter Enterprises and was able to leave Garrett when Adam was older and not have to worry about supporting myself, then maybe I could focus on the love part.

Maybe by then I could look at myself in the mirror, and my son would respect me. Maybe I could even convince Michael that I had some semblance of dignity left.

[17]

I stood in the doorway of Garrett's office for several moments, watching him squint at the computer screen. Finally, he sighed and sat back.

"How long are you going to stand there staring?" he asked without looking at me.

"How long are you going to squint at that computer before putting on your reading glasses?"

"They make me feel old," he confessed.

I entered his office and walked around the desk. Sitting on the edge, I held out his glasses. He snatched them but didn't put them on.

"I need you for five minutes."

He grinned. "I may need ten with foreplay."

I frowned at him. "We have some things to discuss about our son."

His interest in me instantly diminished. "I'm working, Mara. I'm sure you can settle whatever it is."

"Five minutes."

He sat back, clearly resenting the intrusion. "Three."

My irritation with him grew. "You're negotiating the time it takes to talk about Adam?"

"I have a very important call to make in less than an hour. I need to get my head together."

He didn't need to say more. Even if I did fit this conversation into a three-minute summary, his head wouldn't be in it.

"Okay. My aunt is taking Adam for the night."

"Didn't he just have a sleepover with...*someone*?"

"Yes, but she wants to take him to the zoo tomorrow, so he's going to stay with her." "Cancel whatever plans you have. You're spending the evening with me tonight."

A slow smile spread across his lips. "I am?"

"Yes. You are. So whatever girl is on the line for tonight, cut her loose. You're having dinner with your wife. And if you're good"—I leaned in as if I was going to kiss him but pulled back at the last second because I needed to keep him somewhat interested in giving me what I wanted first—"maybe I'll let you have dessert."

He drew a deep breath. "Dinner at seven. Wear something sexy."

I slid off his desk. "Of course." Leaning down, I kissed him lightly before leaving him to do whatever he was up to.

The town car came to a stop in front of a high rise—the one where I had discovered Garrett had more than just the King Incorporated apartment for business purposes.

The building had a high-class restaurant, but I had yet to

find something on the menu I enjoyed. The food was never cooked properly and tended toward the bland side, but the restaurant more than made up for it with the trendy décor that made it a hotspot for the well-to-do.

I turned my head to my husband as the doorman opened my door. "You know I don't like the food here."

Garrett gestured for me to get out of the car. "Just trust me, please."

I accepted the doorman's hand and thanked him for helping me out of the car. I stood, looking around at the boutiques nestled between the name brands and restaurants that filled the city street. Garrett tipped the doorman and guided me into the building...and past the restaurant to where the elevator would take us to the apartments higher in the building.

Goddamn it. I should have known.

"Garrett," I said on a sigh. "When I suggested dinner tonight, I actually meant *dinner*. I want to talk to you about Adam."

He kissed the back of my hand. "And we will."

"Good evening, Mr. and Mrs. King," an attendant said.

I smiled but then focused on Garrett while the uniformed man rushed to summon the elevator.

"I think he's getting old enough to see more than we realize."

Garrett patted my hand, and I was tempted to slap him with it.

"Let's have dinner before we get too deep into this, darling."

Stepping into the elevator, I actually bit my tongue to stop from lashing out. I hated how he dodged every parenting issue I brought to him. At some point, he was going to have to step up and be a father to his son. Instead, he'd taken my request for a private dinner for two to mean I wanted to hide away and fuck his brains out. Typical Garrett.

The elevator stopped, and we stepped out. With his hand on the small of my back, I let him lead me to the apartment we kept for business purposes—and occasional romps away from home. He opened the door and stepped in, holding it for me to enter. I did and walked into the living area without waiting for him—then I came to a sudden stop.

Garrett flipped the light switch off, and the flames of dozens of candles flickered, lighting the room in a dim glow. Much like our home, the apartment was crisp and clean and contemporary. But the candles' glow eased the sharp lines of the tempered glass table and the straight-back sofa and chairs. Soft music filled my ears, and the soft scent of lilies from the multiple bouquets tickled my senses. Like the Bird's Nest, the city below was hidden behind near-shear curtains.

Garrett slipped his arms around my waist and kissed my neck. "Do you like it?"

"It's beautiful." Turning in his arms, I met his satisfied grin with a curious one. It wasn't like Garrett to romance me. He was more of a wham-bam-fuck-me-and-go-away-ma'am type. Then the lightbulb in my mind lit, flickered, and exploded like neon fireworks.

What had I told Jake? I wanted to be seduced. I wanted to be romanced.

Looking over my shoulder at the table in the corner confirmed what I'd suddenly realized. A private dinner...for *three*. Of course. I rotated my jaw, but I couldn't quite stop the clip in my tone.

"I was hoping the seduction would come off a little less premeditated."

Cupping my face, he kissed me lightly. "Premeditated sounds so sinister. Consider this well-thought-out. For instance, I picked up sushi and Koshu wine from that place you like downtown earlier today because I *do* know you hate the food downstairs. Jake arrived half an hour ago to light the candles, turn on the music, and set up dinner. All for you."

I stared at him. I should be flattered. It was a rare occasion that Garrett actually showed me any consideration. But then again, it was all part of a ruse to get me into bed. With Jake.

Taking my hand, Garrett lifted my knuckles to his mouth and kissed them, then used my hand to turn me toward the table. Jake was there now, and when I met his gaze, he offered me a warm smile that eased some of my frustration. I knew Garrett's motives were all about his own pleasure, but Jake seemed to genuinely care about mine.

I'd told him my expectations of this scenario, and he'd followed through. He'd listened. I had no doubt he was to thank for the candles, the music, the food, and anything else that was about to take place.

Stepping to him, I kissed his cheek. "Thank you."

"Of course." He slid out his chair as I sat. Putting his hands on my shoulders, he lightly massaged the muscles and leaned down to whisper in my ear. "This is about you, Mara. If you want out, just tell me."

I nodded. And he stepped away, taking the seat next to me. Jake lifted the lid off a platter, and I smiled at Garrett after seeing the dish was filled with salmon rolls. He knew my favorite?

"Don't look so surprised," he insisted.

"Well, I am."

He rested his hand on mine. "I, too, see more than you realize."

I laughed softly. "We'll discuss that another time." I wasn't going to debate my concerns about our son when my husband and lover had set up an obvious attempt to get me to make good on my promise. And the way my heart hadn't stopped racing implied their attempt was succeeding.

I sipped the wine Jake poured as the men filled their plates. I wasn't quite sure of the protocol for this type of dinner. Usually, we talked business while Megan blatantly threw herself at Garrett and Jake and I smirked at each other, knowing what would happen later. This was different. An elephant sat squarely on the table in front of us, and I didn't know how not to notice it.

But leave that to Garrett. He started rambling about the next deal they should try to steal from Carter Enterprises.

"And we have Mara to thank for closing the deal with McCullough Corp.," Garrett said, toasting me with his wine. "Very nice work, darling."

I smiled. "They just needed a lighter touch than you were bringing to the table."

"And if anyone is good with a light touch, it's my wife."

He winked, and I held his gaze as I took another drink of wine. My glass somehow remained full throughout dinner even though I was drinking steadily, and it was still full when dinner ended and the conversation shifted from business to sharing stories and laughing. Between the wine and the casual conversation, all the anxiety seeped from my bones, leaving me completely relaxed.

True to their word, neither pushed—neither made me feel that the only reason they were there was for the very reason they were there. The conversation was genuine. The dinner was delicious. And the wine...the wine was going down a bit too easily.

When we left the table for the sitting area, Garrett helped me stand, as he would at any other dinner. He guided me to the sofa, where he sat me down. But then he moved to sit in a chair across from me.

A moment later, Jake sat close to my side. My heart skipped, and my stomach rolled. I'd officially just become Jake's date for the evening. The handoff had happened, and they were so very subtle about it.

As the men talked, I debated how this was going to transition into what we all knew it would. Was there some clue I was supposed to give that I was ready? Would one of them give me the cue? Maybe I should go to the restroom and come back naked. That'd shock the hell out of them—or not, considering the circumstances—but that wasn't how I'd imagined this playing out. Well...not the *only* way I'd imagined this playing out.

I had run a dozen scenarios through my mind since

giving Jake the go-ahead to plan this evening. Everything from sweet and sensual to rough and rowdy had danced through my mind in the last few days. But in all those daydreams, I hadn't considered how to get from point A to point B.

I took another drink and closed my eyes as the wine slid down. I wasn't drunk, but if I kept drinking from the glass that never seemed to empty, I would be soon. I didn't want that. I didn't want my judgment to be clouded or my memory of this evening to be foggy.

Leaning forward, I put my glass down to stop myself from drinking more. When I sat back, I leaned into Jake and jolted. He'd clearly moved to get in my way.

I didn't mind. Now that I knew he was there, I sat back against him, and he wrapped his arm around my shoulder and let his hand dangle, moving his fingers back and forth over my nipple. I dropped my hand to his knee. Looking to Garrett, I searched his eyes, seeking any sign that he was unsure of what was happening right in front of him. There wasn't one. The conversation never missed a beat.

My heart nearly pounded out of my chest when Jake's light touch turned into him cupping my breast and squeezing my nipple between his thumb and forefinger. And Garrett just sat there. Several moments later, Jake pressed his face into my neck, kissing me, still groping. And Garrett still just sat there. Then his other hand moved to my thigh, traveling higher, pushing the hem up until I was exposed.

And that bastard *still* just sat there.

Any notion that this wasn't going to happen ended when

Jake's hand reached the apex of my legs, and my breath left me in a rush.

Garrett smirked, and I think I hated him a little in that moment. Wouldn't a normal man—a man who loved his wife—be jealous? Closing my eyes, I blocked him out of my mind and focused on Jake.

Dropping my head back on his shoulder, I reached up and fisted his hair while he kissed my neck. Opening my legs, I invited him to touch me in the ways that he knew I liked. He slid his hand into the leg band of my panties and rubbed over me, tweaking my clit before slipping several fingers inside me.

Finding his way inside my shirt, he pinched my erect nipple, sending waves through me. Then he pulled his fingers from my skirt and licked them clean before tracing my lips. I opened my mouth and sucked them in and dared to look at my husband.

Holding his gaze, I sucked three of Jake's fingers into my mouth down to his knuckles.

"Fuck," Garrett whispered when I moaned.

Jake jerked my face to his and kissed me hard as he squeezed my breast. Then, like the well-practiced lovers we were, we worked on removing each other's clothes. Leaving only my strappy high heels. Just the way he liked me.

Jake rolled on a condom, lifted me up, and brought me to straddle his lap. He slid into me with one hard, deep thrust that caused me to gasp. He lifted me again and slammed me down as he slammed up, making me cry out at the mixture of pleasure and pain he knew I loved. After several times, he finally let me drop my knees to the cushion.

Wrapping our arms around each other, we kissed hard—tongues dueling, lips smacking, teeth nipping—as we pressed our bodies into each other's.

We knew this routine. We knew what would happen next. We fucking loved what happened next. I ground into him as he held me to him, almost restraining my moves, letting the friction build. And just as the anticipation was about to kill me, he released his hold, and his hand crashed down on my ass.

I cried out and threw my head back. He squeezed my stinging cheek, I moaned, and his hand found my ass again, sending the sound of flesh smacking flesh to my ears. I rode him faster, harder, determined to find that sweet release he always brought me.

But he didn't let me finish. He lifted me up off his lap. He loved taking me from behind with my knees on the sofa, my back arched, my ass out for him to fondle. But he stopped me before I could take that position. Instead, he pushed me to the floor, on all fours.

I was looking my husband in the eye when Jake slid into me from behind. I bit my lip, ground my hips, and moaned at the feel of his body against the sting in my ass.

As before, Garrett sat there, watching. I stared into his eyes as Jake took me to the brink. Finally, unable to stand another moment of Garrett simply staring at me, I leaned back onto my knees and reached for him. He was on the floor in front of me immediately. I fisted his hair and pulled his face to my tits. He instantly latched on to my nipple.

I could have sworn he growled as he bit my sensitive flesh. That was what I needed. That last little twinge of pain.

Someone rolled a finger over my clit, and I screamed out as my lover grunted. Jake pulled out of me, and Garrett pulled me into a deep kiss, then scooped me up and had me on my back on the floor. Then he was between my legs, tasting the juices Jake had produced from my body.

While Garrett licked, pulling moans and gasps from me, Jake plucked at my nipples, rolling them, sucking one and then the other.

I lifted my hips up to meet Garrett's mouth, and his fingers slid in me, fucking me as he moved his mouth over me, and Jake played with my breasts. I could have sworn I saw stars as the sensations hit me one after another.

Dear God, why hadn't I given in and done this years ago?

When Garrett climbed over my body and thrust his cock in me, I cried out. I don't know where his clothes went, and I didn't ask. I just needed him inside me. Deep inside me. And then I met his gaze, and we both came undone.

I woke with a start when fingers trailed down my back. I had to blink a few times to realize where I was. In the bed of the King Inc. apartment, sandwiched between my husband and my lover.

I only needed a moment to realize Jake's fingers were the ones tickling my spine. Turning my face into his bare chest, I kissed him.

"You stayed," I whispered.

"I promised I'd look after you, didn't I?" He kissed my head.

I smiled. "You did."

"How are you this morning?"

I took a moment to gauge my physical and emotional well-being. "I'm good. You?"

"Good."

I slid on top of him and planted a quick kiss on his lips. "I need to use the little girls' room, though." Slipping into the bathroom, I used the facilities, then dug out three of the toothbrushes and a small tube of toothpaste that was kept on hand for guests.

Wrapping myself in a provided robe, I went back to the bedroom and sat next to Jake. "Coffee?"

"Please."

Leaning down, I kissed him. "Freshen up. I'll get it started."

In the kitchen, I brewed coffee and smiled when I found a platter of fruit in the fridge. Obviously, the men had planned on staying overnight. I was spooning strawberries and melon onto a plate when Jake slipped his arms around my waist and hugged me against him.

"There are croissants as well."

"Oh, you and your temptation." I accepted a buttery Viennoiserie pastry, even though I had sworn off such treats. Not that it mattered, I guessed. Not after the dietary sins I'd committed with Michael as of late.

Jake kissed my neck, and I forced thoughts of the other man from my mind. Turning, I smiled as I accepted Jake's lips on mine before carrying my breakfast to the sofa. He sat next to me with his drink and picked at the fruit with me.

When the plate was empty, he pulled me back against him. "I like this a little too much," he whispered.

"What?"

"Sharing my morning with you."

I cuddled closer to him. "This is nice."

He brushed his fingers over the area of my exposed chest. "Garrett and I talked for a while after you fell asleep last night."

My stomach tightened a touch. "About what?"

"You. Megan."

I sat up enough to look back at him. "Don't even suggest—"

His quiet laugh cut off my protest. "No. Not like that. Okay, not *just* like that. I won't deny that the idea was tossed around."

"The answer is no, so just drop that now."

He hugged me back to him. "Dropped."

"What else did you talk about?"

He put his hand back to my chest. "I just told him he could have a little more respect for you without outright saying it."

"And how did that go over?"

"I think he heard me."

I rested my hand on his knee. "How do you know?"

"He got quiet. Contemplative. I went to bed to give him time to think."

I bit my lip. "It's never a good thing when Garrett gets quiet. I hope you didn't overstep."

Jake kissed my head. "I was subtle in my observation."

I smiled as he brushed his hand over my nipple. "Just like you're being subtle now?"

"What? This?" He pinched the peak.

"Yeah, that."

"I was going more for suave than subtle."

I giggled. "I'm not sure you achieved either."

He playfully took a handful of my breast. "How about now?"

"Now I think you're flirting with me."

He bit my ear. "I'm definitely flirting with you."

Turning to face him, I debated for a moment before pulling him with me as I lay back on the sofa. Digging my fingers in his hair, I held him close as I kissed him deeply. He ran his hand up my thigh, pushing my robe aside as he situated between my legs.

"Condom," I muttered against his mouth as he pressed our bodies together.

He cursed at the reminder. Stretching over me, he reached and patted along the end table while I flicked my tongue over the nipple that he conveniently hovered over my face.

"Ah-ha," he said a moment later.

Sitting back, he covered himself as I opened my robe all the way but didn't take the garment off. He didn't bother removing his either. Matching white terry cloth protected us from the cool air in the room as he slid into me.

I gasped, and Jake stopped moving.

"Okay?" he asked.

I exhaled. "Yeah. A little tender."

He withdrew more slowly. "We'll do this later."

"No." I wrapped my leg around his, stopping him from leaving me. "Just go easy on me." Lifting my mouth to his, I kissed him as he entered me. Though our sex was usually heated—even a bit rough—I thought slowing things down was just as good. I clung to him as he moved. Putting my hand to his face, I held his gaze as he thrusted in and out. The build was slow but as strong as any other time we'd been together.

Resting his forehead to mine, Jake exhaled slowly. "Jesus, Mara. What you do to me."

I lifted my head, capturing his mouth again. Ending the kiss, he buried his face in my hair as he shoved into me one final time.

He laughed softly, sounding a bit embarrassed. "I think I beat you to the finish line."

"You can make it up to me next time," I whispered.

Brushing my hair back, he looked into my eyes, and my breath caught. Something there was a bit too tender, a bit too intimate.

Looking away, I shifted and lightly pushed him back.

He climbed off me and closed his robe as I sat and did the same.

"Shower?" he asked.

"I need a bit more coffee in my system," I said. "Go ahead."

He disappeared into the bedroom, and I sipped my lukewarm drink. I was just finishing my first cup when Garrett emerged from the bedroom buck-naked.

Refilling my mug, I chuckled. "I'm not sure Jake will appreciate your nudity."

He took a mug from the cabinet and set it beside mine. "I'm not sure I appreciate him making love to my wife."

I stopped pouring to look at him. "Isn't that why you invited him?"

"No. I invited him to fuck you. There's a difference."

I creased my brow, and he reached across me for the coffee pot.

He topped off my cup and filled his own, then leaned against the counter. "Do you deny that's what happened on the couch this morning?"

"He was being gentle. I'm a bit tender after last night."

Threading his fingers in my hair, he pulled me to look at him—not roughly, but he certainly got his point across.

"He was making love to you. That's *my* job."

I scoffed. "When's the last time you made love to me, Garrett? I'm only good for a quick fuck and a threesome these days."

He actually looked hurt. Releasing his hold on me, he lifted my cup and handed it to me. I hesitated in taking it, but when I did, he took my hand and pulled me behind him to the bedroom. I wasn't exactly in the mood for whatever he had in mind, but I felt bad. Maybe even a bit guilty.

He was right. I could deny it, but he was right. The look in Jake's eye, the tender way he'd said my name—that didn't feel like him simply having sex with me. That felt deeper.

Garrett set his mug down and tugged the sash of my robe free. I let him remove the covering, expecting him to fondle me. And I'd probably let him if for no other reason than to appease my guilt and keep the peace.

But he surprised me. Instead, he eased into the bed and

leaned against the headboard, then gestured for me to join him. I sat next to him, and he pulled the blanket up, covering me.

I handed him his coffee and waited. Instead of pushing for sex, he asked me about my plans for the day. When I told him I was hoping for a quiet day since Adam would be with my aunt, he brought my hand to his mouth and kissed my knuckles.

"Let me take you shopping."

I laughed softly. "You hate shopping."

"I'll make an exception today."

My smile faded. "You don't have to—"

"I want to."

I glanced toward the bathroom. The shower was still running, but even so, I whispered. "If this is about Jake—"

"This is me asking my wife to spend some time with me. If you don't want to, just say so."

"That's not what I'm saying."

"Doesn't sound like you're saying yes."

I drew a breath. This was definitely about Jake. Garrett didn't feel insecure often, but when he did, it was best to placate him. Smiling, I squeezed his hand. "I'd love to spend some time with you. But you and I both know shopping is about as enjoyable for you as a root canal."

He didn't argue. He actually looked relieved. "So what do you suggest?"

"This. Just this. We'll see Jake off and have some breakfast and just relax. No phones, no computers, no outside world. At least for a while. Sound good?"

"Sounds perfect."

I kissed him lightly. I didn't care if his attention was jealousy-induced and likely never to be repeated. I couldn't remember the last time he wanted to spend time with me just for the sake of being with me. He always wanted something in return.

So I'd take what I could get and pretend we both believed it actually meant more than what it was—Garrett restaking his claim on me.

[18]

I leaned against my headboard when Garrett entered my bedroom carrying a wicker basket and tartan blanket. Just like he had carried into my office on the night he'd proposed.

He closed the door behind him and held out his gifts. "Tell me this is still romantic. I can't keep up with the trends."

I couldn't help but smile. He'd been so much more attentive since the night we'd spent with Jake. Granted that hadn't even been a week ago, but the change in Garrett was welcome. He'd eaten dinner at home each night. He'd played cars with Adam while I sat watching, soaking up the moment. And now, he was bringing me a picnic dinner—at nearly ten p.m.

"Yes," I said despite the late hour. "This is still romantic."

"Thank God." He spread the blanket out, as he had done that night so long ago, and gestured for me to join him.

I did, closing the files on my laptop before pushing the blankets aside and crossing the room in my light-pink nightgown. Easing to the floor, I smiled as he unpacked a meal much like the one we'd shared the last time we ate like this. Meats, cheeses, crackers. And champagne.

As he filled our flutes, I remembered that night. How much hope I had for our future. How in love I was with this man. How fucking blind I was to the truth.

"Mara," Garrett said.

I had to blink several times to return to the present. Forcing a smile, I accepted the glass he held out to me.

"Thank you."

"What's wrong?"

"Nothing."

"If you could see your face, you'd disagree. What did I do?"

I took a breath and let it out slowly. "I was just thinking of the night you proposed."

"I'd like to think that's a happier memory than what your expression implies."

I laughed softly but without any amusement. "It was a wonderful night, Garrett. It was perfect."

"So why do you look so miserable thinking about it?"

I frowned, no longer able to hide my real emotions. Not that I had been, apparently.

"I was so naïve back then. It's hard to believe that girl was me."

"I loved that about you."

"Of course you did. I was so easy to manipulate." I closed my eyes when I realized what I'd said. Slowly opening my eyes, I sighed. "I'm sorry."

"Don't be."

"That just came out."

He shook his head as he sorted through the food he'd brought.

"The last few days have been wonderful," I said. "But sometimes it's hard not to fall back into snapping at you."

He chuckled. "That's second nature for you, darling."

I grinned slightly. "Well, you do make it easy."

He handed me a plate. "You were naïve, and I loved your innocence. Not because it made you a target—you were too smart for that—but because it was refreshing to find a woman who wasn't out to bed me. You couldn't have cared less about me and my position or my money. It made me want you more than you can ever imagine."

"And now that I'm no longer naïve?"

He smiled as he brushed his hand over my hair. "Darling. You're still so innocent. So much more than you could ever know."

His comment stabbed at me. I wasn't naïve. I knew exactly what kind of man he was behind his charming smile. I knew what it was to lie and cheat. To betray. I stopped being innocent a long time ago.

"I'm not."

He smirked as he eyed me, and I gawked at him.

"I'm *not*."

"Okay. You're not," Garrett said gently and held out a glass of champagne.

I hesitated before accepting and taking a sip. The crisp bubbly wine lit my taste buds.

"That's wonderful," I said after swallowing.

"It should be for what I paid for it. I was saving this

bottle for our anniversary, but I thought it might serve a better purpose tonight."

I eased back and looked up at him. "What's so special about tonight?"

He took a drink and sighed before looking up at me from beneath his thick lashes. "I have a proposition for you."

A proposition? From Garrett? That was guaranteed to be a dangerous thing. I'd already practically masturbated in front of Albert for a business deal. I'd fucked Jake in front of him. What more could he ask?

"I want us to start fresh, Mara."

I creased my brow, not understanding his intent. "What?"

"We're a family, but I haven't been the husband that you deserve."

Usually, I could hide my emotions a little better, but he'd thrown me for yet another loop, and I stared at him.

"Honesty time," he said quietly. "I never thought you'd utilize our agreement. When I realized you had, it hurt. I couldn't believe that you could want any other man. Then I got a reality check. That's how you'd felt all along. How could I possibly want someone else? So I worked to accept that you could still love me and have sex with someone else because despite it all, Mara, I love you and *only* you. I even convinced myself that we could live out this fantasy I've always had—sharing you with another man."

Heat flared low in my stomach at the memory of Garrett and Jake kissing, sucking, touching me at the same time, and I shifted.

"I'm not trying to make you uncomfortable," he said quietly. "I know you did that for me."

I didn't challenge his assessment. I didn't confess that I wanted that to happen again. Next time, I wouldn't be so shy. Next time, I wouldn't be so timid.

Next time would be so much better.

"Everything you do is for me," he said. "I know that now. I see that now. And I am so lucky to have a woman like you. Who cares so much about my needs and my desires. I took you for granted for too long. I want to rectify that."

I creased my brow. I don't know who wrote this speech for him, but I didn't believe for a moment this was my husband speaking. Body snatchers? Brainwashers? Or just Garrett being Garrett and playing me. He usually used sexual manipulation to get his way. Emotional manipulation was new.

"What do you want?" I whispered, dipping my toes into whatever pile of shit he was laying before me.

"I want us to have a real marriage."

My heart seized. My God. He wanted *what*? The only thing I'd ever wanted from him? The words had just left his mouth. I choked out a sound.

He smiled timidly as he touched my cheek. "I'm sorry. I'm so sorry for all the hurt I've caused you. I see now how deeply I've cut you. I don't want to do that anymore, Mara."

"What...what are you saying?"

His smile grew a bit, became a touch more confident. Leaning over, as he'd done the night he proposed, he reached into his pocket and pulled out a ring. Instead of a gigantic diamond, this one was a wide band of diamonds. He slid it on my finger, and it fit perfectly around the ring already there, as if they were made to go together.

"You're my queen." The same words he'd said when we got engaged. "Now and forever. And I promise, I will start treating you like it."

I stared at the band for some time. I wanted to trust him. I wanted to believe him. I wanted to fall into his web and pretend it wasn't going to be the death of me. I swallowed because I knew that I couldn't. I couldn't trust him or believe him, and this *could* be the death of me. I looked at him, and he leaned forward to kiss me. I put my fingertips to his lips before he could.

He held my gaze.

"What do you want from me?" I whispered. "Just tell me," I insisted when he started to protest.

"I want us to try monogamy."

I laughed softly and shook my head. "You don't know the meaning of the word, Garrett."

He tugged my hand. "I do, Mara." He lowered his face, and I frowned.

He couldn't even pretend to want to be exclusive for the length of this conversation. Heavy silence filled my bedroom as he sat up. He downed what was in his glass and set the empty flute aside before finally meeting my gaze again.

"I'm not perfect, Mara. I have weaknesses. I tried to hide them from you. When you found out and you left me, I felt a fear like I'd never known before. Not just because you were pregnant but because I loved you." He put his hand over his heart. "Never, in all my life, have I loved someone the way I love you. You are a part of me, and when you came back and we came to an agreement, I wanted so much to believe you had come to terms with me—the real me. But deep down, I knew better. I knew eventually you'd push back because that's who you are, Mara. And that's why I love you."

"You love me because I tolerate your infidelity."

"No. I wasn't betraying you, Mara. I was protecting you."

I creased my brow, not understanding his justification. "Protecting me? From what?"

"From me. From the things inside me that I can't escape."

I scoffed. "What *things*?"

He traced his fingers along my knee to where my thigh disappeared beneath the slit of my nightgown. "You're precious to me. I love your strength. I love your boldness. I love that you challenge me. Push me when I need it. You are beautiful and brilliant and everything I have ever wanted in a woman." He flicked his gaze to mine, and his eyes suddenly seemed hard. "But the truth is, in the bedroom, you'll never be able to satisfy me."

My heart dropped.

Heat sparked in his eyes as he gripped my thigh so hard it hurt.

I sat up straight, tried to pull away, but he tightened his grip. I knew Garrett could be a viper in the boardroom, but this was the first time I'd seen a menacing look in his eyes directed at me. And his words. How could he be so cruel?

"How dare you?" I spat at him.

"Because it's the truth, Mara. I've kept those women because...because I do things to them that I could never do to you. Because I could never tie you to a bed and shove my dick so deep down your throat you couldn't breathe while another man rammed his cock in your ass."

I'm sure my eyes widened, shocked at the image he'd created.

"Do you know what an O-ring is, Mara?"

I didn't. But the way he was looking at me when he said it made me swallow. I didn't know if I was more curious or more terrified.

He released my thigh only to cup my face and press his thumb between my lips and deep into my mouth. I tried to pull back, but he held me.

"It's a strap of leather with a hard round bit that goes in your mouth and holds it open for as long as I want it to be. To do whatever I want to do."

This time, when I pulled my head back, he released me only to grip a handful of my hair and jerk me to him. He used his other hand to grab my hand and put it to his crotch. He was hard.

"Do you see what the thought does to me?" he asked through clenched teeth. He forced my fingers around his erection and pumped our hands as he held my face millimeters from his. "Do you feel that? How much it turns me on to think of you like that? Strapped down and forced open for me?" He moaned and closed his eyes as he used my hand to stroke him. "You'd look so fucking beautiful." His breath crashed against my face as he tightened our hold on his dick and moved our hands faster.

I pulled to free myself from his grasp. I was shocked, but mostly at myself because the image he was creating wasn't nearly as offensive as it should have been. I'd let Garrett King take so much of me already, I wasn't about to let him take what was left of my dignity...even if he had piqued my sexual curiosity in ways I'd never admit to him.

Finally, he stopped forcing my hand over him and opened his eyes. The heat there as he looked at me was enough to catch the room on fire, and he exhaled slowly as he eased his grip on my hand. He didn't release his hold on my hair, though.

He held me close so I was looking right at him as he said, "You think I'm betraying you, but I've rarely had my way with another woman and not pretended it was you. But I respect you, Mara. I respect you, and I would never ask you to do those things for me."

Tears filled my eyes. I felt the sting. How had I not seen this side of him before? The things he'd tried to slip into our lives—public sex, anal sex, pinning me down until my hands went numb—were nothing compared to what he'd been hiding all this time.

He eased his hold on my hair and my hand, and I pulled away from his hard-on.

"When you started working at King Inc., I knew you were different," he said. "Every other woman threw themselves at me and the other executives. You barely noticed anything going on around you. You were so dedicated. To me. To the company. God, how I admired you, and I swore you'd be mine. I thought I could be the man you needed. I wanted to be that man, Mara. I tried. But my needs didn't change. You couldn't quench this thirst I have. I wouldn't ask you to. I would *never* ask you to. You may not believe it, but I was so broken when you left me that night." He smiled slightly as he touched my hair. "But then you came back and offered me the best of both worlds, and I jumped at the chance without considering what it would do to you. I'm sorry for that."

I licked my lips, but my voice still trembled when I said, "What makes you think your needs have changed now?"

"My needs haven't changed, Mara. *You* have."

A soft laugh left me. "If you think you're prying my mouth open—"

"Shh." He put his fingers to my lips as I'd done to him. "No. Nothing like that. I'd never ask you to do something so extreme." His breath quivered as it left him. "But I saw the fire in your eyes when you were with Jake. I saw that you liked that little bit of pain he inflicted. You liked that I was there. Watching. You liked it more when I came to you and we were both touching you."

My cheeks immediately began to burn, and I had no doubt my lightly tanned face was bright red.

He smiled and traced my lips. "You're new to pain. I could tell. He was so gentle with you. It was beautiful." Lowering his hand, he brushed my nipple, which was standing at attention. "I could take you to heights you've never known, Mara. I could blow your mind."

I swallowed. "From the sounds of it, I wouldn't hold your attention for long."

"But you would." He inhaled slowly. Deeply. "I can't stop thinking of the things I could do to you now that I know your mind is opening."

Threading a strand of my long hair around his finger, he

pulled gently. Meeting my gaze, he eyed me with a hunger I hadn't seen in him since we were dating.

"I've always respected you too much to push your boundaries. You are my queen, after all. But if you are willing, I can teach you the joy of pain." He gave my nipple a sharp but gentle pull when I started to protest. "Within the confines of your comfort zone. I would never ask for anything you don't want to give. I would never push you more than you want to be pushed."

"And you think that would keep you satisfied?"

"I want to try." Pulling me to him, he brushed his lips over mine. "Can you imagine how happy we could be if we both finally got what we always wanted from the other?"

Yes. I could imagine. I'd been imagining that very scenario for the last six years. I didn't protest, so he kissed me. Hard. Demanding.

When he finally broke free, he brushed his lips over mine as he whispered, "I want to try something. If you're willing."

I stared at him. Frozen. Not knowing if I was willing or not. I was intrigued, I can admit that. But also terrified. Not of him hurting me—I believed him when he said that even if I didn't believe anything else the man said. I trusted that he wouldn't cause me physical pain against my will—but was I willing?

He brushed his mouth over mine again, feather-light as his breath heated my face. He cupped my breast and rubbed his thumb over my nipple. I closed my eyes and swallowed hard, uncertain of where this was leading. He rarely seduced me like this, and I didn't want him to stop even though I knew he was going to push those boundaries he'd mentioned earlier.

He pushed the strap of my gown down, tugging at the satin until my nipple was exposed. He tweaked the pebbled flesh, pinching and pulling, gently at first, but his manipulation was getting noticeably harder each time. He licked my lip before lightly sinking his teeth in, and my brain sparked, not sure which sensation to pay attention to.

I gasped as my breathing increased—a quiet panting as I sat, letting him have his way. He tugged my hair, and then his mouth was on my neck, his kiss so hard, his whiskers dug into my skin.

I inhaled sharply but didn't stop him. Before I realized what he was doing, he pushed me onto my back and was between my legs with his mouth on the nipple he'd been teasing. The skin was sensitive now, so the flick of his tongue sent sensations rolling through me.

He moved up my body, grinding his erection against my lace panties. His mouth met mine with an open kiss, hot and demanding.

Then he gently stroked my cheek. "If you want me to stop, just tell me."

I stared into his eyes for a moment before giving him one nod of agreement.

He ran his hand down my thigh as he held my gaze, gently lifting my leg up to wrap around his. And then an unexpected sting hit my skin as he slapped the underside of my ass.

I jumped, gasped, wriggled, but then he pressed his hand

to my skin, rubbing over what he'd done, soothing the pain as he ground into me again.

He repeated the process, and I bit my lip to stop my breath from quivering. The pain, then the soothing, then the pressure against my center. After the third time, Garrett sat back on his knees and gripped my hips. He flipped me onto my stomach, pushed my gown up, and lifted my hips enough to make my ass perk up for him.

"God, I wish you could see this," he growled as he ran his hand over what was surely a bright-red handprint. He stroked it, dipped his fingers between my legs, and exhaled heavily again. "Your pussy is so wet."

I bit my lip as he tugged the crotch of my underwear aside and shoved two fingers deep inside me and quickly withdrew them. The sound of his lips smacking caused my breath to catch, then a moment later, his hand was on me again, stroking.

And then he spanked my previously untouched cheek. A hard, crisp slap that left needles prickling my skin. I jumped, gasped, and let my breath out slowly as he eased the sting. He was being as gentle as I imagined he could be considering his confession, but the pain was starting to get more intense than I wanted.

Before I could tell him to stop, he fingered me again, making me forget how much my ass hurt. He touched my clit, and I forgot how to breathe. My entire body seemed more aware of his touch somehow. He had touched me there a thousand times. I knew his hand as well as I knew my own. But this was different. This was...more.

He fingered me hard, shoving deep and fast, but before I

could finish, he pulled his hand away and sucked his fingers again. I exhaled, partially with disappointment and partially with the excitement of knowing this wasn't over.

When his hand found my skin the next time, he returned to where he'd originally spanked me. The pain was even more intense. He rubbed me, soothed me, fucked me with his hand, eased the sting, only to give me more.

Finally, I pulled away, letting him know I couldn't take more. But he wasn't done, and I didn't stop him when I heard his belt releasing. I swallowed. Held my breath. Closed my eyes tight—fear and excitement mixing. But he didn't take the leather to my skin. He pushed his slacks down, pulled me to my knees, and shoved his cock in me.

There was nothing sweet about the move. He was demanding to enter me, demanding to give me pleasure. And I fucking loved it.

I arched my back, cried out, and all but begged for more. The only thing that stopped me was that I would *never* beg Garrett King for anything. But I didn't have to. He seemed to be able to read my mind. He gripped my hips hard as he pulled me back and took what he wanted with a kind of ownership I should have been offended by.

But I couldn't be offended. I was in heaven.

He was deep inside me, and my skin was alive with a million starbursts of light every time his thighs crashed into mine. Everything he was doing to me was so wrong but so fucking right. He fisted my hair and pulled me back to him, and I didn't even protest. No, I let him. And when my back was against his chest, he put his hand to my clit, and I cried out. He grunted out a sound I'd never heard from him before—something deep and primal and almost frightening.

Then I felt something I hadn't in so long—Garrett came deep inside me.

I closed my eyes. Cursed him. I didn't want him uncovered inside my body. I had no idea how many women he'd been with, or who. Pulling away from him, I turned and shot an accusing glare his way as I pushed my nightgown down.

"You didn't wear a condom."

He smiled, his face red from exertion. He closed the distance between us and put his mouth on me, another demanding and possessive kiss.

"You said I had to do that when I have other women. I haven't been with another woman all week."

I swallowed. "Not nearly long enough to know whether or not you've caught something that will rot your dick off."

He laughed softly. "Darling. Not only do all my women have to have a clean bill of health, but I would never touch one of them without the proper protection. You're my wife, Mara. That provides you certain privileges."

I scoffed. "Having your cum in me is a perk?"

"Many women would think so."

Before I could respond, he was on me, kissing me lightly. "You enjoyed this," he whispered.

I couldn't deny it if I'd wanted to. He was there. He'd seen me.

Running his hand tenderly over my cheek and brushing my hair back, he smiled sweetly. "This is only the beginning of the pleasure I can bring you. I can give you so much. All you have to do is tell me you want it." Pressing his lips to mine, he brushed my hair again. "Tell me you want it."

Why did I always feel like I was walking into a trap where Garrett was concerned? Why did I always feel deceived?

His hand moved down my side, and I gasped at the feel of his fingertips sliding over my sensitive skin. The pleasure overrode my common sense, as tended to happen with Garrett, and I nodded even though I knew I'd likely regret it.

$$[\ 19\ ]$$

Jake sat back and watched me cross his office, but I didn't go to him. I went to the couch I'd admired the last time I'd visited him. Sitting back into the plush gray cushion, I crooked my finger, gesturing for him to join me.

He grinned wickedly as he did, leaning down and kissing me fully on the mouth before falling onto his back and putting his head into my lap.

I smiled as I stroked my fingers through his wavy brown hair. I loved his hair. Loved how it blew in the breeze when we sat on the balcony of the Bird's Nest. Loved gripping it as he had his face buried between my legs. Loved running my fingers through it as we basked in the afterglow.

"Uh-oh," he said as he looked up at me. "This isn't a quick fuck kind of visit, is it?"

I shook my head, and he sighed as he sat up.

Putting his elbows to his knees, he sat quietly for a moment. "You're ending things."

"I'm sorry," I whispered.

"No. We couldn't go on like this forever, could we?"

"It'd be nice if we could."

He looked at me. "Why now? After we…"

"Made love," I finished. "We made love, Jake. And he saw us."

He laughed softly. "He's making you do this."

I licked my lip. "He said there was an emotional connection between us. I told him it wasn't like that. That we were just being easy because I was tender. But that's not true. Is it?"

"I care about you, if that's what you're asking. I cared about you before we had an affair."

Leaning forward, I put my fingertips to his cheek. I held his gaze, stared into his eyes, then closed the gap. The kiss was light, sweet, tender. Emotional. Our lips moved slowly, taking the time to really feel each other. And when he parted his lips and slid his tongue over my lips, it wasn't a fevered, sexual demand. He was tenderly probing at my soul with his.

Pulling back slightly, just enough to look into his eyes, I whispered, "We made love."

He sat back and ran his fingers through his hair as he exhaled slowly. I turned, pulling my left leg beneath me so I could face him. I had to smile. He looked so perplexed.

Running my hand down his chest, I sighed too. "We can't pretend that didn't happen."

"Nor can we pretend why." He clasped my hand before kissing it. "We're good together. Too good in some ways." He smiled sweetly. "If we'd met first…"

I nodded. "It's a nice thought, but we didn't meet first.

We're married to other people. And neither of them is particularly kind when they feel betrayed."

He narrowed his eyes a bit. "Did he hurt you?"

Technically... I flashed to the scene that had played out—me on my knees and Garrett's hand finding my ass over and over. "No. Actually, he wants us to be monogamous. I know, I know," I said when he laughed. "But I have to try, Jake. That's all I ever wanted from him."

"He's asking for this because he wants you to end things with me."

I nodded. "I know that as much as I know this will never work. He'll cheat again. I'll be hurt again. I'm used to his kind of hurt." Squeezing his hand, I frowned. "But I don't want you and me to hurt each other. The only way to avoid that is to stop before we get too far into this thing. What we had was good. I want to remember it that way."

"Me too." Leaning over, he kissed me. "You're an amazing woman, Mara King. And if you ever need a quick fuck, you know where to find me."

I laughed. "Good to know." Tugging his hand, I grew serious. "Thank you, Jake."

"For what?"

"For everything. For being a friend and a lover and not being an asshole."

"I hope, for your sake, Garrett gives you what you need. But when he doesn't, I'm here for you. And not just for sex. If you ever need anything, you call me, and I'll come running."

"If that skank wife of yours starts giving you fits, you let me know," I said. "I'm happy to fake sex with you anytime she needs to be put in her place."

He grinned. "I just might take you up on that."

"I'm here for you, Jake. I mean that."

Cupping my face, he stroked my cheek. "So do I, Mara. Be careful. Please. This deal you have with Albert Carter could be dangerous. Please, watch your back."

"I will." Leaning forward, I kissed him again. The moment lingered, but it wasn't heated or sexual. It was two people ending an affair before it got too tangled to do so.

"What's troubling you now?" Aunt Victoria asked, sounding bored.

I didn't answer. Adam was underwater, holding his breath as long as he could. And I was debating how long before I needed to check on him. He resurfaced, and I realized I'd been holding my breath too. Exhaling, I eased back.

"You have got to learn to relax, Mara. He's right there." She set her glass down much harder than necessary. "What is eating at you?"

I glanced around the pool patio. "Garrett has suggested we try monogamy."

My aunt stared, then giggled and shook her head.

I sighed, then frowned.

"I agreed we should try," I said.

"When did this happen?"

"Last night." Which was why I wasn't in the pool with

Adam. Garrett had left me bruised in places a bathing suit didn't hide. "Jake had let me know he was at his office this morning, so I went to him and ended things. I'm a little sad about that."

"Oh, Mara." The disappointment in her voice was obvious. "You really bought this line of shit?"

I smiled at Adam when he called out for me to watch what he could do—a flip off the diving board that ended in a belly flop.

"I want to believe him. I'm *trying* to believe him."

"You know he can't be faithful. No man can. It goes against their very nature."

I bit my lip to stop myself from justifying that I'd been a prude in the bedroom. That I was becoming more aware of my sexuality. That maybe, just maybe, I could please my husband now. If I even attempted to take some of the blame for Garrett's behavior, my aunt's lecture would never end.

Besides, I didn't owe her an explanation. Yes, she was my aunt, but this was my marriage and my sex life and none of her damned business. She was far too nosy about the subject as it was.

"Even if it doesn't work out, it was time to end things with Jake anyway."

"*Why?* He's sexy as hell." She shook her head and said, "Oh, Mara," with that same disapproving tone. "You fell in love with him."

"No," I snapped. "No, I didn't. But I care about him more than I should. And we...we fit together more than we should."

"Fit? I hope you mean physically, because you should

never get emotionally invested in a lover. Don't get to know them. Don't bond with them. Fuck them and go home."

I rolled my eyes. "Aunt Victoria, *please*. That is awful."

She chuckled. Just like Garrett, she simply loved getting a rise out of me. Speaking of Garrett, he came strolling out of the house carrying a tray and headed right for us.

"How are the two most beautiful women I know?" He kissed Victoria's cheek as he set the tray down.

"Not buying your shit," she said flatly.

He chuckled. They could pick at each other all day, but they seemed to have an underlying affection for each other despite my aunt's insistence that Garrett wasn't worth the time I put into him.

He moved to the chair beside me, pecking my cheek before sitting. "And my lovely wife?"

I smiled at him. "Wonderful. You?"

His smile said he was happy too, and Victoria snorted with disgust.

"Lord, just take her upstairs now," she muttered.

He brought my hand to his lips for a kiss. "Gladly. Though she likes to pretend other people don't know we have sex, so we'll have to come up with some other reason to excuse ourselves."

I shook my head, trying to fight the smile that was tugging at my lips, but as soon as Aunt Victoria threw out another disgusted sound, I laughed. Garrett laughed too, and before long, even my cranky old aunt was smiling.

Adam climbed from the pool as soon as he noticed Garrett and came running. Despite being soaked, Garrett pulled Adam into his lap and pointed to the tray full of fresh lemonade and a plate of cookies. He filled glasses while Adam passed them around, then they dished out cookies.

The scene was so normal, so familial, that for a moment I let myself believe this could be real.

I KNEW ON SOME LEVEL THAT GARRETT'S PROMISE TO BE a committed husband and father was a show. He was convincing, though. Convincing enough that I let myself start to actually hope he meant what he'd promised.

Just a few days had passed since I'd ended things with Jake, and here I sat at the park on my usual bench watching Garrett chase Adam around the slide. Our usual Wednesday morning trip to the park had never included Dad before, so this was new for all of us, but I was content to sit back and watch as I always did. I was taken aback when Garrett opted to join in Adam's fun.

I snapped a picture when Garrett scooped him up, causing Adam to scream. All the times I'd sat here watching Adam play, this was the happiest I'd ever seen him. He hadn't stopped smiling all week, and I hadn't stopped capturing the images on my phone. I had about a gazillion images that I'd saved of my time with my son. Painfully few of them included my husband as well. When Adam looked back on his life after his parents were gone, the first six years were going to be fairly absent of his father.

I didn't want to think about what would happen when Garrett grew bored of this role he was playing. His face would again disappear from my pictures. I would again be the main provider of fun and discipline and everything else Adam needed. And Adam's resentment would undoubtedly continue to grow.

I was so focused on my little family that it took me a moment to notice the little bundle of energy making a beeline for the slide was Will Redmond. I turned just as Michael sat next to me, though with noticeably more space between us.

"Never thought I'd see the day that he acted like a father," he said watching Garrett coach Adam on going down the slide headfirst. The clipped resentment in Michael's voice was clear as day. I didn't call him out on it. Part of me resented Garrett's presence too.

This was my time with Michael and Will, and I hadn't even considered how precious that time was to me until realizing that Garrett was intruding on it. Instead of agreeing with his unspoken bitterness, I focused on the boys. Even so, I could sense Michael's resentment suffocating me, and I started to feel guilty.

I had done this. I had brought Garrett to the park.

"Adam invited him," I justified out of some sense of obligation. It was the truth. Adam had been sucking up Garrett's attention like a little sponge. Now that his father seemed interested in him, he wanted him to be part of everything. Instead of "Mommy watch..." or, as it had been lately, "Mr. Redmond watch..." every other phrase from my son had turned into "Daddy watch..."

I hadn't felt the maternal jealousy kick in because I was so happy for Adam, but I guessed it would be sooner or later if this kept up. For years, I was the one who watched his stunts, made him laugh, and put bandages on his boo boos. It was sweet for Garrett to finally step up, but it wouldn't last. I knew it wouldn't. Even if Garrett did stick by his intent to be a family man going forward, this would bore him soon enough.

Much like my need to clarify that it was my six-year-old who wanted his father to join us, I felt the need to explain why.

"Garrett is going to try being more hands-on."

Michael seemed to stiffen as he gave a curt nod. "That's good."

"It is. Adam needs that."

"A boy should have a father who is invested in him."

I took a slow breath but decided not to respond. When I looked back toward the slide, Garrett was headed our way. He sat next to me, sliding his arm around my shoulders.

"I got the shaft," he announced.

I smiled. "Yes, that tends to happen when his best friend shows up. Those two are peas in a pod these days."

"I guess that means you two are as well," Garrett commented. His words, even his tone, were friendly enough, but I felt the underlying accusation of his words.

"Only on Wednesdays," I lied. "The rest of the time it's the parental drop and run." I glanced at Michael, hoping he didn't out me. I didn't need to justify my time with him to Garrett.

Michael kept his gaze on the boys, but a smirk tugged at his lips. "I don't mind. Gives you two plenty of time to see each other without Adam tagging along. Quality time together is important for a marriage."

His words were a jab. An intentional poke with a sharp stick. And they hit the mark.

I swallowed and took a deep breath as I returned my focus on the kids.

"Well," Garrett said, oblivious to the slap I'd just been given, "that's what nannies are for. But it sounds like Adam would rather be with Bill—"

"Will," I corrected a bit sharper than intended.

He shrugged casually. "Whatever."

It was then that I knew he was aware of the tension on the bench. Of course he was. Garrett King didn't miss a thing. Nor did he miss an opportunity to pick at someone else's wounds. He always had taken pleasure in someone else's misery.

He leaned forward enough to look around me at Michael. "How's the new nanny working out?"

Michael tensed again. "She's great."

"Mara has a special talent for finding help. Don't you, darling?" Hugging me closer, he kissed my temple in a rare show of affection. "She has a lot of special talents, actually."

I cut a look to him, but he just winked and smiled wider.

"How is old Albert doing these days?"

"He's plugging along," Michael said.

Garrett casually dropped his other hand to my thigh. The movement was subtle, but Michael lowered his gaze enough to take notice. Garrett smirked and brushed his thumb along my knee.

"We really should take time to schedule that playdate at his beach house like he suggested. It'd be great fun watching the boys build sandcastles while the adults sat around drinking champagne and...bonding."

I swallowed. He was clearly referencing the events on the yacht. Did he really think I'd play the same stupid game for him again?

"Though last time, Mara had a bit too much sun." He hugged me, squeezed my knee, and chuckled. "She got a bit overheated, and the bubbly went straight to her head. Albert and I had to help you cool down, didn't we, darling?"

I forced a smile, but I was sure my discomfort was obvious. I had never told Michael about the events on the boat, and I doubted Albert had either. He didn't seem the type to watch and tell.

"It was a bit embarrassing, I admit."

"Nonsense." Garrett patted my knee and smiled at Michael. "It was our pleasure."

Michael practically jumped to his feet. "I'll talk to Albert about scheduling something. But I really have to get back to the office." He did his customary whistle, and both boys immediately came running. We'd taught them the signal for lunchtime, and they responded like Pavlov's dogs.

"Can we have McDonald's?" Will asked.

"Burger King," Adam countered.

Garrett scoffed. "Neither." He smiled at Michael. "Why don't you two come to our house for lunch? Let the boys play a bit more while we"—he put his arm around my waist and pulled me closer to him—"get to know each other better."

I held my breath. What game was he playing? It was obvious he was playing one. I just couldn't quite put my finger on it.

"Like I said," Michael answered flatly, "I need to get back to the office."

"Aww, Dad," Will started, but he cut his whine short when Michael cocked a brow at him. He turned his pout to me.

"Next time, buddy," I said. "Dad's got a busy day ahead."

"We always have lunch." Will kicked his toe to the ground.

Adam's face sank with disappointment too. It seemed I wasn't the only one who felt as if Garrett's presence had ruined the playdate. Adam had been thrilled to have his dad around, right up until our routine had to change.

Garrett would never approve of chicken nuggets and chocolate milk for lunch. No. Most likely we'd head home, and he'd have a sandwich or some form of salad or we'd stop at a restaurant that had slim pickings on the kids' menu—if there was a kids' menu at all.

I brushed my hand over Adam's head. A silent show of support in his frustration.

Michael held out his hand, and Will took it, but not before the boy cast another glance my way. He didn't say anything, but it seemed he didn't like Garrett touching me any more than his father did.

I offered him a smile, but he turned away. Which stung almost as much as Michael's brush-off.

"What the hell was that about?" I asked as we started for the car. Adam was trailing behind us, still pouting about his playdate ending earlier than usual.

"What?"

"Don't play innocent with me."

He jerked me to a stop as he turned to see if Adam was within earshot. He wasn't. He'd stopped to poke at something on the ground.

"Why don't you tell me what the hell that was about? I could feel the tension between you two before I even got to the bench." He narrowed his eyes at me. "Are you fucking him?"

I clenched my jaw. "We agreed to fidelity. Remember? I'm not fucking anyone."

"*Were* you fucking him? Is that why he was shooting lasers at me with his eyes? Because he lost his little side piece?"

I scoffed and shook my head. "Adam! Let's go."

Garrett jerked me by the arm before I could resume the walk to the car. "Answer me."

"No. I wasn't fucking Michael Redmond. Not that it is any of your business if I had been."

"Then what was that all about?"

"You were imagining things."

He shook his head.

"Mom," Adam asked as he neared us. His pout was heavy and determined. "Since we didn't have lunch with Will, can we have dinner at his house?"

"Not tonight, Adam."

"But we—"

"Not tonight, Adam," I said more forcefully.

His little lip quivered, and tears filled his eyes. "I haven't played with him all week." He stormed off in an unusual show of discontent.

I watched for a moment before facing Garrett again. "I

told you they are best friends. That means I spend time with Michael. Not to fuck or plot or whatever else your twisted mind is thinking. The boys play. We sit and watch. End of story, Garrett. That little show you put on to stake your claim did nothing but make everyone uncomfortable."

"I'm not stupid, Mara. And I'm not blind. He was pissed because I was here."

"And you automatically assume that's because I'm screwing him? We just undermined yet another Carter Enterprises deal. That's three in the last six weeks, Garrett. I'm sure he's feeling the heat that we're putting on him, don't you?"

Garrett stared at me as if gauging my reasoning. I didn't waiver in my stare—didn't blink. Didn't let him see I knew exactly why Michael was furious or that it had nothing to do with Carter Enterprises.

"If that's his problem, why wasn't he glaring at you?"

"Because like every other man on the planet, he doesn't take me seriously."

Finally, Garrett backed down a bit. I doubted his suspicions had been put to rest—they rarely were—but at least he seemed less angry. I followed Adam to the car, and as I reached in to buckle him, which was completely unnecessary now, I smiled and winked.

"We'll see Will soon, okay?"

"Promise?"

"Promise." And I meant it. I had a word or two I needed to say to Michael about his behavior as well.

$$[\ 20\ ]$$

I was wet before Garrett even put his hand on me. I knew what was coming the moment he walked into my office and locked the door behind him. I watched, fascinated, as he crossed the room with hunger in his eyes.

He grabbed my hair and held me as he bent down and kissed me hard. No words. No demand. Nothing but him taking what he wanted and me sitting there giving it to him.

He pulled me to my feet and stared into my eyes, daring me to challenge him as he tugged my skirt up. He didn't ask if I wanted him or the pain he'd discovered I was so fond of. He simply smirked and turned me around, pushing me forward until I rested my forearms on my desk.

I closed my eyes as the cool air caressed my skin when he pulled my panties down. All the way down, over one high heel and then the other. I widened my eyes and started to protest when he pressed his hand, my underwear wrapped around his palm, into my mouth, and hushed me.

The only sound he'd made since walking into my office. "Shhh."

I obeyed. I let him press my underwear into my mouth. In fact, as soon as I took a breath—smelling my scent—I realized having him silencing me like that wasn't as horrible as it should have been. I rolled my eyes closed when his other hand touched my bare ass. He rubbed, soothed, teased. I waited...and waited...and waited...

And then I gasped when he crashed his hand on me, and a thousand sensations overcame me—the pain, the sting, the scent from the lacy material against my mouth. I jolted, but he put his hand to my back and pushed me onto my desk and smacked again. I took what he gave me until I couldn't take any more. I was just about to break, but then he released me. The pressure on my back eased, and he pulled the lace from my face.

He rubbed the material deep between my legs, and I felt my moisture spreading. My clit practically danced when he finally touched it. But that was all he did. He rubbed my panties over it and left it wanting. Left me wanting.

"I'll keep these for later," he whispered in my ear as he tugged my skirt down, making me whimper as the cotton slid over my freshly spanked skin.

I wanted to protest, but he jerked me around, kissed me hard, and headed for the door. I stood there, my body needing the release he'd denied me. At the door, he stopped and turned, making a show of smelling the black material in his hand before tucking my underwear in his pocket.

"We'll finish this tonight," he said. "No cheating, Mara. Trust me. The wait will be worth it." And then he was gone.

I was stepping out of Albert's office when I nearly bumped into Michael. He hadn't returned a single one of my texts or phone calls. My attempts at talking about his actions at the park had been rebuffed. This was the first time I'd seen him in three days.

Funny how I hadn't even noticed that spending time with him and Will had become such a regular part of my week. So much more now than just Wednesday at the park and Friday night dinners at his house. Our "playdates" were several times a week now.

At least until this week, when he decided he didn't have to respond to my messages. I tilted my head and cocked my brows at him.

He lowered his gaze and sighed.

"Michael," Albert practically sang. "What are you doing here at this late hour?"

"Finishing up a report. I'm about to head out. I just wanted to run this by you." Finally, he looked at me. "Mrs. King. What brings you by so late?"

"Charity," I lied. Because I sure as hell wasn't going to tell him the hefty check in my purse was to hire a contractor to renovate the warehouse properties we'd just purchased.

"You sure do a lot of charity work," Michael commented. "When do you find the time?"

I smiled. "In the wee hours of the evening. Obviously." I turned to Albert. "Thank you again for your donation."

He bowed slightly. "My pleasure, Mara."

I faced Michael, expecting some kind of farewell, but he simply stared at me. I rolled my eyes at him. Right in his face.

"Good night, gentlemen. Don't stay out too late."

I refused to focus on Michael's cold shoulder. Refused to give it a second thought. Refused to be hurt by the sudden withdrawal of his friendship. Refused to be upset that he wasn't speaking to me.

What the hell did I have to apologize for? My husband was at the park with my son. I didn't have to apologize for that. I didn't have to apologize that *my husband* put his hands on me. Michael was the one that was acting like an ass first. Garrett just responded in kind.

I didn't have to apologize for that. Michael should be apologizing to me. And to our boys, because his childish behavior was getting in the way of rescheduling a playdate for Adam and Will.

Stupid jerk.

Stupid, sensitive, overly dramatic jerk.

I made it all the way back to King Inc. before realizing that my determination to keep Michael from my mind was in vain. Thoughts of him had dominated the entire drive back to my office. I was chastising myself as I rode to the top floor. I went straight to my office and punched in the code to unlock the drawers. Inside one locked drawer sat a long, flat safe-deposit box. I punched in a different code to open that and put the check inside.

I had a meeting the next morning to go over the final plans for what was going to be my first project for Carter Enterprises—the first step to ultimately gaining control of his company. I was giddy. But my excitement was overshadowed by Michael's snotty attitude. I drew a deep breath and let it out slowly, determined to shake off the discontent he'd left me with.

Garrett had promised we'd finish what we'd started earlier, and I needed that. I needed my mind to go someplace Michael Redmond couldn't reach. I doubted Michael had ever smacked a woman's ass the way Garrett had taken to smacking mine. No, I imagined he was the tender lover type. Which was nice. I wouldn't mind that. But I also couldn't deny I was looking forward to Garrett's promise to make tonight worth the wait.

I glanced at my watch and determined he'd had plenty of time to make the calls he insisted he had to make when I went to make excuses on why I needed to run errands before we left for the day. He had dismissed me with a wave, and I was glad he hadn't pressed the issue.

I pushed his office door open, but before I could call out to him, I stopped in my tracks. My heart did a little flip before falling to my stomach. I don't know why. I wasn't exactly surprised to find his secretary on her knees before him. This was a scenario that I'm sure played out several times a week. I just hadn't been unlucky enough to walk in until now.

And I had no doubt that was intentional. Garrett knew I was going to be back. He knew I wouldn't knock before entering. He knew I'd walk in and find him just like this. Or at the very least, it seemed, he'd hoped.

Why? I didn't have to ask why. For a week, he'd been a good husband. An attentive lover. A devoted father. That was about a week too long for Garrett.

I'm sure he was expecting me to walk in and raise hell. Throw a fit. Scream and yell. Maybe even cry. I didn't. I simply crossed his office unnoticed and sat in the seat on the other side of his desk. My stomach rolled at the sound of him moaning and her slurping.

Jesus.

He needed to teach her to swallow her spit. I wasn't exactly escort-level in the sex department, but at least I could give a blow job without slobber running everywhere.

I leaned back, watching and wondering what the hell Garrett got out of this scene. The power I assumed. The power over that girl on her knees. Over me. He knew I couldn't leave him. That I was trapped. That he could do this every night of his life and come home to me. And what would I do about it?

Fall into his *let's be a family* trap, apparently. But I hadn't fallen into it. I had known it wouldn't last. I just gave him enough credit to last longer than one week.

Garrett gripped her hair as he thrust deep. She gagged, tried to pull away, but he held her and shoved deeper until he sighed and let her go. Stupid, stupid girl. That's why I never gave the man head. He couldn't be trusted.

"Oh my God," she gasped, but it wasn't pleasure. She'd finally noticed me, and her drool- and semen-covered chin dropped as her eyes widened.

"Give her your handkerchief, darling," I said flatly, "before she gets that shit on the floor."

Garrett stood for a moment before digging in his pocket and handing her a folded bit of material.

Pulling her to her feet, he shoved her away. "Go home."

She didn't say a word. She just rushed from the room, wiping her disgusting little face clean.

He didn't say a word as he pulled his pants up and tucked in his shirt.

"This just happened," he finally said.

I held up my hand, and he actually stopped speaking. "I don't care, Garrett. I honestly don't care. You had me fooled for about two seconds. You knew what I wanted for us, and you played on that, and I bought into it. But I knew it was only a matter of time. It's been a great week. Thank you for that. But now it's done, and things can go back to normal." I stood and took several steps toward the door before facing him again. "It's almost a relief, isn't it? To not have to pretend to give a shit about me and your son any longer?"

"Mara—"

"I want to make one thing very clear to you, Garrett. We're done. The game is over. We have nothing left but a business agreement. You will not come to my room. You will not proposition me sexually or romantically. Other than public appearances when you are being a gentleman for show, you are not permitted to ever touch me again. Do you understand?"

He stood. Unmoving.

I nodded. "Good night. Oh, Garrett," I said as I reached his door. "Fire that whore and hire one who can swallow. She's ruined your pants."

He looked down and cussed at the stain on his slacks.

I should have gone home. I should have had a glass of wine and a hot bath and decompressed, but as I drove out of

King Inc., my car seemed to steer itself and didn't stop until I parked in front of Michael's house.

I told myself not to do it. I was on fire. Ready to spit nails. So, naturally, I climbed from the car and banged on the door. I was ready to let loose, but his new nanny, Talia, opened the door.

"Good evening, Mrs. King," she said and stepped aside. "I'm afraid Mr. Redmond isn't home yet."

"Oh. Well, is Will still up?"

She stepped aside. "I'm afraid so. He refuses to sleep until his dad gets home. Sometimes that's much later than it should be."

"Where is he?"

"Probably in the kitchen defying my orders."

"Uh-oh."

"He's been a handful this week. I don't know what's going on with him."

"Well, we haven't been able to coordinate playdates. I'm sure he's just full of energy."

He darted into the foyer, his eyes wide and a big smile on his face. "Is Adam with you?"

I put my purse on the table. "Not tonight, buddy. I just wanted to pop in and see your dad so we could schedule some time."

Will visibly sank. "He's been working late all week. I'll never get to see Adam again."

"Oh, that's a little dramatic," I said. I put my hand on his head and nodded to dismiss Talia. She didn't hesitate in leaving me with Will. "Have you had a snack yet?"

He sighed and lowered his face. "No."

I chuckled. "Wow. You are going to trip over that lip, little man." Taking him into the kitchen, I lifted him up on the counter as I'd seen Michael do countless times. "Apples?"

"No."

"Animal crackers?"

"No."

"Ice cream?" I said with a conspiratorial whisper.

"Yeah!"

I helped him back down, and he ran right for the freezer while I pulled out two bowls. I scooped while he dumped on more toppings than either of us needed, but I didn't stop him. It'd been a rough week for both of us, apparently.

We were sitting at the counter, him rambling on about some dinosaur show he'd watched, when the atmosphere in the room changed. Will slowly lowered his spoon, and the excitement in his eyes faded.

I turned to find Michael standing in the door, his arms crossed, and his eyes full of anger.

"Isn't it a bit late for junk food?" said the man who didn't seem to have any dietary restrictions.

"That's my fault," I said.

"She told me to have apples," Will defended, his little voice sounding defiant. "I didn't *want* apples."

"Go to bed," Michael ordered.

I'd never seen him be short with his son, but there was something going on that I didn't know about.

Will stared, his lips pressed together. Finally, he looked at me.

"Good night, Will."

He dropped his spoon and lurched toward me. I caught him in a tight hug and kissed his head before easing him down. He huffed before storming off, not even acknowledging his father.

"I'm sorry," I said. "I overstepped."

"Yes. You did."

I opened my mouth, intent to counter, but sitting with Will had soothed the anger that had flared in me earlier, and all that remained was the sting. The sting of Michael's cold shoulder. The sting of Garrett's manipulation. The sting of my stupidity for daring to have even the slightest bit of hope that my marriage could get better.

I laughed softly as I grabbed the bowls. I put them in the sink and washed my hands. I was drying them when my eyes started to burn. Turning, I faced him, but I could only see his outline through the tears in my eyes.

"Are you seriously punishing me because my husband decided to play Dad for a day?"

I wished I could see his face, but when I attempted to blink my tears away, my vision just got worse. My God. I didn't cry. I wasn't a crier. I'd put a wall around my emotions long ago. It seemed the only time I cried these days was with Michael. Which was stupid.

Turning my back on him, I wiped my eyes, sniffed, and dried my hands on the towel again.

"Forget you," I muttered as I headed for the door.

His big, stupid body was in the way, and he didn't move. I glared up at him. I could see him now. And his face was something I couldn't read, but I didn't care. I'd made a mistake coming here, and I just wanted to leave.

"Move."

"Why are you here?"

Looking away, I rotated my jaw. "Because you're an asshole who won't return my calls."

He didn't respond, so I shoved my hands to his chest, but he didn't budge. Much like when we'd had our epic pancake battle, my tiny frame was nothing when it came up against his towering one. I pushed again, but other than his torso leaning back a few inches, he didn't move.

"Goddamn it, Michael. Move!"

He hesitated for a few seconds but then stepped aside. I started by him, but he wrapped his arm around my waist to stop me.

Startled, I looked at him, but he hesitated in meeting my gaze. When he did, I had to swallow. He was looking at me with a tenderness I rarely saw these days. The kind of look that let someone know a person actually cared.

"He doesn't deserve you. You know that, don't you? If I hadn't known it before, I knew it after watching him intentionally make you squirm at the park. I don't know the underlying meaning of all the things he said, but I know he said it to embarrass you. To remind you that you are beneath him and to make sure I knew that you were his."

"I can't leave him," I whispered. "You know that."

"So he gets to keep jabbing you with a hot poker while wearing that damned smirk of his?"

Another tear fell. "Yes. And I get to keep my son."

He lowered his hand, and I swallowed. I only managed to take one more step before he put his arm around me again.

"That's our time," he said softly. "The boys. And ours. I didn't like him intruding."

"I know."

"I didn't mean to be such an ass the other day. Or tonight. I'm just... I'm trying to reconcile what that means."

I creased my brow as I looked up at him. The look in his eyes—guilt, shame, confusion—was familiar. It reminded me of how Jake looked as we debated having an affair. I couldn't stand seeing that look in Michael's eyes. It made me want to lean in and kiss him. And never stop.

Instead, I lowered my face and stepped to him. His arms enveloped me as I buried my nose in his chest. Taking a deep breath, I inhaled the faded scent of spicy cologne and wrapped my arms around his waist. He rested his cheek to my head and held me.

"It means that we are friends," I said. "Good friends. And having him there put a kink in our usual plans." I leaned back and looked up at him. "That's all that means."

The temptation was there. Beckoning me. I was nearly enticed, but I sighed heavily and pulled myself from his embrace.

"I should go."

"Mara," he called as I left. "I meant what I said. Garrett doesn't deserve you."

I smiled, touched by his words. "I'm glad you think so."

[21]

Jake ran his hand over my back, bringing me to the conversation we were supposed to be having. "Hey. What's on your mind?"

I cleared my throat. "Nothing."

He stared at me with his soft amber eyes, and I sighed.

"Garrett's already cheating. Didn't last a week."

"He told you?"

"I caught him. He wanted me to. I'm sure of that. He had all the fidelity he could handle, so he made sure I saw him." I gave him a half smile. "He just wanted me to end things with you."

He put his hand to my face, but I caught it before he could either pull me closer or touch my lips like he always did before kissing me or whatever else he may have had planned.

"It was time for us to end things, Jake. You know that, right?"

He sighed and dropped his hand. "I suppose."

"I care about you," I said softly. "More than I should. That's dangerous for all of us."

He nodded and pulled his hand away. "Yeah. It is. Megan has been in one seriously foul mood since Garrett told her he was going to focus on his wife."

I chuckled. "Oh, he did. For about five minutes."

"I'm sorry."

"Don't be. I knew it wouldn't last."

Clearing my throat again, I put my hand on the blueprints we were reviewing. Though Jake wasn't helping with the warehouse project for Carter, he was advising me. He had helped me hire another company to do the work, but he really was the one guiding me through, weighing every decision.

I had confidence in my choices and my abilities, but if I failed at this warehouse project, I would lose my stake in Carter Enterprises, and I *needed* that stake to secure my life when I was able to leave Garrett. I couldn't screw this up. Having Jake by my side, even in the shadows, was comforting.

I trusted he wouldn't intentionally steer me wrong.

"There's more?"

I blinked the moment Michael started trying to push his way into my mind. He'd been doing that all day—his sad eyes, his soft touch, his warm embrace. He'd been there, lurking, demanding I give the memory of the night before more attention than it deserved.

"I have a lot riding on this deal with Carter. I guess now that it is happening, I'm starting to doubt myself. That's all."

"Mara King doubt herself?" Jake asked with amusement. "That's something new."

I laughed softly. "Not as new as you think." Pointing to the blueprints, I said, "Tell me again why we can't put the plumbing here."

He stared at me for a few seconds before giving in and dropping the subject. We discussed plumbing and electrical and structural integrity, and I took notes like a madwoman. Our brainstorming didn't end until his secretary buzzed that his next appointment was waiting.

While I rolled the blueprints and put them back in the cardboard tube, he let her know he was wrapping things up. I was putting my things back in my bag when he gently tugged my arm and pulled me to face him.

He looked in my eyes for a moment, and I almost feared he'd kiss me. Feared because if he did, I wouldn't stop him. In fact, I'd welcome it. I missed him more than I should, and if we continued our affair, one of us was going to get hurt. Considering my history with men, it would probably be me.

"Don't doubt yourself, Mara. You've gotten yourself caught in Garrett's web, but you can get out. You are doing the right thing by setting the foundation for your escape now. You can survive this. Once Adam is old enough, you can leave, and you'll have Carter Enterprises to fall back on. Garrett won't win. He won't. Just keep going."

I let out a slow breath as I threw my arms around his neck. I needed to hear that more than I had even realized. Hugging him tight, I closed my eyes and committed his words to my memory. I could do this. Garrett *won't* win. Just keep going.

"Thank you," I whispered. I leaned back and offered him a slight smile. "Do me a favor and remind me of that from time to time. Okay?"

He kissed my forehead. "As often as you need it. And, Mara," he called as I gathered my things.

I looked at him.

"You're right. We were getting too invested in each other. And it was getting dangerous." He smiled that sweet, lazy smile of his. "But I happen to like danger."

I laughed softly and gave him a kiss at the corner of his mouth. "I think I'm married to all the danger I can handle. But, if I change my mind, you'll be the first to know."

IF I COULD AVOID MY HUSBAND FOR THE REST OF MY life, I would have. But I couldn't. He'd given me a day to cool down, and when I walked into my office after meeting Jake, Garrett was leaning against my desk with the largest bouquet of roses I'd ever seen.

He was mistaken if he thought flowers would change my mind after his latest round of deceit. I stared at him for a moment before walking around my desk and putting my briefcase down.

Finally, I met his gaze. "They're beautiful. You should give them to someone who will be impressed."

He pouted and eased the oversized vase down on my desk and walked around. "Will you give me a chance to explain?"

"No."

He traced his hand over my hair, but I pulled back and pushed his arm away. His eyes widened a bit. He was used to me playing hard to get when I was angry. He was used to me falling for his fake apologies. He was used to me bending to his will.

Not this time.

"Get out of my office."

His eyes hardened. "This is *my* office, Mara. I just let you use it while you play businesswoman."

I smirked. "Fine. I'll go."

He gripped my arms before I could step away. He held my gaze for a moment before trying to put his mouth to mine, but I turned my face away.

He rested his head to mine and sighed heavily. "I just lost control. I was so crazy for you. I couldn't control myself," he whispered.

I scoffed. "If that's supposed to be a compliment, it isn't. You promised me that you were done with all that. I let you touch me in ways I never would have if I'd known you were going to let the first whore who asked suck your dick." Turning my face, I glared, making sure what little space there was between us was ice cold. "You ruined the last chance I was giving you. You will never touch me like that again. You will never see me like that again. I certainly hope her sloppy little blow job was worth it."

"I fired her."

"Good. The last thing you need is to walk into a meeting with stains all down your pants. I'd suggest a swallow test with the next hire. Think HR would approve that?"

"Mara," he whispered.

I tilted my head and smirked. "Get out of *my* office and go back to playing businessman, Garrett. I have deals to close on your behalf. One of us has to keep the business running so we can pay all the staff you're fucking."

He met my icy stare with his own before releasing me with a slight shove. "Mind yourself, Mara. You may be my wife, but there is only so much shit I'm willing to take from you."

"That goes both ways, Garrett."

He stopped halfway across my office and faced me. "I told HR I wanted my next assistant to be male. I promise you, no more secretarial blow jobs after hours." He smirked. "Unless I find myself attracted to him. And if my wife keeps giving me the cold shoulder, that is possible."

I didn't smile at his joke.

His smile fell, and he left.

I looked at the roses for a moment before carrying the vase out to my secretary. "Find a nursing home to send these to. They're making me sick."

I cringed as Will jumped into the pool, nearly landing on top of Adam. "They are getting so rough with each other."

"They're boys," Michael said before taking a drink from his tea. "You didn't answer my question."

I glanced at him just for a moment. I'd found it incredibly difficult to look at him this evening. Not because I was working with Albert behind his back. Or because he was asking questions I'd rather not answer. Or because I was an idiot who had trusted her liar of a husband. But because I was finding it incredibly difficult not to confess that I hadn't been able to stop thinking about the few seconds we'd shared in his kitchen the night before.

"I was evading," I said. "A gentleman would have let me get away with it."

He grinned. "Lucky for you, I'm no gentleman. Why were you so upset when you got here tonight?"

I reached for my glass but put it down before taking a drink. "Because... Garrett told me he wanted a real marriage. He promised he was going to quit cheating. And I believed him."

The heavy silence said what I hadn't. That his promise was already broken.

"I know better than to believe him," I said quietly.

"I'm sorry," he said just as gently.

I shook my head and took a breath so the memory of Garrett getting sucked off in his office didn't invade my mind. "Don't be. This is my mess to work through."

"I know you feel trapped—"

"I am trapped." Finally looking at him, I shrugged. "And I set that trap. This is my fault."

"No." He put his glass down and jabbed his finger into the tabletop. "Real men, men who love their wives, don't behave like this." The spark in his eye was not one I'd seen before. Anger, but not the kind I'd seen previously. This wasn't a reaction to feeling hurt by Garrett's interference with our time together. This was a protective kind of anger.

I smiled and reached across the table, putting my hand

on his. I stroked his soft skin until he sighed and relaxed. "Marriage isn't like that in this world, Michael. Everything is a business deal here. I let my heart lead me instead of my head. When I tried to take control, I didn't think things through. I was emotional, angry. I made this deal with him. I set the terms. I can't blame him for accepting them."

"He doesn't have to behave like that, Mara." He squeezed my hand between his. "You're enough. For any other man, you'd be enough."

I swallowed at the way he was looking at me. Sweet. Sincere. Tender.

"*Mom!*" Adam yelled frantically from the pool, breaking the spell between us. "Mom, help! Will's drowning!"

My heart dropped, and I jumped up, sending my chair flipping over in my haste. Michael reached the pool first. He dove in as I reached the edge and dropped to my knees. I grabbed Adam's arm, pulling him to me and lifting him out.

As soon as Michael broke the surface with Will in his arms, I grabbed the boy's limp body. "I've got him."

Will started sputtering and spitting water as I pulled him from the pool and hit his back several times with the ball of my hand. I tilted his face so the fluid ran from his mouth as Michael climbed from the water.

Will collapsed against me, taking a big breath and then coughing.

"Talk to me," Michael demanded, crawling to where we sat. "Will, talk to me."

Several more hacking coughs left Will, and I sat him forward so the water left his lungs.

"I'm okay," he panted. "I'm okay."

"What happened?" I asked Adam as Michael pulled Will from me and into his arms.

"We were seeing who could hold our breath longest. He waited too long. He took a big gulp of water."

"That was stupid," Michael chastised.

I ran my hand over Adam's hair when his lip trembled. "It's okay, buddy. He's fine."

Michael scooped Will even closer against him and held him tightly.

Will immediately started protesting. "Dad. Dad, I'm okay."

I sighed as Michael buried his face in Will's hair. "Adam, go grab your towels. You're done swimming." When he walked away, I put my hand on Michael's shoulder. "It wasn't nearly as bad as it seemed."

"Here, Will," Adam said, holding out a towel.

Will wriggled away from Michael.

I wrapped the towel around the trembling boy's shoulders and gave him a reassuring smile.

"All better?" I asked.

He nodded and tugged the towel more tightly around himself.

"You guys go sit in the sun and warm up. Your dad and I need to put on some dry clothes." I watched the boys walk off before reaching for Michael. He looked up, and the fear in his eyes made my heart ache. "He's all right."

"Mr. Redmond?" His nanny came rushing out with a handful of towels.

He waved her off, but I accepted them. "Talia, keep an eye on the boys, please. Don't let them get back in the water."

"Yes, Mrs. King."

"Hey," I whispered, wrapping a towel around Michael's shoulders. "You okay?"

"You told me to get him in swim lessons."

"No. Michael, don't."

"Why didn't I listen? If anything happened to him..."

"It didn't. He's okay." Using another towel, I dried my face before running the material over his hair and patting his cheeks dry. "Come on. He doesn't need to see you like this." Standing, I gently lifted Michael and guided him into the house.

Once inside, he turned and pulled me against him. I hugged him back, ignoring how his drenched clothes were getting me even wetter than Will had. By the time he finally eased back, the front of my shirt was nearly as wet as his, and a puddle had formed at our feet.

"You need to get out of these clothes," I said softly when he shivered.

He looked down at me. "You too. I don't have anything—"

"I've got my gym bag in the car. Are you okay?"

"Yeah." Looking out the window, he watched the boys for a minute. They were laughing like nothing had happened, like Will hadn't very nearly drowned. "Nothing fazes them, huh?"

"Not much, no."

"I'm sorry. I didn't mean to snap at Adam."

"I know." I gave him a soft smile as I cupped his face. Stroking my thumb over his cheek, I looked into his eyes. "Don't worry about it. Let's get dried off, huh?"

"Hey." He grabbed my hand to stop me from leaving. "You just keep saving me. One of these days, I'll repay you."

"No repayment necessary. Go change." I grabbed my car keys on the way out. My alarm chirped as the doors unlocked. With my gym bag tossed over my shoulder, I headed back inside. I used the guest bathroom to change, then handed off my wet clothing to a maid and headed back outside.

"Talia, has Mr. Redmond come out yet?"

"No, ma'am."

I watched the boys running for a moment, increasing my confidence that Will was just fine. "Would you take the boys in and get them rinsed off and dressed, please?" I glanced at my watch. "Go ahead and get them something for dinner when they're ready."

She nodded and rounded up Adam and Will. I smiled at them as they headed inside, debating what movie to watch after they finished eating.

"Can we have chicken nuggets again, Mrs. King?" Will asked.

"Please, Mom?"

I wanted to argue they'd had that for lunch, but I didn't. They may not have realized how shaken they should be, but I certainly did, and if they wanted chicken nuggets, then they could have chicken nuggets.

I put my hand on Will's head and smiled. "Sure thing, buddy."

"I'll let the cook know," Talia said.

"Thanks." I looked around the backyard for a few moments before heading inside.

Upstairs, I could hear the boys laughing as Talia encouraged one of them to get into the shower. I knocked on the door across from Will's. I didn't get an answer, but easing the door open and poking my head in, I saw Michael sitting on the bed with his head in his hands. I sighed when I realized he was still in his wet clothes.

Sitting beside him, I ran my hand over his back. "Baby, he's okay."

"I'm sorry," he said and sniffed. "This is stupid."

"No. It's not. That was pretty terrifying. I had to take a few minutes myself."

He tried to be discreet, but he clearly wiped tears from his cheeks. "Where are they?"

"Talia's getting them cleaned up and dressed. They want chicken nuggets."

He laughed, but the sound was flat and unfeeling. Giving his head a hard shake, he rubbed his fingers into his eyes. "I can't get the image of him sitting at the bottom of the pool out of my mind. He just looked...dead."

"He's not, Michael. He's across the hall laughing and making a mess while Talia tries to wrangle them into the shower."

A strangled sound left him, and I wrapped my arms around him. I didn't know what to say. I imagined if it'd been Adam who we'd pulled from the water, I'd be inconsolable. I'd probably still be sitting by the pool, rocking him as I reassured myself that he was okay. The thought made my words cut off before they could leave me to once again tell him his son was alive and well. He deserved this time to come to terms with his son's mortality.

"I'm going to get you all wet again," he said after a few moments of my holding him.

I pulled him closer. "I don't care, but you do need to get out of these clothes. A warm shower wouldn't hurt either. Come on."

He grabbed my hand when I stood and started to walk away. My breath caught, and my heart skipped a few beats when he pulled me back to him. Standing between his legs, I held his gaze as he stared up at me. Finally, he lowered his face and rested his cheek against my chest as his arms slid around my waist.

I wrapped my arms around his shoulders, half-relieved and half-disappointed that he only needed a hug. Dropping my face, I kissed the top of his head and ran my fingers through his hair, whispering reassurances.

His hold on me shifted after a few moments. He moved his hands to my hips and pushed me back a step. He looked up, his eyes filled with obvious confusion.

Cupping his cheek, I met his uncertain gaze with my own.

Debate silently waged between us. I pulled away. "Get a shower. I'll keep an eye on the boys."

He nodded, and I left him sitting there.

$$[\ 22 \ ]$$

THE BOYS MADE it through dinner, and we were just getting settled in Will's room for the weekly showing of *Cars* when Michael finally rejoined us. Will looked up and smiled, but he didn't seem to have any idea of the gravity of the day's events.

That was a good thing, I'd decided. He was too young to accept his mortality. He had a few good years of innocence in him, and that didn't need to be stolen by one bad moment in the pool. Michael, on the other hand, was more than aware of how easily life could be cut short. The scars of losing his wife were visible as he curled up next to Will and kissed his head.

I leaned into Adam, feeling my own sense of parental gratitude.

Today wasn't the right time, but I would take steps to make sure Will got swim instructions. I was sure Michael wouldn't put it off any longer. Looking at the man in question, I smiled when I noticed him looking at me. The boys laughed at something on the television, giving me a reason to break the intense eye contact.

Leaning down, I gave Adam a kiss on the head. "I better head home, guys."

"Bye, Mom," was the extent of Adam's farewell.

"Bye," Will echoed.

"I'll see you out," Michael offered.

We both struggled to get off the pile of pillows and blankets the boys had spread out to watch the movie. Finally Michael made it to his feet and took my hand to lift me up. He pulled the door closed behind the boys and grabbed my arm when I started for the stairs. Instead, he pulled me across the hall to his room.

My heart thundered, immediately pounding.

He pushed me inside and closed the door.

The sun was setting outside, illuminating the room in an orange glow through his white curtains. We shouldn't do whatever was about to happen. I knew it and could see in his eyes that he knew it too. Even so, he tilted his face down, and I lifted mine. Our mouths crashed together. I parted my lips as his tongue pressed into my mouth. His hands slipped under my T-shirt, and I started tugging his shirt up.

He leaned back, stopping me and resting his hands on my hips. "You should tell me this is a bad idea."

"This is a terrible idea," I answered just as quietly.

He scanned my face and shook his head. "I don't care. I want you so much, Mara."

I exhaled slowly as his words nestled in my chest and filled me with warmth. "Say that again."

"I want you. So much."

I smiled and lightly traced his mouth with my fingertips. "I want you too."

He seemed to consider my words before locking the door and stepping back. I laughed when he lifted me up against his chest, but my laugh was cut short when he kissed me as he carried me across the room. God, I'd spent so much time convincing myself that I didn't want this. Now I didn't think I could possibly get enough...and we'd just begun.

Michael kissed my ear as he set my feet to the floor. "Last chance to back out."

I considered stopping. This seemed to be the only relationship in my life that wasn't built on some form of lies or deceit, but I dismissed the thought quickly. I fisted his hair in my hand and kissed him, then somehow I was on my back on the bed and he was between my legs without the passionate kiss breaking. He snaked his hand up my shirt, cupping my breast as his mouth worked down my neck. He leaned back, removing his shirt, and I half-sat to do the same with mine. Then he was on me again.

"I don't like this thing," he said, tugging at the strap of my sports bra. "I can't get around it."

I smiled. "It's not meant to get around." I managed to wriggle my way out of the tight material while he released his belt. He slid his shorts down, and I stopped moving as he revealed himself to me. "Very nice," I whispered at his naked body.

"Yeah?"

"Yeah."

"Let's see what you've got." He reached for the waist of my yoga pants and gave them a swift tug. Dropping them along with my underwear on the floor, he lifted his brow and sighed with contentment. "You're perfect."

I smiled. "I bet you say that to all the girls."

He chuckled. "Not *all* of them."

I inhaled sharply as he climbed between my thighs and nuzzled my neck.

Catching his mouth with mine, I pulled him into a deep kiss, alternating between tangling tongues and nipping his lips. Finally, breathless, I pulled back. Dropping my head on the bed, I looked up into his eyes and my heart flipped in my chest. This was so perfect. *He* was so perfect. Being with him like that couldn't have felt more right.

"Do you want to stop?" he whispered.

"No. I just... I can't decide if I should make love to you until you cry or fuck you until you cry."

He smirked. "Either way, I'll apparently end up in tears, so let's just wing it."

I laughed. He always made me laugh. I loved that about him. Stroking his face, I kissed him again, but this time much more tenderly.

"It's been a long time. I won't last long once I'm inside you," he confessed. "And I want this to last. I've wanted this for too long to not let it last. Do you mind if I take a few moments to worship your body?"

"Do whatever you need to do. *Within reason*," I amended when his eyes lit in the way they tended to do before he said something outrageous.

"I have a feeling"—he kissed me lightly—"my idea of reason and yours are completely different. And I suspect yours is far more reasonable than mine."

"Very likely," I panted as his fingers brushed over my skin. "I imagine we'll have to test each other's boundaries to determine our limits."

He kissed my shoulder. "That could require a bit more experimentation than I can handle in one evening."

"I suppose we could do this again, if necessary."

"Oh, it will be necessary." He lowered his body until he was face to tit with me. Taking his time, he ran his soft hands over me, teasing me with his feather-light touches until finally he sucked one nipple into his mouth.

I sighed, swallowed, and braced myself as his fingers trailed lower. He didn't go straight for my center. He ran his hands over me, teasing me, slowly letting my need for him come to a boil rather than trying to turn me on high immediately. And, surprisingly, I was finding this to be much more enticing.

He moved his attention to my other breast, loving it as he'd done the first. Then he was kissing my stomach, and my breath—and my body—was getting incredibly difficult to control. I wanted to buck, beg, cry, pant. But I forced myself to be still, to take what he was giving because despite the torture of it all, his light kisses and touches were the most sensual thing I thought I'd ever experienced.

His next kiss, as light as all the others had been, landed between my legs, making me jolt. He didn't pull my center apart, searching for the spot to make me lose my mind. He didn't thrust his fingers in, desperate for a reaction. He simply kissed. Traced. Inhaled. Kissed again. Then he gently opened me and, as if to test my response, kissed the newly exposed parts.

I moaned. Bit my lip. Silently begged for the patience to let him have his way instead of throwing the man down and having mine. I needed him to lead me down this path. Otherwise I'd make a beeline for the finish line, and I was certain I'd miss something spectacular if I did.

He dragged his tongue over me again, pressing just a bit harder. "Like I said," he whispered, "perfect."

I was so ready for him to enter me, and I was certain he was about to when he slid up my body, but he rolled beside me and started that damned sensual tracing of my contours again.

"Michael," I begged on a whisper.

He pressed a kiss to my temple. "Shh. First things first."

Moving his hand between my legs, he finally touched the nerve bundle that he'd barely acknowledged. I very nearly jumped from his arms, but he tightened his hold. He didn't press just on my clit, he moved his hand over the entire area —coaxing my entire center to respond.

"Sadism," I whispered. "You're into passive-aggressive sadism."

I couldn't see his smile, but I felt his mouth move and could imagine his dimples appearing as he grinned.

"I just want to give you the best experience I can."

"Passive-aggressive sadistic overachiever."

This time he laughed softly, but my amusement ended with a gasp as he gently moved his fingers inside me. The ball of his palm continued his previous torture while his fingers started something altogether new. Threading the fingers of his other hand in my hair as he kissed my head. He didn't pull, didn't act aggressively in the slightest, he caressed with such gentleness that he sent me over the edge.

I gasped, writhed, and breathed his name as I came. I was still riding the waves when he slid between my legs, filling my body with his in one smooth stroke. He lovingly cupped my breast, rubbing his thumb over my peaked nipple before trailing his fingers down my side and gripping my thigh.

I closed my eyes as he slowly pulled back and then entered me again in a long, deep stroke that seemed to reach my soul. He pulled me close to him, wrapping himself around me, stroking, murmuring how much he needed me as he moved.

Part of me wanted to demand more, harder, faster, deeper—like I normally would—but my heart wouldn't let the words leave. His movements were too precious, too giving, too tender, and when he entered me again, I gasped as something inside me cried out.

Leaning back, he looked down, stroking my hair and placing sweet kisses along my forehead, my cheeks, and lips, and I realized what this feeling was.

Cherished.

This was what it was like to feel cherished.

This was what it was like to really feel like someone's queen.

Garrett could call me that all day long, but he had no idea what that actually meant. He'd never once made me feel like more than a well-respected escort in the bedroom. And

I'd accepted that as enough. For far too long, I'd believed that was enough.

With just a few kisses, a few moments of making love, a few whispered words, Michael had shown me what I'd been missing all my life.

Realizing how deeply he was touching me—emotionally, not physically—sent me spiraling. I clung to him as my entire body tensed. He moaned in my ear, a sweet-sounding agreement on how damn good we felt in that moment. I leaned back and blinked in a vain attempt to stop the stinging in my eyes from surfacing. The tears welled and fell anyway.

Damn it, why did this man always make me cry?

Michael's face instantly turned to concern as he wiped my eyes. "What is it?"

I didn't have the words to tell him, so I wrapped my arms around him and lifted my hips, moving his body deeper into mine.

"Mara?"

I shook my head. "I'm fine."

"I thought I was the one who was going to cry?"

I giggled. "We're not done yet."

He smiled, but his eyes still held the same concern. I leaned up and kissed him, hoping to get him back to loving me instead of worrying.

He put his forehead to mine and sighed. "This was wrong."

"No. Please don't. It isn't. This isn't wrong. It's...everything." I kissed him again, pulling his attention back this moment. I shifted under him, silently encouraging him to continue. "Please, Michael," I whispered against his lips. "Please."

Relief found me as he moved deeper again. He put his mouth to mine as he started loving me again. Focusing on the sensations, ignoring the emotions, I let my body fall and clung to him as a lesser but still amazing orgasm rocked me.

"You ready?" Michael asked when I started to relax.

"For what?"

"We just made love. I'd say it's time for the other, wouldn't you?"

I laughed softly as I lightly ran my nails over his skin. He'd had his way with me. I was about to have mine.

"I think I am."

"You're looking a bit mischievous, Mara. Am I going to need a safety harness for this?"

"Now that's an idea," I whispered. "Next time, hmm?"

Shoving up with my hips, I pushed him over and straddled him. Putting my hands on his, I held him down as I looked into his eyes.

"Ready?"

"I'm a little scared."

Sitting back, I put one hand to his stomach to brace myself and the other between his legs. He gasped and jumped the moment I gripped his balls, shoving himself deep inside me in the process.

"What was that?" he panted.

I squeezed again. "This?"

"Shit. Mara. Don't do that again."

I massaged his testicles as I ground into him. "Don't do what, Michael?"

He thrust up, gripping my hips as he moved. "Holy shit. Holy shit."

I started moving faster, grinding harder, gently tugging at his intimate parts as I did. He groaned, panted, cursed, squeezed me tighter. But when he started grunting out my name, I lost control.

Releasing my hold on him, I fell forward and crashed my mouth on his, thrusting harder and faster. He met my movements as he wrapped his arms tightly around me. The sound of our bodies slapping together filled my ears. His skin, burning hot now, rubbed against mine, and his cock throbbed deep inside me as we came together.

I didn't mean to doze off, but apparently I had because I jolted at the feel of the bed shifting. I yawned as I looked at the clock. It was after eleven. I hadn't just dozed off. I'd passed out. I sighed with contentment as Michael curled behind me and kissed my shoulder. His hand roamed down my side, and I couldn't help but smile.

"What are you doing?" I asked, my voice thick with sleep.

"Admiring how perfect you are."

I laughed softly as he kissed my neck again. "It's getting late."

He gently pulled me onto my back as he looked down at me. "Do you turn into a pumpkin after midnight?"

I chuckled. "More like one of those ugly squash with all the bumps."

"Cucurbit warts."

Lifting my eyelids and creasing my brow, I stared at him. "What?"

"Those bumps are called cucurbit warts."

I sighed. "You would know that."

He grinned in that way he did when he thought I'd said something silly and kissed me softly. "I know a lot of things. About botany. Frogs. Wine. What I'd like to get to know more about," he whispered as he slipped his hand under the sheet, "is your anatomy."

Biting my lip, I threaded my fingers in his hair as he kissed my neck and cupped my breast. "Have you checked on the boys?"

"They're sound asleep," he said between kisses.

I lolled my head to the side as he lowered his hand and his kisses. This was the most perfect moment. The peace and contentment in my heart ran deep. A little too deep, so I tried not to think about how being here with this sweet man about to make love to me while our children slept across the hall was so very wrong.

I bit my lip and laughed softly. "Michael. We had sex with our kids right across the hall."

"Mmm. I know."

"I'm feeling a little guilty about that. Aren't you?"

"No." After a moment, he worked his way back up so he could look down at me. "Why would you feel guilty? Parents have sex with their kids in the house all the time. That's how younger siblings are made."

I giggled. "Yes, but usually those parents are married."

He ran his hand down my arm and curled his fingers around mine. "Or at least living together."

I was about to point out that we aren't even dating, but

my throat froze when he looked into my eyes and I realized he wasn't simply making a comment.

"What?"

"Leave him," he whispered. He squeezed my hand and gave me that crooked smile of his. "Move in with us."

My voice cracked. "I can't. Michael, you know I can't."

His jaw muscles twitched as he pressed his lips together. "The way he treats you and Adam... He doesn't deserve you. Either of you."

Sitting up, I pulled the sheet up to cover myself, suddenly feeling weak and vulnerable. "I know that. Believe me; I know that. But the agreement I signed made it nearly impossible for him to divorce me, and vice versa. There is no way out of this marriage unless I want to lose everything, including my son."

Taking my hand, he kissed it. "I'm not as powerful as Garrett, but if you put the two of us together, there is no way he can beat us. You'll get what you're due, including full custody of Adam."

I shook my head at him. "No. I won't risk losing my son."

"So what are you going to do? Hide me like a dirty little secret? Like he hides his other women?"

"Garrett and I have an open marriage." Putting my hand on his cheek, I smiled reassuringly. "Honey, he can't stop us from seeing each other."

He pulled my hand from his face. "I don't want to just *see* you, Mara. I don't want to be your weekend affair. I want us to be a family. I want every day to be like this." He closed his eyes and scoffed. "Okay, today isn't the best example considering Will could have drowned, but you know what I mean. Look at us. We're already a family. We spend so much time together. We just need to make it official."

"*Official?* Michael—"

"What are you going to do, Mara? Spend the rest of your life as your husband's second choice?"

I gasped. "I'm not—"

"You *are*. You've said it to me a dozen times. You're tired of being an afterthought in your own marriage. Do something about it. Stop wringing your hands and crying about it."

Tossing the sheet aside, I rolled from the bed and reached for my clothes. "It's late. I need to go."

"I would never treat you like that," he said from behind me. "I would never cheat. I'd never lie. You and the boys would be the most important thing to me. I'd give you the kind of marriage you should have. The kind you want. I'll be a good father to Adam. I'll actually be there for him, Mara. I'll take care of you. Both of you."

I pulled my underwear up and turned to him. "Stop it. Michael, I can't leave him. He would obliterate me in court. He would take my son from me just to hurt me."

"So what the hell was this? What the hell have we been doing? What did we do tonight?"

I swallowed as I looked at the hurt starting to overtake his fury. "I didn't..." Stepping into my yoga pants, I pulled them up as a distraction, a way to get my head together. Finally, I looked at him and sighed. "I didn't know you... I thought you understood. I can't give you more than this."

The pain on his face was plain to see. I crawled onto the bed and sat on my knees in front of him. "Listen. We can have this. Nothing has to change. Adam and I, we can still spend our evenings here. We can still have pizza night and S'mores and ice cream." Smiling, I brushed my hand over his hair. "We can still have each other. But I can't divorce Garrett. He wouldn't stop until he ruined me. He'd go after you, too. You know he would."

He stared at me for a few moments before scoffing. "Okay. So. He breaks the contract."

I creased my brow. "What?"

"We convince one of his mistresses to come forward. She tells the world everything, and you're free."

I gaped at him. "You can't be serious. You want me to ruin him?"

"He ruined himself the first time he cheated on you. It's just time to give him what he has earned."

I didn't like this side of him. In my eyes, Michael was pure. He was honest and good. He was above the sneaking and cheating and lying. I didn't want to see this side of him. I didn't want this side of him to exist.

"No. My God, Michael. *No*. I'm not setting him up."

"Setting him up would be *making* him sleep with someone else, Mara. He's already doing that."

"No. This could backfire. He could find out what we'd done. We can't cross him. He's dangerous."

He glared at me for a moment before shaking his head and scoffing. "You know, all this time, I thought you didn't deserve the way he treated you. Maybe I was wrong."

My face fell at the anger in his tone as much as his words. "Excuse me?"

He rolled out of the bed. "You want Garrett's leftovers? You want to be his doormat? That's fine. Go home, Mara.

Go. But don't come whining to me the next time he's spending his nights with some whore instead of his wife."

I stared at him, disbelieving. Finally, I found my voice. "Fuck you." Snatching my shirt, I put it on as I walked away. Stopping at the door, I turned to him. "I'm taking Adam."

"Good. Maybe Garrett will be home by now. He can be reminded what his son looks like."

I wanted to retort, but he walked into the bathroom and slammed the door behind him. Creeping into Will's room, I gently shook Adam awake.

"Hey, big guy. We need to go."

"I'm spending the night."

"Not tonight, buddy. Come on. Let's go."

"*Mom.*"

"Don't argue."

He rolled out of bed as I grabbed his bag. I looked down at Will, and my heart ached. I hadn't noticed how much the little guy had won me over until earlier in the day. Seeing him sleeping, so peaceful, while his dad was in the other room fuming at me, made my shoulders slump under the weight of the sudden change between Michael and me.

I had a pretty good thing going—this life had actually felt right for a while. I'd blown it. The way Michael had looked at me, I knew I'd blown it. Leaning down, I kissed Will's head.

He opened his eyes and looked up at me. "What's wrong?" he whispered.

"Nothing. I just wanted..." I kissed his head again and stroked his hair. "Go back to sleep. I'll see you soon."

He smiled and closed his eyes. "Night, Mrs. King."

"Night, Will." Standing up, I turned and noticed

Michael leaning against the doorframe. The fury in his eyes hadn't lessened.

"It's better this way, really," he whispered as I passed him. "You'd only disappoint him too."

Putting my hand on Adam's shoulder, I steered him down the stairs. We slipped into our shoes and out the door. By the time I was climbing into the car, hot tears were sliding down my cheeks.

[23]

"Are you going to sulk all evening?" Garrett asked as he shoved a glass of wine into my hand.

I looked away from him and scanned the crowd. The ballroom of the country club had high, white-paned ceilings that did little to mute the constant chatter. It seemed the more people who came into the room, the louder each one seemed to speak until the room had come to a loud crescendo that was unintelligible.

Albert was there. He'd silently toasted me, but I had yet to see Michael. My stomach was in knots. I knew he'd be there. This was a charity fundraiser for a new wing at the hospital. He had to be seen. I doubted Albert would tolerate his VP not showing his face at such an important event.

"I'm not sulking."

"You've been sulking for days."

"How would you know? I've been avoiding you for days."

"That's how I know."

I scoffed. "How's your new assistant doing? Has he come to terms with all you expect of him?"

He smirked. "Keep putting me off, Mara, and you just might walk in on another scene like that. Male assistant or not, my balls are turning blue."

"Aw. Call one of your whores, darling. They're always ready and willing to take your cock."

He put his arm around my waist and pulled me closer to him. "The only whore I want ready and willing to take my cock is you."

I cut my gaze to him and rotated my jaw.

"Careful, sweetheart," he warned. "Your fangs are starting to show."

"Well," Megan Decker's bitter voice said, "if it isn't the Kings. Look, Jake. It's Mara and Garrett."

I turned my face and smiled sweetly at her. "Oh, I'd love to stay and catch up, Megs, but I need to speak with your husband. I'm sure you won't mind keeping Garrett company, will you? He gets so bored when he's left on his own."

She actually softened her rigid posture a bit and looked at the man who was digging his fingers far too deeply into my skin. "No. I was actually hoping to get a chance to speak with him tonight."

"Take your time," I said as I put my hand to Garrett's chest and pushed him away. He finally released me, and I reached for Jake's arm.

"What the hell was that?" Jake whispered as we walked away.

"We're not on the best terms right now."

"Yeah. Noticeable."

I lowered my gaze and took a breath. "I just needed an excuse to get away from him. Sorry to drag you away from Megan."

He chuckled. "Please. She's been about as warm to me as it appears you've been to Garrett."

I laughed softly as I skimmed the crowd. "He pushed me too far this time, Jake. He just pushed me too far."

"Well, that's been a long time coming."

Nodding my agreement, my heart tripped over itself at the sight of a dark-haired man moving through the groups of people. It was Michael. No one else had that carefree shaggy style. I turned my gaze to where Garrett was chatting with Megan.

He was smiling, but his eyes had filled with his don't-fuck-with-me warning as she looked up at him with wide eyes. They were thoroughly distracted.

"Excuse me," I said to Jake, leaving before he could respond.

Working my way to Michael, I looped my arm through his and started pulling him away from the gathering toward the oversized French doors that were propped open. He didn't protest. He couldn't without making a scene.

We were on the stone terrace before he pulled from me, but I kept walking. And he followed me down the stairs and along the pathway until we were surrounded by immaculately trimmed bushes and trees.

I faced him, begging with my eyes. The sun had set, but the garden path had lampposts filled with bright bulbs that reflected off the sequins that covered my gown.

This was the dress I'd intended to wear to the last fundraiser before I let Garrett manipulate me.

"You look beautiful," Michael whispered. A smile touched his lips and relief touched my heart.

He didn't hate me. Thank God, he didn't hate me.

"I'm so sorry for what I said," he whispered just as quietly. He reached for me, put his hand to my face, and though it was stupid to be seen with him like this, I leaned in and let him kiss my forehead. "I didn't mean it. I swear."

"It's okay," I breathed. I touched his cheeks, ran my fingers through his hair, and leaned back, meeting his gaze. "It's okay."

"It's not. I shouldn't—"

I rested my fingertips to his lips, stopping him. I couldn't stop my body from falling into his. I'd been sick to my stomach with fear that he'd meant what he said, that he didn't want to ever see me again. I could see in his eyes now how that couldn't be further from the truth. He wrapped his arms around me, and all the stress melted from my body.

"I promised I would never hurt you, and then I did the moment you didn't give me what I wanted." The guilt in his voice was more than I could bear.

Leaning back, I shook my head. "I hurt you."

"You're in an impossible situation," he said. "I know that. I made it worse."

I smiled at him. "No. You made it bearable." Pulling back, I glanced around. "I want to see you. Just us, so we can talk. Lunch tomorrow?"

He nodded and cupped my cheek again. He brushed his

thumb over my cheek, and it was like he was healing all the wounds in my soul.

"I have to get back inside," I whispered, "but please know I'm thinking of *you*."

He smiled and nodded again.

"We'll talk tomorrow." I left him standing there. I was practically walking on air, my heart was light, and I couldn't stop the smile that had found my lips after days of frowning. I had expected to have to beg and explain and justify, but he understood. I should have known he'd understand. He would never do anything to risk losing Will, and he wouldn't expect me to risk Adam.

My mood stalled when I walked back into the ballroom. The crowd parted for me and everyone started, some even whispered or gasped as I walked toward where I'd left Garrett and Megan.

"Mara," Albert called, his voice echoing through the eerily quiet room.

He reached me just as the rest of the attendees moved and Megan and Garrett came into view. My heart dropped.

Garrett's back was poker straight, his face hard and unwavering. He was furious. Beyond furious. The only time he became so lacking in emotion was when he intentionally refused to tip his hand.

"Oh, look," Megan said, her voice loud and patronizing. "If it isn't *Mrs.* King."

"Stop," Garrett warned. His voice sent chills down my spine, and his warning wasn't even directed at me. "You can attack me all you want, but you will not disrespect my wife."

Attack me? For what?

Instead of letting my confusion show, I joined forces with my husband. We would always produce a united front. Always. That was what kept our business alive and thriving and our farce of a marriage going. I straightened my shoulders, braced myself for whatever was coming, and let my survival instinct kick in.

This was going to be ugly, but I'd be damned if I'd walk out of here with my head hanging in shame.

Megan smirked as she took a step in my direction. Garrett started for her, but I lifted my hand, silently telling him to stop. He did. He was perfectly aware that I could take care of myself.

"Isn't it sweet how old Albert Carter tried to come to her rescue?" She tilted her head and smirked at me. "Wonder why."

I didn't respond. I still wasn't completely on to her game.

She looked at Albert. "You aren't special, you know? She's fucking more men than I can count."

"Well, that's not very many, is it?" I asked, and several people snickered.

Her cocky grin fell into a disgusted stare. "Tell me, Mara. How is my husband in bed?"

I smiled. "If you want to compare notes, we should have tea sometime."

"You can have Jake," she said flatly as she turned her wicked stare to the man who had somehow materialized at my side.

I was too focused on her to notice him until she moved her attack in his direction.

"I don't want him," she spat in his face. "He's pathetic in

the bedroom." She smiled, but none of us responded. So she looked at me again. "And Albert. The thought makes me sick."

I simply smiled.

"Who else are you fucking, Mara?" she asked, and my heart did a little flip. And then she laughed again.

I glanced over my shoulder. Michael had come to stand by my other shoulder. Flanked by lovers on either side.

Megan smirked, and I knew she was about to deal her final blow. I wouldn't let that blow come at Michael's expense.

"Do you know why I let Garrett take you as his lover, Megan?" There were a few gasps, but the cat was out of the bag. I had no choice but to get control of the damn thing before it tore my life to pieces. I wasn't going to let some little tramp ruin my life or embarrass me in front of all my business associates and fake friends.

She smirked. "Because you're weak."

I tilted my head down to look in her eyes, giving her a sad, sympathetic look. "Because I'm a lady, and I make my husband treat me like one. Even in the bedroom. So when his needs are more...*primal*...he takes that elsewhere. I would never let him do to me what he does to you. I mean really, Megan, the thought of sleeping with a respectable man like Albert Carter makes you sick, but letting a man tie you up and cum down your throat doesn't?"

This time when the room filled with gasps, I was the one who smirked. Megan leaned back, her mouth agape, clearly shocked that I knew about her sexual appetite. I hadn't known for certain, but I suspected based on what Garrett had told me and how Jake had treated me, Garrett never would bother with a lover who wasn't fulfilling him the way he'd said I wasn't, and Jake never would have spanked me without thought had his wife not allowed that treatment. He would have asked first. No, he'd been taught how to do that. And I'd guessed it was Megan—now I knew.

"You have my permission to fuck my husband, Megan, but you have no claim on him. *I* am his wife. I wear his wedding ring. *You* wear an O-ring that he's used on countless women."

She gasped and stepped back, but I leaned toward her. I had a good inch and a half on Megan, and I used it to my advantage as I stood just a breath from her face.

"The only pearl necklace I've ever let him give me is actually made of pearls." I smiled as I touched the necklace I was wearing. It was, indeed, made of pearls, but it had been a gift from Victoria. Megan didn't need to know that.

I had her by the proverbial throat. She'd tried to humiliate me—and she had to some extent—but now the world knew she liked to be treated like the whore that she was. While men would flock to her door, the women of our society would look down their noses at her. And probably at me, to be honest, but they always had. And they knew the score.

There wasn't one of us who wasn't aware that our husbands took lovers. And most of us knew why. But I'd just told them all that Megan Decker was one of those whores their husbands turned to.

"My husband loves me. He uses you. And when he's done, he tosses you aside and comes home to me."

"After you're done fucking my husband."

I laughed softly. "Well. Someone had to keep him satisfied."

She reached up to slap me, but Jake grabbed her wrist.

"You've humiliated us all enough," he said harshly.

She glared at me before turning to Garrett. "Good luck finding someone to replace me. You fucking pervert."

We all watched in silence as Jake practically dragged Megan from the room. I looked at Grace Carter. "I've never slept with your husband, and I don't intend to. No offense, Albert."

Grace wrapped her arm through her husband's in a show that she believed me.

I looked to where I'd last seen Michael, but he was gone. I'd have a lot of explaining to do, but first I had to save face. Looking to Garrett, I frowned as I would at Adam for disobeying.

"Looks like someone owes his wife a shopping spree and a trip to Paris."

The room filled with uneasy laughter. Mostly because we all knew how these embarrassing little situations were resolved.

Garrett held his hands out as he closed the distance between us. "Sorry, darling."

He slid his arms around my waist and tugged me closer. He leaned down for a kiss, and I turned my face away and glanced around the room, judging the audience.

The women rolled their eyes and shook their heads—likely because they'd been there and were already bored with the scene. The men were all smiles, probably mentally patting Garrett on the back.

"I suggest you leave a hefty donation to make this scene up to the organizers," I said quietly.

"Yeah. I will."

I continued looking at the crowd. Most were already finding other things to do besides stare at us. The gossip wouldn't die down soon, but they were likely already talking about other affairs and their resolutions. Our circles were ripe with confrontations between men and their lovers, though they didn't usually play out so publicly.

I'd have to call Jake and check on him. He'd taken as hard a hit to his pride as I had tonight. But I was more concerned about Michael. We'd just made up. We'd just agreed to talk things out. Now he was gone and I couldn't go to him. I couldn't leave. Not now.

Now, more than ever, I was Mara fucking King, and I would stand by my husband. Because anything less would be more detrimental to my social standing, and I couldn't have that. Not now. Not when I was working so hard to make my own way.

[24]

"I figured you'd show up here sometime," Michael said as he leaned against his front door. His tie was undone and hanging loosely around his neck. His hair was disheveled, reminding me of how it had stood on end when I'd run my fingers through it as we made love.

I hadn't bothered to change yet, either. Tomas let us out, and I went right to my Lexus. I didn't tell Garrett where I was going, and he pretended he didn't notice I'd made a beeline for my car.

We'd stayed at the fundraiser as long as we needed to soothe some ruffled feathers and laugh off Megan's embarrassing episode as if we didn't have a care despite her exposing our agreement to the world. I held his arm, he patted my hand, and we smiled like the fucking social royalty we were. And when we got in the car, Garrett turned to glare at me.

"You didn't have to tell the world I like rough sex."

"And you shouldn't have let her get so out of control."

He shook his head. "We're even now."

"I suppose."

After a moment, he had sighed and put his hand on mine. "We both had affairs. We've both been exposed. Our agreement is null and void."

"Good. I'll take Adam and leave."

He laughed softly. "You even think about taking my child, and I'll ruin you, Mara."

I returned his laugh. "Doubt it. I'm just as well respected in this town as you."

"You're tolerated," he said. "Because I say so. Do you really think there's a man in this town who would give you the time of day if he weren't trying to get in your pants or my good graces?"

I smirked. "There could be a few."

My smile fell when he grabbed my hair so hard it hurt, and not on the sexual pleasure-pain way he'd slipped into our sex life. He glared at me.

"You leave if you want. I'll pack your fucking bags. But if you even think about taking my son with you, I'll destroy everything you touch for the rest of your life."

I pushed his hand away from me. "Gee, Garrett, it's almost like you care about him."

He shook his head and looked out the window. "We have to come up with a plan to show the world we're more than what Megan said. We have to watch every step we take. We need to be more calculated. More dinners in public and romancing. We'll take that trip you mentioned. Paris or wherever you want to go. But we have to be even more united than we were before. We have to show them there are no cracks in King Inc."

I looked out my own window. No cracks in King Inc. Not in our marriage. Not in our lives. Not in Adam's world. In King Inc.

I frowned and took a slow breath. "We had a good start tonight. Laughing it off was the best thing we could do. There's not a couple in that room who isn't or hasn't indulged in adultery. I'm sure they knew the score the moment she started throwing a fit."

"Oh, she made sure they knew. She was quite upset that I was choosing my prudish wife over her."

I grinned. "Is that what she said?"

"Verbatim."

"Good. That plays into what I said. Let them all think that. That will stop half the women there from throwing themselves at you and at least two or three men from trying to sleep with me now that they know the door is open."

"That's going to be the hell of it, isn't it?" He laughed softly. "Prepare to be wooed by stuffy old men, darling."

I sighed heavily. The only wooing I wanted was from Michael. And that was never going to happen now.

"QUITE A SHOW YOU PUT ON TONIGHT, MRS. KING."

He said my name with such contempt, I knew the ground I'd gained with him was lost.

"Michael."

He chuckled as he pushed himself from the door. "I'm such an idiot."

I followed him inside, easing the door shut and glancing up the stairs just to be sure we were alone. He ran his hand over his hair, and I noticed the bottle of what appeared to be whiskey in the other. Oh boy. Maybe I should have waited until morning.

"What was I supposed to do? Shrink back and let her humiliate me?"

"Sounds like you humiliated yourself." He laughed. "You know, more than once I thought there was something between you and Albert—"

"There isn't."

"Liar!" He glared for a moment. "You fucking liar. I've seen you with him. I've seen the conspiratorial smiles. The sideways glances. The way he looks at you. My God, Mara." He pulled his mouth tight as if he were about to be sick. "He's like...ninety."

I laughed softly. "I'm not sleeping with Albert."

He shook his head. "Bullshit. I've seen you with him."

"Really? You've seen me with him, Michael. And that's enough to confirm that I'm sucking his dick in his office?"

"What about Jake?" he yelled.

"What *about* Jake?"

"Are you going to deny fucking him?"

I shook my head. "No."

"And then you climb into my bed. You fucking slut."

I stared at him for a moment before laughing. "You know you have always been so quick to believe the worst about me. From day one. You remember that day in the park, don't you?

The day you tried to rub my face in Garrett's affair with Jake's wife?"

"And all the while you were screwing him, too."

I shook my head. "No. No. My affair with Jake started after that. In fact," I said a bit more coolly than intended, "I should thank you. It was that scene you made that finally pushed me over the edge. See, I'd never cheated on Garrett before. I'd always sat at home pretending I didn't care what he was doing behind my back, but the truth was, I did care. It did hurt. And Megan was exposing that wound with her behavior, but you, Michael, were the one who really dug in and ripped my heart out."

His anger eased a bit as he listened to my accusation.

"I needed somewhere to go. Someone to take the pain away. But who's a girl to turn to when she has no one? So, yeah, I took Jake into my bed, and for a while, it was good. It was *so* good to give Garrett a taste of his own medicine. But you know what I learned about myself in the process?" I blinked away tears, and I hated that once again this man had done that to me. "I learned that I can't just fuck someone and walk away. I can't not care about someone I'm being intimate with. So I ended things with Jake, because if I didn't, I was going to get my heart broken. Well, if I had a heart, right?"

Michael lowered his face.

"Besides that, there was this other guy who kept dragging me over for cookouts and ice cream and chocolate chip pancakes. I couldn't keep up with Jake when I was always here, could I? When *this* was where I wanted to be."

He shook his head, and I stepped to him. Stroking his hair, I waited for him to look at me.

"This is where I *want* to be," I whispered.

He took a shaky breath before letting it out slowly. "You never slept with Albert?"

"No." I considered telling him about the scene on the yacht, but that didn't matter now and would only make things worse. Nothing like that had happened since, and it wouldn't happen again.

"And you left Jake?"

"Yes."

He put his hand to my hip and his forehead to mine. "And you'll leave Garrett now?"

I leaned back. "No."

The anger flashed in his eyes again. "You said if any of his lovers came forward, you could leave him."

"Yes, Michael, but Garrett's affair wasn't the only one exposed. Mine was too. Any leverage I had is gone." Slowly, a realization came to my mind. "Oh, dear God, Michael. Tell me you didn't put Megan up to that. Please tell me you weren't responsible for that scene."

He ran his hand over his hair. "Had I known you were fucking around too, I might have reconsidered my plan."

A sense of betrayal washed over me. "I told you that plan would backfire. Damn it. Why didn't you listen to me?"

"Why didn't you tell me you were sleeping around too?"

"Because it was none of your goddamned business!"

"None of my business? You were here, in my house, building a life with me and my son. Acting like you wanted this life, but all the while you were screwing someone else."

I shook my head. "Building a life with you and Will? Michael, we were friends."

"Friends?"

"Yes."

"I... I was falling for you," he whispered.

My heart dropped and lifted with hope at the same time. I reached for him, but he knocked my hand away.

"I thought..." He laughed a flat, slurred sound. "I thought you were some trapped little rabbit that I needed to rescue. Turns out you were a fox. A vicious and cunning bitch in a deceiving little package. Worming your way into my life, into my home, knowing you were never going to stay."

My eyes widened. "He will take Adam."

"Stop. Stop using that sweet little boy as an excuse. You like it," he said harshly. "I saw you. I saw the look in your eyes when you went in for the kill. You were getting off on hurting her."

"Oh. And she wasn't enjoying the humiliation she was inflicting? Yes, I see your point. I should have wilted like a little flower. I should have whimpered and cried and begged for mercy."

"You enjoyed hurting her," he said again. "Just like you enjoy the games Garrett plays with you. You play the victim so well, Mara. I fell for it. But I see you now, lady." He pointed at his eyes as if to emphasize his point. "I see you for what you really are."

"And what am I?"

"Some kind of emotional masochist. You play these games with him to use people. Just like you used me."

"I never used you."

"You used me!" He leaned close. "I loved you. I loved you, and you used me."

"What did I use you for?"

He didn't have an answer. He just smirked. "I see you now."

"I think you do," I whispered. "You keep saying I wormed my way into your life. You know what I think, Michael?"

"I don't give a fuck what you think."

"I think you feel guilty. For loving me. For wanting a life with me. For letting Will get attached to me. You're afraid I'm replacing her."

He glared.

"That night you came home and I was with Will in the kitchen, you were so angry. So furious. Not just with me but with him. I didn't understand it. But I see you too. I see the guilt and fear in your eyes. You're scared he's letting her go because of me."

"Get out of my house," he whispered.

I smiled. "That's it. That's what this is really about."

He closed the distance between us, looming over me, but I didn't back down. "You could never replace her."

"But I was, wasn't I? Little by little, I was filling Rebecca's shoes. And you aren't ready for that, and you certainly aren't ready for Will to be ready for that."

"Leave my son out of this!"

"I can't leave Garrett," I said softly. "He reminded me of that tonight. Of how powerful he is and the lengths he will go to if I try to take his son from him. But I can be here, too. We can keep going as we've been going until the boys are older. Until I can leave and he can't take my son from me.

We could come here, be a family. A real family. Without hiding."

"Do you really think I want a woman who hides me and my kid in the shadows?" he whispered.

I closed my eyes and sighed. "That's the best I can do."

"It's not enough. *You're* not enough."

"Daddy?" Will called, and we both looked up the stairs. There, on the landing, his little dark-haired boy stood wide-eyed, watching us. "I heard yelling."

"It's okay," he said, putting the whiskey on the table and out of view.

"Are you fighting?"

"No, Will. We're just saying goodnight."

He looked at me. "Where's Adam?"

I gave him a fake smile of reassurance. "He's at home. In bed, just like you should be."

"Go to your room, Will. I'll be up in a minute."

Will didn't budge.

"Go to your room."

"Mrs. King?" he said weakly.

"You're scaring him," I whispered.

Michael grabbed my arm, but I pulled free and marched up the stairs. "Come on, buddy. Back to bed."

"Are you fighting with my dad?"

I sighed. "Yes, Will. We're fighting."

"Why?"

"Because I did something, and he thinks it was wrong."

"Was it?"

I pulled back his covers and hopped into his bed. I pulled the covers up and sat next to him. "Maybe. I don't know.

Sometimes grownups don't always know right from wrong either."

"Are you guys going to make up?"

I inhaled slowly before shrugging. "I don't know. But even if we don't, I promise you and Adam will *always* be best friends. He can still come visit, and I hope you'll come see me sometimes."

His little lip trembled. "Don't go away."

I put my finger to his mouth to shush him. "I'm here for you. Whatever you need. Talia can help you call me, okay?"

"Dad's sorry. Whatever he said. I know he's sorry."

Leaning down, I kissed his head. "I love you, Will. Bunches and bunches. And I promise no matter what happens between me and your dad, I *will* see you soon. Go to sleep, okay? The faster you sleep, the faster you wake, and then we'll see what tomorrow brings."

He nodded and stared for a moment before closing his eyes. I stroked my hand over his hair and kissed his head, as I'd done the night I left after Michael and I had made love. I left his room, easing the door shut, and walked down the stairs. Michael had exchanged his whiskey for water and his anger for shame.

"I didn't mean to scare him."

"He's okay."

"Thank you for taking care of him."

I nodded. "Of course. You should get some sleep too."

"Mara. I can't. I can't live half a life with you. I can't see you with him and not feel the sting. That might work for you, but it doesn't work for me. And it's not what I want for Will.

He needs someone who can give him everything. I'm sorry. But... No."

I swallowed. I was expecting that. "Well, I told him he can play with Adam whenever he wants, and I meant that. If you don't want to see me, I understand. I can send him over with the nanny. But we can't let this hurt them."

"No, we can't." He smiled slightly. "We should, uh... work out some kind of shared custody thing, huh? You get Wednesday at the park. I get Friday campouts."

I smiled, though tears had filled my eyes again. "Yeah. We'll work it out." Stepping to him, I put a soft kiss on his cheek. "Goodbye, Michael."

"Goodbye, Mara," he whispered as I left.

[25]

I DIDN'T WANT to get out of bed. Not only did I have a world of damage control to do to recover from Megan's scene at the party, but I had to face my first day knowing Michael wasn't going to be there. Knowing he really did hate me.

But when Garrett came into my room with a tray and a sweet smile to soothe my anger, I sighed and sat up. By the time he made it to the bed, I was leaning against the pillows and waiting for his tenth apology.

"I know you like to eat a light breakfast, but I thought you deserved something a bit more filling after last night." He lifted the dome to reveal a fluffy yellow omelet with cheese oozing from the ends next to a pile of crisp hash browns.

I did love a good omelet. But then the scent of egg filled my senses, and my stomach rolled. Not just rolled but lurched. My eyes bulged as I shoved the tray aside, not caring about the mess it would make.

Garrett called out my name, but I didn't stop. As soon as

my feet hit the floor, I ran to the bathroom, barely making it to the toilet before the bile in my stomach forced its way out.

I held my hair, gagging, vomiting, and panting until there was nothing left in my stomach. I sat for a moment, making sure I was done, and finally Garrett took my arms and helped me to my feet.

He filled a glass of water, and I rinsed and spit.

"Better?" Garrett asked, taking the drink from my trembling hand.

I nodded. The nausea was as good a reason as any not to meet his demanding gaze—I closed my eyes against the waves rolling through me—but the truth was what kept me from looking at him.

"The last time you were sick like this, you were pregnant," he said after several long moments of heavy silence.

I didn't react. There was no reason to. We both knew what he'd said was true.

He brushed his hand over my hair before tucking his fingers under my chin and lifting my face.

Finally, I opened my eyes and met his gaze in the mirror. His eyes were blank. Like they'd been with Megan last night. That frigid fury that filled him.

I cleared my throat and licked my lips. "I remember."

"Are you pregnant, Mara?"

"I-I don't know. I guess I need to call the doctor."

He stared at me—calculating—before dropping his hand from my face. He left me standing there.

My heart started pounding. Garrett wasn't the only man in my bed, though we'd had unprotected sex not long ago, I'd also realized after my romp with Michael that we hadn't taken time to use protection. Stupidity on my part, but I'd been caught up in the moment like a stupid teenager.

I took a few moments to collect myself before following Garrett to the bedroom. He was staring out the window but glanced at me when I stopped by his side.

"Do you know that Jake and Megan don't have kids because Jake *can't* have kids? They considered adoption a few times, but he isn't confident Megan would be a good mother. He told me all this over drinks one night." Turning from the window, Garrett crossed his arms and looked at me. "Did he ever tell you that?"

"No."

He moved his head in a slow, thoughtful nod. "After you came to me with your proposal all those years ago—the open-marriage contract that I signed—I wanted to make damn sure I never got another woman pregnant and lost everything over some fling. Do you know what I did, Mara?"

I held my breath and swallowed hard. "No."

"I lied about being out of town for a business trip and had a vasectomy."

I didn't visibly respond, but my heart dropped to my stomach. *Michael.* The baby was *Michael's.*

The very contract I'd put into place to protect myself was about to be my undoing. Garrett sat on the bed again. This time I didn't hesitate to meet his cold stare. I would not allow him to see how terrified I was.

"If you are pregnant, I'm not the father. Nor is Jake Decker. Which leads me to wonder who else you've been fucking, Mara." He smirked when I didn't answer. "I'm pretty sure I know. All those playdates with little Will

Redmond weren't just playdates for Adam, were they? You used my son to whore around."

"No! Garrett…"

"What?"

I drew a breath and let it out slowly. "We slept together once. After the incident with Will in the pool. We were both emotional. The boys had no idea—they were watching a movie. It was nothing."

"Well, it *is* something, darling. A boy or a girl, I would assume."

I sank back, less than amused by his observation.

"Does he know?"

"I didn't even know until ten minutes ago."

Garrett stood and paced to the window.

I lowered my face and bit my lip. I wasn't going to beg or cry or plead for forgiveness. But I'd be damned if he took my son. I had to convince him not to take sole custody of Adam. The company and houses and cars be damned. I just needed to keep my little boy.

"Garrett—"

"Shut up," he snapped.

My breath caught. "Just listen—"

"No." He faced me. "*You* listen to me."

I couldn't read his eyes. Hurt. Calculation. Anger. All mixed together into something I couldn't quite understand.

He lowered his face for a moment before meeting my eyes again. "I know you wanted more children. So did I."

I watched him, creasing my brow with confusion.

"But you were right in what you demanded of me. I wanted a lifestyle that didn't fit your idea of marriage, and you were right to take steps to protect yourself. So I took steps as well. As Adam grew, I regretted not having more children with you. So we'll make another deal. This one on my terms." He sat next to me and nodded his head as if confirming what he was thinking. "I'll give you three choices here, Mara. You think about it and let me know which one you're going with."

I swallowed hard, certain I wasn't going to like any of the choices he was about to give me.

"One: you take that bastard child and walk out of here with nothing—including our son—per your agreement. Two: you abort that child and take the same steps I took to make sure nothing like this happens again."

"And three?" I whispered.

"Three. Option number three is that from this moment forward, that child is mine. No one will ever know he isn't. Not even Michael Redmond. We go on with our lives as we have. One beautiful, happy, and growing family. You'll be my wife and the mother of *my children*. You'll give up your role at King Inc. You'll be too busy raising our kids to keep up with the demands of a corporate job. If you get bored, you'll take on charity work, but you'll no longer be by my side in the workplace. I've tolerated that to make you happy, but you'll now move into the role most corporate wives take."

I inhaled as I looked down. I'd always detested that role, and he knew it. But my other options were to lose my children.

I scoffed. "We don't even know for sure that I'm pregnant."

"It's Friday," he said. "I think I deserve some time off,

don't you? I'm going to take Adam to the zoo. A little father-and-son excursion. When we return, you'll be gone, you'll no longer be pregnant, or you'll congratulate me on becoming a father again. Choose wisely, darling." Leaning forward, he kissed my cheek.

He walked away as if he hadn't just locked me in a cage. But then I realized I'd always been in this cage. From the day I first met Garrett King. He'd opened the door, and I'd walked in willingly. I'd even helped him lock me in by making him sign that damned open marriage contract.

I put my hand low on my belly where another man's child was growing.

AUNT VICTORIA FROWNED AS SHE SAT BACK. SHE'D given me this same look over six years ago when I'd gone to her to tell her I was planning to divorce Garrett. She was wondering how she'd raised such a mess as the one who sat before her.

I sniffed, dried my tears, and took a breath as I stared at the pregnancy test in my hand.

"Abort," she said without hesitation. "Just abort it and forget this entire mess, Mara. You need to focus on proving to the world that you aren't going to get pushed around by the likes of Megan Decker." She shook her head as she stood up. "This is my fault. I didn't properly prepare you."

"Prepare me for what?"

"I thought you were smart enough not to get yourself pregnant, girl! Goddamn it, do you have any idea the mess this will make? Do you think the father—and don't tell me his name, I don't want to know—won't demand a DNA test? Do you think the world won't whisper behind your back? This on the heels of Megan's little fit last night? You'll never sweep this mess under the rug if you've got a baby on your hip to remind them of what you've done."

God. What was I thinking coming to her for support?

Pushing myself up just as dramatically as she'd done, I bit my lip. "Thanks for listening," I said before heading for the door.

"Mara," she called after me. Her eyes softened. "I had a child once."

My heart sank to my toes. Victoria had a child?

"A beautiful little girl." Her smile was wistful. I'd never seen her look so happy and sad at the same time. "I loved her father. I thought if I kept her, he'd come around. That he'd realize he loved me and our child."

"What happened?" I asked softly.

"When I told him I was pregnant, he slapped me across the face and cursed me for ruining his life by having that abomination. He told me I could ruin his life, and that wasn't going to happen. He gave me options—much like Garrett gave to you. But I wasn't the wife. I was the mistress. My options were to abort or to disappear. I didn't do either. But then I got fired from my job, and I couldn't get another. And I knew why. He was pulling strings, keeping me from taking care of my baby. But I was smart," she said with a curt nod. "I knew what I had to do. As his secretary and his lover, I knew things about him and about his partners."

She lowered her face for a moment before meeting my

eyes with the resolve and confidence I recognized. "I gave my daughter to a couple that could care for her—who could provide her the family I couldn't. And I got my revenge. I blackmailed that son of a bitch and married one of his partners. I had the money and the standing, and for the rest of his life, he wrote a check to me that I gave to my daughter's family to care for her."

I creased my brow. "She's an adult, then? Where is she? Why haven't you connected with her?"

The sadness returned. "She has a family, Mara. You of all people know what that means. I wouldn't dream of taking that from her. I take care of her the best I can. She doesn't know, but I love her, and I'll do everything to protect her."

I crossed the room and smiled before hugging her tight. She hugged me back, and I buried my face in her shoulder.

Leaning back, I cupped her face. "You would have been an amazing mother. She's lucky to have you looking out for her. I cherish everything you've done for me."

She searched my eyes for a few moments before smiling. "Fuck them, Mara. Fuck them all. If you want this baby, you have this baby. Fuck the world and what they think. You're Garrett King's wife. The DNA test will say whatever Garrett pays for it to say. But understand it's one more barrel that man has you over. He'll never give you room to breathe now. He has you cornered like never before. But I'll help you. I'll help you cover the truth and make this life the best you can for you and *both* your children. If that's what you choose."

I pressed a firm kiss to her cheek. "I love you."

"I love you," she whispered back.

I met Adam and Garrett in the foyer when they returned from the zoo. Adam ran straight for me, throwing his arms around my hips and hugging tight. Then he let go and started rambling excitedly about the elephants he'd seen.

Garrett held my gaze, clearly wondering what choice I'd made. I hadn't left, obviously. Not that I'd ever walk away from Adam. He knew that.

Kneeling down, I smiled and ran my fingers through my son's hair. He looked so much like me. No one could ever doubt he was my child. One of the fears that had plagued me throughout the day was that if I had this child and it looked more like Michael than me, the world would know—or at least suspect—it wasn't Garrett's.

Both men had dark hair, but Michael's olive skin and sharp features were a stark contrast to Garrett's all-American-boy looks. But Adam—he was all me. He had the same strong Norwegian features my aunt and I shared.

Aunt Victoria was right. As soon as Michael found out I was pregnant, he'd demand a DNA test. And I'd have to consent or fear him taking me to court. But Victoria was right about another thing—the test would say whatever Garrett wanted. If I was going to keep this child and pretend to be a big happy family, I'd have to keep Garrett happy or he'd make sure the results were real and he'd have grounds for divorce.

And to take Adam. If I wanted this baby, I was going to have to go all in. There was no wavering. There was no backing out. There was no changing my mind. Keeping

Michael's baby was a huge risk—not just now, but for the next twelve years until Adam was an adult and I couldn't lose custody of him.

I'd spent all afternoon weighing my options. Debating what to do. Really, I wasn't sure until I looked at Adam and the words left me. "I have a surprise for you and Daddy," I whispered when he took a breath.

The elephants were immediately forgotten, and his eyes grew even wider. "What?"

Taking his hand, I stood and held my other out for Garrett to join us. I entwined my fingers with his and, walking between my two men, led them to the dining room. There on the table was a small white box with a gold bow.

I put my hand to Adam's head. "Open it."

He tore into the package as Garrett put his hands on my shoulders. I was tense, but he gently dug his thumbs in, lightly massaging the muscles as we watched Adam pull the tissue paper aside.

He made a face, clearly disappointed as he pulled out a pair of booties. "What's this?"

"Shoes."

"For who?"

Garrett wrapped his arms around my shoulders and hugged me to him as he whispered, "Good choice, Mara. Very good choice."

I forced my smile to remain. "For the baby."

Adam scrunched his little face. "What baby?"

Garrett scooped him up and ruffled his hair. "Looks like somebody's going to be a big brother." Putting his other arm around me, he pulled me into his embrace and kissed me. "If ever there was a doubt that I love my family, it will be put to rest now. My wife and my *children* mean everything to me. And I'll do whatever I have to do to keep them."

I smiled, though I heard this threat clear as day.

Just like I'd done six years ago, I'd walked right into Garrett King's trap.

ALSO BY MARCI BOLDEN

STONEHILL SERIES:

The Road Leads Back

Friends Without Benefits

The Forgotten Path

Jessica's Wish

This Old Café

Forever Yours

THE WOMEN OF HEARTS SERIES:

Hidden Hearts

Burning Hearts

Stolen Hearts

Secret Hearts

Cheating Hearts

Runaway Hearts

OTHER TITLES:

California Can Wait

Seducing Kate

A Life Without Water

ABOUT THE AUTHOR

As a teen, Marci Bolden skipped over young adult books and jumped right into reading romance novels. She never left.

Marci lives in the Midwest with her husband, kiddos, and numerous rescue pets. If she had an ounce of willpower, Marci would embrace healthy living, but until cupcakes and wine are no longer available at the local market, she will appease her guilt by reading self-help books and promising to join a gym "soon."

Visit her here:
www.marcibolden.com

facebook.com/MarciBoldenAuthor
x.com/BoldenMarci
instagram.com/marciboldenauthor

www.ingramcontent.com/pod-product-compliance
Lightning Source LLC
Chambersburg PA
CBHW031435200726
48289CB00001BA/218